COLD
COAST

COLD COAST

ROBYN MUNDY

Published in 2021 by Ultimo Press,
an imprint of Hardie Grant Publishing

Ultimo Press
Gadigal Country
7, 45 Jones Street
Ultimo, NSW 2007
ultimopress.com.au

Ultimo Press (London)
5th & 6th Floors
52–54 Southwark Street
London SE1 1UN

A catalogue record for this
book is available from the
National Library of Australia

Cold Coast
ISBN 978 1 76115 021 0 (paperback)

Cover design Sandy Cull
Cover photograph Mark Folstad Photography
Author photograph Kirsty Pilkington
Text design Simon Paterson, Bookhouse
Typesetting Bookhouse, Sydney | 12/17 pt Adobe Caslon Pro
Copyeditor Deonie Fiford
Proofreader Rebecca Hamilton

10 9 8 7 6 5 4 3 2 1

Printed in Australia by Griffin Press, part of Ovato, an Accredited ISO AS/NZS 14001
Environmental Management System printer.

The paper this book is printed on is certified against the
Forest Stewardship Council® Standards. Griffin Press holds
chain of custody certification SGSHK-COC-005088. FSC®
promotes environmentally responsible, socially beneficial
and economically viable management of the world's forests.

Ultimo Press acknowledges the Traditional Owners of the country on which we work,
the Gadigal people of the Eora nation and the Wurundjeri people of the Kulin nation,
and recognises their continuing connection to the land, waters and culture.
We pay our respects to their Elders past and present.

This project has been assisted by the Australian
Government through the Australia Council,
its arts funding and advisory board.

For Ingrid Crossland, adventurer and friend

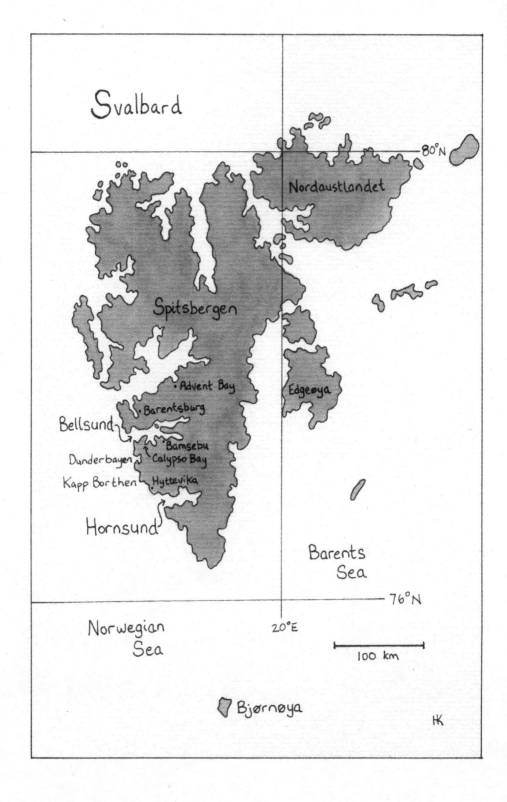

Svalbard

Nordaustlandet

80°N

Spitsbergen

• Advent Bay

Edgeøya

• Barentsburg

Bellsund

Bamsebu
Calypso Bay

Dunderbayen

Kapp Borthen

Hyttevika

Hornsund

Barents
Sea

76°N

20°E

Norwegian
Sea

100 km

Bjørnøya

HK

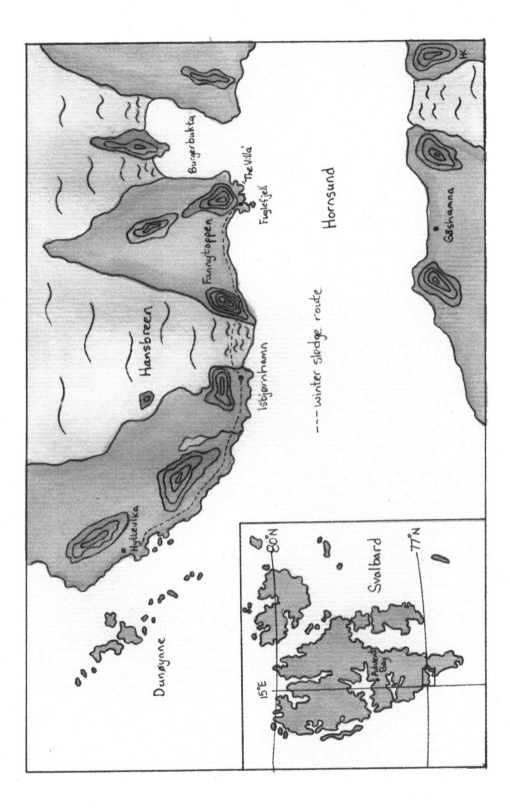

Author's note

WANNY WOLDSTAD, BORN 1893, was Svalbard's first female trapper and hunter, overwintering in Hornsund in 1932–33. While *Cold Coast* is a work of fiction, it draws on field and archival research, personal encounters on Svalbard, and is informed by Wanny's own account from her published memoir *Første kvinne som fangstmann på Svalbard / First Woman Trapper on Svalbard*. Wanny died suddenly in 1959.

A glossary of Norwegian and Arctic terms appears at the end of the novel.

FOX

food falls from the sky

SIX TO BEGIN, this summer's litter from a pair of fox too smart for the traps. Five kits tawny, the spit of their father; one, the runt of the litter, the coal brown coat of its mother. Unless you know what the change in seasons brings – the summer moult, the prized winter coat that grows thick and glossy in its place – these pelts are worthless.

The vixen roams. Dog fox sleeps in the sun near the opening of the den. Below him, kits bound amongst the rocks. The largest leaps upon its brother's back. A third, woken from its nap, flicks its tail and joins the game, the three tousling and nipping, a wriggling knot of fur that tumbles down the snow slope, limbs and tails akimbo. A yip from the kit pinned beneath. An odd sound. Not a cat's cry. Not the yelp of a dog. A sound akin to a bird, to the cry of kittiwake gulls who make their summer home in lofty heights above the den, the swirl of air a heaven of wings.

The runt of the litter knows this: food falls from the sky.

Its mother holds no expectation for the runt beyond its time in the den, even her larger kits' first winter alone holds the prospect of a summons with death. Why let it follow, this underweight youngling whose colour and form mirrors her own? She smells the runt at her flank, senses its effort to keep pace. She wishes it gone. They angle sharp up the slope to trawl the base of bird cliffs.

On gravel amongst the moss beds, a bird egg has smashed, mother and kit lapping at a yolk already gelling in the Arctic sun. The vixen sights a second egg cushioned amongst tufts of pink campion, intact, though the egg has plummeted an impossible distance. The mother shunts the kit aside and takes the egg whole in her mouth with the tenderness she uses to pull her newborns to her teats. She tracks swiftly across the slope to cache the egg in a crevice within an outcrop of rock. This tract of land is a larder, a memory map in readiness for harder times.

Not only eggs, entire birds plunge from the sky. Broken-winged birds, sick birds, birds weak from hunger, kittiwakes, fulmars, even dovekies whose tiny bones add crunch to a platter of warm flesh, here for the picking along the breadth of slopes.

The breast of a kittiwake quivers even as the vixen splits it apart. The kit sits, forelimbs straight, as her mother sets a paw upon the bird and tugs at entrails. The kit salivates, limbs trembling in wait. The vixen tears meat from the breast. She halts, takes a step back. The runt pushes her muzzle into the bird's cavity; she rubs her snout over guts and fascia strung out on the ground, the savoury stench as exhilarating as the first entrails sliding down her throat, as warm and comforting as mother's milk.

1

Tromsø, late July

'LAND AS MIGHTY as a cathedral,' Anders Sæterdal bellows to the boy pouring beer behind the bar. 'Glaciers with a yawn to swallow you whole. Fjords so vast –' The lad shifts his weight, stifles a yawn. Anders imagines the boy counting down the days until the new season takes this bar full of trappers and their endless stories away with it. 'I tell you this, boy.' Anders leans in, determined to resurrect himself. 'Up there in the north you do not count on God. My word, you do not. A man who stays alive stays living thanks only to himself.'

The boy gives a perfunctory nod, holds the glass aloft, beer foam sliding to the floor. Anders fishes in his pocket and pushes a handful of øre across the counter. Away with the coins goes the lad, dragging his useless leg.

Pitiful to be struck down that young. Pity all round. A trapper without his rifle is a man lost, they say. Said someone. Whoever that might be. Anders slugs the *blanding* without tasting it, his quench for all the things he'd craved in the north grown stale. In his mind's eye is a simple hut of bleached driftwood, clouds pressed upon those pointed peaks from which Spitsbergen takes its name. He looks about the bar of Mack Ølhallen with its stained walls and ceiling yellowed with tobacco, the air a choke of smoke and a throng of voices that has him beg for solitude, the cry of eiders arcing overhead. *Time, Anders. Time to be gone.*

Anders Sæterdal has downed a skinful to match every other trapper at Mack's beer hall. The yabbering and skiting rise to a pitch to make you think they've all amassed their fortunes this winter gone. Unless you're Henry Rudi seated quietly in his corner, the canny old trapper who holds the touch of magic when it comes to hunting bear or fox, any creature with a pelt worth flensing, for the rest in this place, the truth falls dismally short. Some years the pelts pay well enough; other years a trapper like Anders makes scant more than to settle last season's loan, secure the one ahead and live high as a king in the weeks between. Ah, but life is short, is it not, the promise of the future sweet as cloudberry, he'd said once too often to the wife when he came home buoyed up with tales of daring and adventure and little else to show. Her glower fierce as storm, a woman turned frigid as a winter blizzard. *Out on your ear, Sæterdal. Out on your arse, boy, and a long time coming.* Anders downs the dregs and sets down the glass. He pulls his cap from his pocket and punches it into shape. The north frees a man. No time for maudlin thoughts. Loneliness never. No other life comes close.

He moves in the direction of the doorway. These last weeks every prospect who has frequented Mack's – the place to find a partner, a man fit for the Arctic who works hard and keeps his wits about him, who doesn't drive you mad with mindless chatter or moody temperament – is spoken for; the rest in this room drunkards, layabouts or off to the boats to stake their chances on the herring.

The bar is several steps below street level. The lintel above the stoop was never built for men of height, though Anders has ducked through it unscathed a hundred times. But now, up on the street, he spies a woman in a uniform and cap resting on the bonnet of a taxi, arms folded, ankles crisscrossed as slender as a set of ski poles. As if this whole damn town is hers for the taking. Anders feels the onset of a grin. *Smack!* against the lintel. He checks his forehead for blood, rubs at his skin, pain dazzling his vision as he collects his fallen cap. He staggers up the steps to the night air beyond.

'Are you all right?' calls the woman, though now he sees two of her wincing at his mishap, two pairs of pins sliding from the bonnet of the car.

'All right?' he says, determined not to pass out. 'Never better, my sweet.' Other nights he walks the distance through town to his lodgings; tonight, he is too sauced with beer and battered into silliness. 'Where do you intend to take me in that fine machine of yours?'

'Where would the gentleman like to go?' says she. Does he detect a flirty glint? My word he does. A wager on it. Cabs are new to Tromsø, she as big a novelty: the town's only woman chauffeur, the Ford her own vehicle, he's been told. A talking point amongst those who can afford the fare.

He'd sit alongside her, but she holds the rear door and in he dives, the leather of the seat aromatic, slippery as an eel, the air within the cab a heady blend of tobacco and cologne. Anders sniffs the floral trace of ladies' scent. Tourists. *The Paris of the North*, they coin this town and throng up here in warmer months. The wealthy kind to take a cab a distance the rest of town would walk. The same kind, Anders checks himself, whose wives are draped in fox, whose fancy floors boast a polar bearskin beside a polished piano. In the mirror he catches the woman's amusement.

'Mr Sæterdal?'

Anders sobers at his name. The taxi still sits parked, waiting for direction. He gives the address of his lodgings, down along the dock. She presses the starter to turn the motor. A purr of engineering.

Mr Sæterdal. She knows his name. No woman would set foot inside Mack Ølhallen. Anders thinks on the volume of beer talk that surely leaks onto the street. Across the crowded bar, the men pay a nod to a glimpse of skirt or a curve of ankle up there on the pavement. As quickly they turn their backs when the shuffling of feet grows agitated, when that gathering of women forms a pearly school of fish that circles back and forth – held back from entry by some impenetrable net. At times a mother with a babe on her hip stops Anders on his way out; those women know a soft touch when they see one. She will beg him, *Please go back in, sir; please call my husband home.* He turns dunderhead before a pretty face.

They move along Storgata, the cab gaining speed. 'I may know of someone suitable,' says the woman.

'Suitable?'

'For your hunting team.'

Team. A grand term for the sum of two. 'You know something of the north?'

'Stories, the life, from those like yourself. They say you are on the lookout for a partner.'

'They would be correct,' says Anders. 'A hunter, this man?'

'Championship shooter. Hard worker. Has shot deer, flensed sheep, cattle. Fished. Farmed. You name it.' Anders registers a note of urgency. 'And quick to learn,' she speaks into her mirror, 'from a man of your experience.'

A man down on his luck, desperate for any kind of work. 'Your husband, is he?'

She sweeps around the corner, shifts gears and motors toward the dock. She answers question with question. 'How are you liking your first cab ride, Mr Sæterdal?'

Is he so obvious? Anders sits back in his seat. 'No complaints from the back row.'

'A first time for everything, they say. First polar bear. Mr Rudi tells me that is something you never forget.'

'If you live to tell the tale.'

Ah, the look she casts him in her little mirror. Here in Tromsø, a hunter is a nobody. A year in the Arctic, come home a prince. 'This man,' Anders says. 'He knows what it means to spend a winter in the north? Away from home.'

'Of course,' she says too quickly.

A man who knows nothing. Anders sighs. This town. Nought for him here. He itches to be gone. Rifles, ammunition, barrels, salt, a new loan secured, a year's provisions boxed and waiting to be ferried to the docks. The same lease as last year, a tract stretching thirty kilometres the north side of Hornsund. Too big a territory to manage alone, even if he were the kind to crave his own company. A half decent partner and they could sail with *Maiblomsten* in two weeks' time. Miss the boat and who knows how many weeks before the next opportunity. He looks to the woman in the mirror. 'Where do we find this mighty hunter?'

She sits taller in her seat. 'Run you by now. Have you home within the hour. No charge, Mr Sæterdal. For any of the fare.'

Never one to pass up an offer. 'Off we go, then.'

She speeds back along the main street and out past town, no more than a lane that runs along the edge of the fjord. She weaves around potholes and he feels the taxi shudder and bump from the rough ground beneath. She flicks on the headlights, though it is neither night nor day. Soft it feels to Anders, this silky in-between, the sky all lilac and butter. 'You know my name,' says he.

'Tromsø is a small place.'

'Not so small that I know yours.' Surely, he'll have heard it.

'Ivanna. Ivanna Woldstad. They call me Wanny.'

'Vonny.' He says it the Norwegian way. *Vonny Voldstad*. Anders winds a handle that lowers the window, soft summer air brushing his face. Twilight colours the fjord, the water liquid glass. On the opposite shoreline stand barns and farmhouses, swathes of pasture, a dotting of boathouses edged along the water. Forest sweeps up the mountain slopes, the outlines of treetops a ragged silhouette. Where the tree line finishes, birch and spruce give way to basalt domes and mountain tarns, to rocky crevices still silvered with last winter's snow. They pass by a boathouse, its roof newly laid with turf. Beyond the rocky shore a *færing* slides homeward, two pairs of oars slicing the fjord as slick and clean as flensing knives.

The taxi slows. They pull off by a newly cut field bordered by dogwood. Not a house in sight. Anders looks around. 'Where are we going?'

'Right here,' Wanny answers Anders Sæterdal, as steadily as she can manage.

She opens his door. A herring gull cries. She steps to the back of the car and unlocks the trunk. The man may be drunk but still she feels his wariness. 'Trust me, sir,' Wanny says to him.

She barely trusts herself.

She extracts her rifle from its sack, aware of Anders Sæterdal watching, aware of the press and sharpness of this violet summer's night, of this field where she'd once lain beneath the heat of a man. A lifetime ago, innocent to how the world would turn. She slows her breath to steady her pulse. *How far, Ivanna, to get the thing you want?*

'Will you join me?' she says. Perhaps it is the measured way she handles the rifle that imparts confidence, or the simple lure of a mystery that has him follow her obediently across the field. Perhaps he thinks her no different from the beet-lipped women who troll the docks at night.

She stands away to load the rifle. 'Fair-sized gun,' she hears him say. Wanny has listened to stories from the trappers. Asked one hundred questions. Has drunk in the life until it pours through her daydreams and wakes her at night. She parted with her competition gun, a last treasured gift from Othar, to buy the Kragen.

'The crooked post.' She gestures to her target. 'Far side of the gate.' She takes aim, the rifle bedded firm into her shoulder. She steps her weight forward, squints to line up the sights. The light dim. *Crack!*

She takes a breath. A second shot. A third. A fourth. She relaxes the fifth and hears it ring through the night. A dog barks.

She checks the empty barrel, slings the weapon back onto her shoulder, looks to Anders Sæterdal, desperate to impress him.

Anders feels clueless to fathom what this is all about. He paces beside her to the target, sixty, seventy metres. He kneels at the fence post. Four of five bullets lodged through the wood in a tidy cluster of shots. 'Not too bad.'

In this light, remarkable.

'My husband taught me. A long time ago now.'

Mrs Wanny Woldstad. He walks beside her back to the cab, waits for explanation as she packs the rifle in the trunk.

'So?' says she.

Anders shrugs. 'You are very good.'

She looks agitated. 'What do you think?'

'Of what?'

'Me. On your team.'

He has had too many beers to make sense of it. 'With your husband?'

She shakes her head. 'I am the person asking to go.'

He wants to laugh but her face is earnest. The obvious seems lost on her. 'You are not a man.'

He sees her tighten. 'As dedicated a worker as any you can name.'

Anders backtracks. Scratches his eyebrow. 'You told me your husband was after work.'

She shakes her head. 'I am widowed, sir.'

Anders turns his gaze to the mountains, tries to clear his mind. A pale moon, a painted sky. 'Mr Sæterdal,' she says quietly. 'I am aware of the undertaking. I am skilled with a rifle. You said it yourself.'

Anders prickles. Deceived. 'Mrs Woldstad. There are no women *fangstmenn* on Svalbard. For sound reason.'

'I will not let you down.'

'The winters are too harsh.' Hard enough for a man. Any trapper would say the same.

She will not be convinced. 'No doubt they are harsh and difficult. But there have been women, yes? On Svalbard.'

He shakes his head. 'Not hunters. Wives, one or two, brought along for . . . companionship. To tend meals, keep the hut.' Hilmar Nøis's wife comes to mind. 'Even then, no good has come of it.' They say Nøis's wife had been alone in the hut when her baby came, the worst part of winter. Had lost her mind with suffering. 'Svalbard is a place to send a woman fully mad.'

She has an answer for everything. 'Not a woman strong of body and mind. I can cook and clean just as capably as trap and hunt. I will follow instruction and learn and do my share of all that is expected from a working partner.'

Hilmar Nøis would say he never lived so well. A hot meal, his socks darned. A woman to keep him warm at night. Anders takes off his cap, rubs gingerly at his throbbing forehead. 'Why? Why the north? You are misinformed to think you will make your fortune.'

'I am not a fortune hunter. I make my own way in the world. Since the age of fifteen I have worked hard for what I have. Adapted to every situation put before me.' She speaks with the same forthrightness as Othelie, his once-wife more capable of running the farm, managing their money, than he had ever been. 'All I ask,' this woman says, 'is the chance to prove myself.'

'Why Svalbard?' he asks again.

She looks to him solemnly. 'Because it is a place of stories.'

'Stories?' His head throbs with trying to make sense of her.

'When a trapper takes my cab. Men like yourself. Not just sunny stories. They talk to me of snowstorms, of dangers and battles, the darkness that can bring the lonely times.' She puts a fist against her chest. 'It leaves me with a longing.'

He wants to scoff but she is not a woman to be laughed at. 'What is it you long for, Mrs Woldstad?'

'To live with nature, experience the place which leaves a deep and aching impression on every man who goes there.' She fixes her gaze on his as if daring him to disagree. She speaks the truth. He turns to the mountains. How did he get himself into this?

'Why not a woman hunter,' she says, 'if she can shoot a gun? If she can do the work. You said yourself I was good.'

No doubt she can cook. Name a woman who can't. A not unpleasant face. A hunter? Look at her. She doesn't reach his shoulder. And she is no spring chicken – well this side of her thirties it looks to Anders, though women and their age are not his strong suit. He grasps for words of reason. 'People speak harshly. An unmarried woman up there with –'

She laughs out aloud. 'Sir, you need have no concern for your honour. Believe me.'

The kind to put you in your place.

'Mr Sæterdal,' she says. 'I am a widow. I have managed a great deal of loss and hardship. I worked my way up to matron at the Grand Hotel. Now I run my own taxi. I stand on my own feet. I have learned the hard way that life is short and wholly without certainty. I haven't the time or inclination to pay mind to gossip.'

They stand in silence, neither budging from the brink of a divide. He has known every kind of partner, small men who prove industrious, large men prone to idleness. With someone untried there is no sure way of knowing. You rely on instinct, pray for luck. 'You are a woman,' he says again, a note of pleading in his voice.

'Yes, I am.' She gives a humourless laugh. 'Though I doubt the foxes and bears of Svalbard will pay mind to that detail.' She stands tight-lipped as she holds open the rear door of her cab. 'Perhaps the concern is your own reputation. That your trapping compatriots will think less of a free-thinking man.' A sniff to seal her disdain. 'Mr Rudi was mistaken when he spoke of you.'

'I make my own decisions.' His head is thick, the knock to his skull blooming to an egg. 'Best made with a clear mind,' Anders says gruffly, 'in the full light of day.'

FOX

a tattoo of scars

EGGS GROW SCARCE, outweighed by plump balls of down. Kittiwake and guillemot chicks tumble to the ground. The fox kits, bigger now, patrol the base of the mountain. They gorge on soft oily meat; they lick and pull at globules of fat lacing flesh to skin. Suddenly they grow wary of a sibling closing in. They gobble in haste, cramming skin and fluff into a bulging gullet before a contender makes a claim. They turn away to retch.

The kits lick their paws. They clean their muzzles of grease. They no longer sleep solely in the den but cross to a ledge or craggy lookout where they sit alone to survey their territory, peering out at ice sliding on the ocean. They crunch on a feather to pass the time of day. They nap then hunt then eat then cache whatever food remains. In slumber, their long tawny brush tails encircle snout and ears. See the eye flick open, the disk of amber. A sound? A scent? Even in sleep, they are alert to the slightest hint of movement.

The runt, the singular chocolate brown kit of the litter, roams farther, higher. Though food at the base of the slopes comes easy, too often she is the target of her siblings. The kits' play has grown fierce, territorial, a bearing of teeth, bites that puncture, a knot of bodies cascading to a brawl. Though they rarely make a sound, they snarl over territory, tear each other for the right to food, their teeth razor sharp.

The runt's back is matted with wounds, her neck a tattoo of scars. She is nearing her full height, agile and bold beyond her size. She climbs higher than her siblings and parents, looks down upon her family stalking the slopes. She squeezes through rocks that have shattered and split from freeze and thaw. Her body is so light she looks to fly, paws barely brushing ground. Daintily she pads along ledges too narrow and perilous for a larger fox. She climbs higher, clears the breadth of a chasm without hesitation or thought for how she will return.

She hears the agitated cry of guillemots along the mountain's narrow ledges. She knows the call of kittiwakes whose nests of seaweed, moss and twigs of Arctic willow are mortared with guano to stud these mountain slopes. Birds that sense a fox is near.

They rise tall, shuffle to the fore edge of their nests to shield their young. Along the guillemots' crammed ledge, the entire enclave grows raucous and panicked at the young runt's presence. Yet the ledge is too high for even an agile fox to reach. This small fox relies on attitude. A game of bluff.

Birds in the air shriek and swoop to divert attention from their young but the fox will not be deterred. She sees chicks on the ledges tremble, bereft of their parent. Birds flap, neighbours are knocked and jostled until one is shunted off balance and forced to take flight. The very air feels ruffled. Chicks cheep beseechingly. Their bodies reach out. The runt halts, her tongue slipping free, pink and wet. She salivates. Watches. A tussle. A tumble. She springs. The snatch. A gratifying crack of bone before the guillemot chick has even reached the ground. She holds the chick fast in her jaw. Feels the beating heart. She looks around for more.

2
———

Tromsø, early August

ON THE MORNING *Maiblomsten* sails, Anders cannot put to rest the workings of his decision which he now finds mystifying. Agreeing to take the woman has already come back to haunt him. The torrent of ridicule from fellow trappers. A turning of backs as if by naming a woman a trapper he has sullied their domain. Henry Rudi the one man to stand apart. A week ago, when he joined Rudi at his corner table, Anders quietly voiced his doubts. One week ago there was time, still, to rid himself of Wanny Woldstad, to pick a different partner.

What kind of man do you need? Rudi had asked.

Anders reeled off his customary list of wants. Someone steady and reliable. An even temperament. A man who could do the work and keep himself alive. What it came down to was a man with fortitude and nous. *She will never have that kind of strength or resilience. Or the common sense.*

Can she shoot? Rudi replied.

Now, this his final Tromsø morning, Anders has risen early, no more than a wink of sleep, to park himself on a bench at the dock – the need to clear his thoughts, the morning sun slow to lift above the hills, a slick of engine oil on the waterline around the timber pier, about him the ever-present whiff of rotting fish and fetid seal. Anders had asked the question of Henry Rudi: *What do you look for in a working partner?*

Much the same features, Rudi said, *though I'm yet to find them within a single man. A good dog*, he said, *now they come close.* The conversation turned to the best and worst sledging dogs they'd known: Greenland pure breeds deaf to every command other than to mush, dogs who run all day and expect no greater reward than a hunk of frozen seal meat and a scratch behind the ears; versus Anders's two young Alsatian mutts, brother dogs he bred up north last season, oversized puppies bigger on brawn than brains.

He and Rudi finished their beers and took their caps from the hook. Rudi off to Greenland's north-east, Anders once more back to Svalbard. A firm handshake to bid each other a safe and prosperous hunting season. Then Rudi stopped him on the footpath. *It often takes a close call*, he said to Anders, *before you can know your partner. Or yourself. A dash of humility is a quality that never goes astray. Nothing you don't already know.*

Advice that offered no clarity at all.

Anders studies his boots. Perhaps it falls to lack of choice. God knows he searched for someone better, finding fault, true enough, with men who sought him out. Perhaps it is this maddening urge to be gone, to rid himself of townsfolk and town living, get himself the fastest passage north. He scratches his head, looks to the hills. As likely it was sheer bloody-mindedness, the need to have the final say. It would not be the first time he has arced up against the strident voice of naysayers, giving as good as he got to those whose very cynicism against a woman trapper Anders himself privately harbours. He wants to think he's come a way since his younger days, his refusal to be harried back then too frequently landing him in trouble. Yet here he sits, older and so-called wiser, gazing at his boots, gulls squawking a mean kind of laughter at his lunacy. *Too late now, Sæterdal.* Half their gear gone ahead on a vessel that had space in its hold, the remainder stowed aboard *Maiblomsten*, awaiting final sign-off from the Customs men.

A different thought ticks through his head. The choice to take a woman: perhaps it falls to witchery. Face it. Somewhere in that strange encounter, following her across a field on a sultry summer's night, a man's rifle slung from that small shoulder – never mind the ale you'd drunk – you were dazzled by the prospect of a self-made woman, filled with bodily glow at where she might be leading you, what was on offer, more in your fancy than what she could do with a rifle. He will not admit to anyone the same tightening in his groin at the first sight of a polar fox padding past the hut, surveying the home territory. Out first thing to scatter titbits of seal meat amongst the rocks, hoping the small creature will pick his place for its den.

A prideful woman, Wanny Woldstad. Every bit as shrewd. *No, Sæterdal, she wanted none of you, except as a means to an end. It was she who chose you.*

❉

Steaming out between the islands on *Maiblomsten*, Wanny feels Anders Sæterdal watching. He is not alone. All five trappers aboard are sizing her up, they and their sledging dogs. Sæterdal's two Alsatians cast her the stink eye; but for her Mira, all are male dogs, whining and barking, pulling at the chains of their deck boxes. Wanny stops herself from kneeling to comfort Mira, curled tight and panting in the corner of her box; a dog who, in her seven years, has never known the sea. Opposite the rear deck towers trapper Schønning Hanssen, his great boots set apart with his knees crooked to ride the sea as if it were a horse, on his way to Hornsund's southern shore. The Italian Alberto Fumagalli, a young man with no more experience than her, is being taken along as Hanssen's partner to learn the trappers' life. The men laugh and joke with Fumagalli, his limited Norwegian no barrier to conversation; rather, a shortcoming that seems to bolster their jovial camaraderie. The trappers share tales with the Italian, offer him advice. Even the bosun has found him a length of rope to practise his knots. None, other than the captain, award Wanny such attention. These men are a brotherhood, fixed and firm.

Wanny listens to their talk, wanting to learn. *Spitsbergen* in one utterance, *Svalbard* the next, names loosely traded aboard the ship when speaking of the archipelago's largest island or the collection of islands. No wonder the Italian looks confused.

Wanny steps out from behind the wheelhouse to breathe in cold air, suddenly overheated in her woollen underwear and woollen trousers and sturdy new boots. Only her old leather coat feels soft and familiar. Her skin grows clammy with the motion. Nothing, not seasickness, not even Anders Sæterdal, can stop her now. She has leased her taxi to cover the loan, packed away her uniform and cap, folded up that neatly pressed version of self. She fretted over Skipper Svendsen's dim assessment of her gear and purchased a smart new trapper's hat from Andresens, the leather neatly stitched, the fur lining soft against her face. Fur mittens, the skipper urged, paw-like things as clumsy as boxing gloves. Sturdy new weather-proof boots. A pair of clogs for inside the hut – insulation from the frozen floor. Wanny baulked at the outlay, finally shamed into telling him she hadn't the means for more. *Reckless*, Wanny. Reckless and headstrong. She fixes her gaze homeward, commands her stomach to settle, the coast of northern Norway blurring into sea. Imagines that small girl in her father's fishing boat, willing him to motor her across the horizon, innocent to the twists and turns of life.

COLD COAST | 19

If Othar could see her now. If he could know the door he opened when he first handed her a rifle. Wanny closes her eyes. She winces at the bittersweet image of her husband unable to conceal his pride at her first championship. She blinks to the sight of Sæterdal scowling in her direction. It should have been Othar, not Anders Sæterdal, here by her side.

The ship's rigging whistles in the rising wind. Mira whimpers. Her dog turns anxious circles in her box. The ship lifts and falls. A shudder runs down its spine. No other trapper but herself and the Italian reach for the railing to keep their balance. Wanny turns to the sea, trains her eyes upon the horizon.

The open ocean, the land gone, is where Anders's Arctic year begins, running the gauntlet across the Barents Sea before the next weather front rolls in. Before him at the railing, the bronze-skinned Italian wears a pallor that bears the old familiar clamminess. Anders points him to the downwind side to retch. He sees the woman close her eyes and wince. She turns to grip the railing. No friends or family to see her off. Nought she gives away. Her expression of remorse serves to confirm his monumental error of judgement, his dread of being shackled. A year spent keeping a woman alive. A loan to be paid in twelve months' time, and he lumbered with the lion's share of work. Quick to learn, she has assured him. Can shoot the heart from a bear, he had skited like a fool to Henry Rudi.

Anders talks down his fears, tries to fathom hers. Is it the magnitude of the undertaking? Was he the same, his first season of trapping? He has scant recollection for feelings. He is not a man to pander to emotion. Ask him to name the features of a place, to list the markers of the land, pinpoint where on his memory map Hornsund's bears and foxes met their maker, he will pore over a map for hours.

Fangstmann Overvintrer 1932–33, the police registration lists the woman, applying the masculine form. *Fangskvinne* is a female hunter. Svalbard's first. Anders closes his eyes to sea spray and an image of women circling the pavement outside Mack Ølhallen, a net raised momentarily to let a single fish dart through.

FOX

days grow pale

DAYS GROW PALE. The dip of light lasts longer, painting the sky with change, languid with each turn. The height of each day clings to the old summer warmth, but vixen and her mate register the shift. Any day this mountainside of chicks will start to fledge. Young birds will follow their parents in a mad flapping of wings as they step out from their ledge to plunge to the water.

In these remaining weeks, vixen and dog fox will scoop up carcases of failed birds, will gorge themselves until their stomachs swell with pain, will cache all they cannot eat before the onset of the hard times, with the mountain barren and silent for winter. Soon, these wily parents will force their young to leave, working in tandem to bar them from the den, setting upon their young with a ferocity at odds with their care to raise the litter. This pair, their third season together, will guard den and territory as, kit by kit their young skulk away.

The vixen pads along the shoreline, past the fading stink of seaweed, leathered and sharp-edged, thrown up on shore. She stops at a sea urchin and puts her snout too near its spines. She steps back to sneeze. The vixen tracks up the gravel beach to a laid-out border of stones, an arched rib of bone. She slows at the empty trappers' hut where she squats and sprays against its wooden door, the brine of aged fox piss her claim upon this dwelling, each nitrogenous layer her measure of the hunters' absence. Each headland bears their mark: rough-hewn wooden frames left idle beneath gatherings of stone. Her kits saunter amongst these objects of men. They lick splintered sticks whose arrowed tips still bear the promise of ptarmigan.

These young know nothing of traps.

❄

The runt finds her mother along the cobbled shoreline beside a runnel of water that springs warm from the ground, winter and summer. The vixen laps, accustomed to its spicy warmth. The runt follows suit but quickly halts, water streaming from her muzzle. She paws at the running water, stamps and splashes, the warmth against her paws a novel sensation. Tentatively, she laps some more.

Onward her mother goes, the runt racing to reach her side. At the far end of the beach the vixen slows. In the distance, hovering low, a flutter of slender wings, kittiwakes aloft. Heavy glaucous gulls commandeer the shallows, the group closing in on a creature slowly floating into shore. A gull cranes its heavy bill to reach the prize. Another gull sets upon it. Squabbles break out until, in unison, the fractious gulls turn skyward to screech at kittiwakes who dart and dive, desperate to snatch the buoyant prize. The vixen lifts her snout to a telltale stench of putrefied meat: the creature a long time dead. Her focus remains on the heavy-set gulls, so intent on their greed they neglect to watch the shore where she and her youngling slink down in slow advance, the runt twitching in anticipation of the hunt.

The runt has taken guillemots that tumble from mountain ledges. She would lunge at these slow gulls this very moment if not for her mother who turns to nip her snout. The runt draws back in pain. The vixen returns her focus to the commotion of birds. She bides her time, still as rock, waiting for a pair of gulls to turn on one another before inching forward on her belly, over gravel, across the desiccated edges of seaweed. The vixen settles on her haunches. She shifts her weight. The group of birds is close. The vixen rises. She pounces headlong, kittiwakes shrieking and taking to the sky, the stealth hunter closing her jaws around the neck of a glaucous gull. She feels the bird struggle. She tightens her grip. Other gulls scatter, the runt running frantic circles, failing to take a single bird. The heartbeat of the gull stills. The vixen loosens her hold.

The runt paws at a creature floating at the shore, a dead fox, its bedraggled coat matted and balding, the fur a deep brown the same as her own. The carcase is neither punctured nor torn; instead, the fox has deflated, its ribs so pronounced that, with its coat plastered flat, its torso sports a pattern of rippled sand. Its eyes steely as dark cloud.

Grudgingly, the vixen shares her catch, the runt tearing scraps of breast meat, a warm strip of thigh. Mother and runt return to the fox carcase, the vixen sniffing its length, the runt perplexed when her mother saunters away.

She follows to where the vixen rests upon a grassy knoll to overlook the bay. The runt drapes herself across the soft round of her mother's back. She noses her mother's ears. The vixen licks the insides of her paws to wipe her muzzle and eyebrows. She grooms the fur across her chest, loose whisps plucked by the wind. The vixen tires of the weight of her youngling and squirms free. She rolls to her side to clean between her hind legs. She combs the underside of her brush with short, sharp strokes. At the prospect of her exposed teats, the runt nuzzles the vixen's belly, searching out her milk. The vixen bares her teeth. She gives a sharp kick to shove the youngling away. The runt yips at the strike. She sits back to wait her turn but her mother wants none of it. The vixen darts away.

3

———

Hyttevika, late August

HYTTEVIKA. HUT BAY. His hut. Anders bends back the nail heads, slides the locking bar free. Gingerly he removes the window shutter, avoiding the tips of nails driven pointed end out to ward off bears. Wood gritty with the sting of salt. Two months he's been gone, his hands grown soft.

He unlatches the hut door and lets his eyes adjust. Behind him he hears the woman's sniff of distaste at the acrid smell of fox piss. A jumble of discarded tins, pots, enamel basins strewn throughout the inside porch.

'A fox has been,' he tells her. Better a fox than a bear inside a hut.

The door to the main room opens to a wan stream of light, to a scent of pine and driftwood that usually fills Anders with verve. He draws in the taint of mould and detritus. Perhaps the hut has always held this stench. Perhaps, left unchecked, a man's senses loosen, wrenched back in line by a woman's disapproving sniff.

He watches her kneel to inspect the stove, seeing anew that the cast iron shows more rust than black, the concentric rings buckled. The stovepipe leans at a gaping angle with soot blown throughout the room. *Feral*, Anders's wife once named him. *No better than an animal.* He'd made himself into the brute she claimed him to be, refused to bathe, had sat down to the table before his children with a foul mouth and the manners of a pig. He'd bellowed it was she, Othelie, who drove him back to Svalbard, a place free of nit-picking women to smear a man for who he was. Sæterdal: forever the man to boast the final word. To own the last regret. Anders looks to Wanny Woldstad turning a fault-finding circle, inspecting the lacking state of this open room where they will eat and sleep and work. His shoulders tense.

The large pot of ice he'd left on the stovetop has turned to water, upon it a skim of grease. The firebox is set with kindling split from last season's left-over packing crates. Atop the stove a pair of matches protrudes from their box, ready to strike, the standard welcome for any *polfarer* seeking refuge.

Anders carts boxes and rolls barrels from foreshore to hut. He sees the woman follow his lead, overly eager to help, which only serves to annoy him. The dinghy from *Maiblomsten*, and a second belonging to the hut, move between ship and shore like passing trams, one empty and swift, the other labouring shoreward, low in the water from boxes, sacks, skis and ski poles, rifles, chain, his new sledge – a glorious, honed construction made by the same Sámi herder who built his first one. By evening, light bronzes the tarred walls, the outside of the hut a barricade of supplies. The woman stands with a broom in her hand. She picks up a basin. 'Shall I make a start?'

'Marking your territory?' He cannot hold the sneer from this voice. Will he ever be able to put aside this grudge?

❄

He and the woman are the last from *Maiblomsten* to be dropped off. First, a party and their dogs sent ashore at Bjørnøya, Bear Island, the first landfall across the Barents Sea. Closer to Hyttevika, Hanssen and his animated Italian are now in residence on the south shore of Hornsund. Anders and the woman row back out to *Maiblomsten* to eat and sleep, the vessel a mile out, anchored amongst the islands. 'Some years,' Anders tells her, 'no skipper of sense would bring a vessel in through these skerries.'

The evening meal is a spread of roasted venison and potatoes – *in honour of Mrs Woldstad*, says Skipper Svendsen, *a lady's final night in civilisation*.

Anders grows weary of the old man's solicitude. From the first day at the dock, the captain has been the self-proclaimed authority on the needs of Mrs Wanny Woldstad. The right kind of hat, the best shoes and coat, *essential for winter above all else*. Had she turned to Anders he would have looked over her things, loaned her what she needed and had the rest make do.

He stands alone on the deck with Storm and Karo, free from their boxes, circling and sniffing and merrily cocking a leg against each of the ship railings. His dogs' second winter at this site. Both born inside that hut. Karo looks to him and gives a happy bark. 'Back home, boy.'

The woman's dog, Mira, refuses his offer of freedom from her box. *No shortage of grit*, the woman had crowed when offering her working dog to seal the deal. Mira rests her chin on her paws, a picture of despondency.

Anders closes his eyes to an image of the rough cobbled shore, the hut set back, stones piled against the windward wall to brace it from the wind. Is there any bolder stake of man than a refuge built in such a place? Rock. Mountain. Terraces of snow. These endless pointed peaks. Shipmen like Svendsen would never understand. Shipmen would think these slopes a wasteland.

He kneels to Storm settled beside him. A scratch beneath the chin, a good brisk ear rub. Anders fills his lungs with the breadth of the land; he bathes himself in gilded light, his breath apace with the lapping beat of ocean. Shreds of seaweed sail by. Shards of ice drift in and bump the shoreline. To the east of Hyttevika the ice tongue of the glacier slicks out across Hornsund's broad waterway. Directly behind the ship are the Down Islands, Dunøyane, dormant until next year's spring when eiders return to nest and breed. Anders tilts his face to the sky. Voice and laughter waft from the stateroom. Svendsen and his crew gone barmy in the woman's presence. He wants to call her up on deck, he wants her to *see*, pay homage to this simple, other world.

He is a man adrift.

❄

A breeze blows, the sky laden with gunmetal cloud, mountains obscured. Skipper Svendsen comes ashore with the final boat-load of supplies. He hands the woman a large package held taut with string. 'True to my word,' he says brusquely. 'A *pelskåpe* to keep you through the winter.' To Anders he hands a promissory. 'Now, you have to be kind to Mrs Woldstad. I expect you to take good care of her.'

'I expect her to take care of herself.'

Anders sees her give a nod of support. The skipper moves out of earshot before she sets down the parcel. 'I thought I had made it clear to him.' She gestures to the promissory. 'That is for me?'

He blinks at the amount. 'Let us hope so.' He passes it over.

He hears her breath catch. 'What do you take it to mean?'

Anders scratches his head. The woman runs her own taxi. Surely she understands the workings of a loan. 'That the coat was bought on your say-so. That you agree to repay Svendsen in twelve months' time. Credit is the way of things up here.'

'Without assurance?'

He gestures to the boxes stacked against the wall. 'The kit,' he says. 'The lease on this territory. All of it bought on credit. To be paid for with what we make in the season.'

'We will make enough?'

She asks this now? Anders shrugs. Hunting, trapping, guessing when the pack ice will form and bring in the bears. 'Only two things are certainties: the long polar night and the long polar day.'

She looks to him, expecting more. 'It depends on how much we catch,' he says, exasperated. 'The grade of fur, our fortune with the bears.'

'On working well together,' she adds.

'That is so.'

She folds the promissory and slips it in her pocket. 'But there is no surety.'

What does she need him to say? 'Myself, other trappers, your Mr Rudi in years gone by, we've had our share of luck in these parts.' The parcel of coat sits at their feet. 'Wanny,' he says, a name too intimate for a woman he barely knows and wishes rid of. But to continually name her *Mrs Woldstad* in the captain's way sounds altogether absurd. She has no place here. Anders circles back his thoughts. 'If a person craves the kind of life where every turn is assured, he . . . she, would never leave the shores of Tromsø. We each do our work; each pull our weight. I repay what is borrowed. Anything on top of that we divide. Equal partners.' *Too hasty, Sæterdal, too late to claim a greater share.* He collects the parcel, weighs the bulk of it in his hold. 'You will not be swept away in the wind.'

Wanny walks with Svendsen along the shoreline. She feels child-like beside his bulk as he jabbers on about this 'godforsaken place'.

She blurts the words. 'I do not need the fur coat.'

His look of surprise. A glimmer of satisfaction? 'You are coming home?'

'I am asking if you will return it to the store. Please.'

No mistaking the flicker of irritation. 'The coat was special order.' Then he softens; a fatherly hand placed on her shoulder.

'I do not have a good feeling about this, Mrs Woldstad. This is no place for the gentle sex. Return to the ship. Sæterdal is a bullock on two legs. He will manage well enough alone.'

Sæterdal watches from the hut. At the shoreline beside the dinghy, the bosun and a crewman wait, glancing her way, impatient to be gone. This presiding world of men. All this space and still she stands contained.

'There is no shame in coming home, no shame at all.'

Wanny wants to scream at the ocean: *This is where I want to be! Where I've longed to come.* If they knew all she has sacrificed to be here, the toll it has taken. Even pushing her case to Anders Sæterdal had felt desperate. The day he acquiesced to take her she'd thrown her driver's cap high in the air, pledged to him: *I will not let you down.*

Wanny steps away. 'Of course I will honour the arrangement, Captain. Just as I will honour my time here.'

❄

The clanging of the anchor chain reverberates across the water to the shoreline where she stands beside Sæterdal. *Sjefen*, Chief, the men call him. They watch as the boat swings out, three warbling horn blasts to signal farewell. A year before they will see another ship. A year away from those she holds most dear. She draws herself firm, raises her arm, imagining how, from out there, she and he are two stick figures, barely human, marooned in frozen vastness.

When the ship motors from view, too late to change her mind, a man's voice comes to her as sharply as the wind that shimmies down the mountain and knocks a fist between her shoulder blades. An aging voice crackling with despair. *No shame?* it beseeches. *Is it not enough to turn your back on the man who has kept you through these years? What kind of mother forsakes her own sons?*

The shrill of wind casts itself across the ocean.

The Chief turns up his collar. 'So.' He rubs his hands. She hasn't seen him grin so. 'Shall we make a start?'

A start. A beginning. Surely she has earned herself this chance. Surely life can credit her this one marvellous thing.

FOX

a parade of antlers

THE REINDEER FAMILY slows at the hummock of beach, a crunch of hoofs sinking into gravel. They barely register the trappers' hut, intent on grazing. They amble beyond to the grassy slope. The largest, the stag, halts to rub its antlers in jolting sweeps across the ground. This maddening urge to rid its bone of velvet, tattered and torn, russet with dried blood.

The runt remains at a distance, curious, lacing the scene into the many scenes which shape her world. She has walked amongst antlers on the slopes, antlers bleached and part buried by tundra that grows higher and lusher than on the surrounds. She has stopped to lick and gnaw at these branches of bone. She raises her snout to the animal that wears them, a creature that is neither bird nor fox. She blinks at the creature's bulk, the spindle legs, set low beneath a stockiness of body, the round of the belly.

The female's antlers are smaller and simple. The calf, unsteady on its feet and clumsy of gait, bumps against its mother as the adult reindeer slow their pace. The family settle to graze, heads down, the male chewing at an awkward angle as if either its ear is painful or the weight of the antlers is too hefty to balance. The sounds of snuffling, snorting, a bovine scent filling the air of Fuglefjell.

The fox studies the three white rumps, the powder puff tails. She sits tall when the female alters her stance, back legs spread wide. The doe continues grazing as a rush of liquid arcs to the ground, splatters on stones.

The runt dozes against a cushion of moss campion, the tiny pink flowers releasing a sweet floral oil. A different scent blinks her awake. She opens her eyes, surveys the scene. The family of reindeer rest on their flanks, back legs splayed, front legs tucked under as they slumber in the afternoon warmth. The male and female sit at a distance, the calf against its mother's side. The runt lifts her nose to track dog fox, her father, circling the animals, approaching the stag from downwind and behind.

Catapulted into action, dog fox bounds toward the stag, nips at its rump, retreats at speed, as if to determine whether the stag is living or dead. The stag twitches awake, turns its weighty head to issue a huff. Begone. After minutes chewing its cud the stag resettles. It closes its eyes, sun shining, breeze ruffling its coat. The stag is once again beset, dog fox a fraction of its size. The runt's father targets the reindeer's rump, digs his canines into the stag's fleshy cheek beneath the puff of tail. The reindeer quivers with pain, staggers to its feet beneath a teetering headdress. Female and calf rise in unison. Dog fox trots away with a carriage that might be skulking or satisfaction. No longer inclined to graze, the reindeer move off around the headland, the vegetation flattened with the imprint of their shape.

4

_____

Hyttevika, early September

WANNY BLINKS AWAKE. Close above her a blur of ceiling boards; below, an empty bunk. The ship gone. Their first morning. She feels thankful to be alone in the hut without the Chief scowling. She closes her eyes to firewood spitting hot inside the stove, the savour of brewed coffee, a lingering backdrop of ammonia – its cloying aftertaste testament to hard soap and scrubbing. She senses a glare of light, sharp from the east through newly cleaned windows.

On the toss of a coin, at the Chief's say-so, she had opted for the top bunk. *There is less of me*, she'd said, deeming it fair that he should take the better bed. Now she swelters inside this itchy reindeer bag, the warmth from the stove rising, the coarse hair of reindeer a furnace on her skin. A loose hair tickles her face. She pouts it away, rubs at her nose. The bunk boards are padded with folded grey blankets, utilitarian things striped down the centre, the kind that were old when she and Othar married. Over the mattress is a cover of fleece, the sheep's wool matted and flat from seasons of use. This earthy blend of animal and scented wood. The sound of the sea. A long deep sleep that brings to mind her childhood home.

She hears sharp yelps from Mira, her dog unaccustomed to being fixed to a chain while the two brother dogs roam free.

Wanny fingers the ceiling. Still the boards feel gritty. *Let it go, Ivanna.* Didn't the Chief say as much in his own gruff way? Yesterday she had inched across the floor on hands and knees, a cloth knotted to keep back her hair, the basin of water too quickly turning cold and scummed with grease. He had walked into the room as she was dragging a meat fork along the joins to prise out dried gut and blubber. She felt caught out by the stiffness to his voice. *The boards will be soaked with innards soon enough.* She hears him out there now, his axe not the rhythmic thudding of logs but agitated strikes. Each packing box smashed to splinters.

Anders greets the woman with a nod, her makeshift tray a plank of pine bearing mugs of coffee, brown cheese and ryebread – a parting gift from *Maiblomsten.* He lays down the broad axe, sweeps the chopping block to make a seat. He upends a crate and parks himself down. 'How did you sleep?'

'A relief not to be rocking around on the ocean,' she says.

She looks different from the woman on the ship, hair tied in tails, shirtsleeves rolled, broad braces buttoning her trousers. She wears a wedding ring as if to remind him of her standing. She need not fret on his account. 'Hard work and fresh air,' he says, the secret to sleep. The ocean glisters, the islands a mirage. 'A night without wind to yank you from your dreams.'

The northern sky is a sheet of blue so piercing that his eyes water; to the south a thick band of cirrus marches this way. 'Weather on the way according to the barometer.' Right now, Anders feels comfortable in a woollen singlet and shirt. A still Arctic day with a warmth that belies its temperature; come afternoon, he'll be reaching for his coat.

She shields her eyes from the sun. 'Too many mountains to count,' she says. 'It beggars belief.'

Anders looks around, expecting to see it as she does. All he registers is the volume of work needing to be done before the days close in. He turns to the hut. 'We can move the boxes into the porch.' He has blocked the hole where the fox tunnelled in. 'The hut has never known such a work-over.' A compliment wrapped in aggravation. The hut now carries the stamp of the world he left. A feral trapper ready to be tamed. He gives a hard laugh. 'I doubt the men who hefted wood from the shore to build this hut would shake my hand today.'

'Me, you mean?'

Anders drains his coffee, downs bread and cheese. *Sæterdal, when did you turn so mean?* He sets down his empty mug. 'You are not expected to wait on me.'

'I am here to learn. Do things as you need them done.'

Stuck with one another is the truth of it. The only option forward is to make the best of it. He feels a new weight of silence. He has offended her. You never have to find your way through a maze of niceties with men. 'Then learn the landmarks,' he says. 'How to find your way back home. Once trapping begins you will often be out there on your own. In darkness and weather. The constant risk of bears. We'll take a walk once we finish our coffee.' She gazes about in a way that reminds him of his daughter the first time he took her to Tromsø, dizzy with it all. Has the woman heard a thing he's said?

'When do we expect to start?' she asks.

'Start?'

'Trapping. Hunting.'

Her eyes spark with thrill, or perhaps a latent kind of fear. He needs someone steady. 'I've never set a trap this side of October twenty-fourth.' Anders taps his nose in superstition. 'Another month for the fox to reach condition. A month more for the pack ice to bring in the bears.'

'How will we fill the time?'

Anders laughs aloud. Where does he begin? Getting in all the seal they can catch, hunting for ptarmigan and the last of the geese before they fly south. A ton of driftwood to gather and split. Whittling countless trigger pegs and bait sticks for the fox traps. He has at least six *selvskudds*, self-shooting traps ready for the bears, to build and bed into place across the landscape. Ahead of them are trips east in the dinghy to ferry gear and provisions to the two satellite huts they will also be using. 'I expect we will find a thing or two.'

She gathers the tray and moves inside. 'Bring a shotgun. Plenty of slugs,' he calls. 'Your coat and rucksack.' He has reverted to a parent.

The landscape is a jumble of stone. Inland the ground sheers upward to the mountains; seaward are stony beaches, rocky bays, wind-ruffled ocean. The Chief with his long legs bounds ahead. Wanny concentrates on her footing across loose scree. She is fit from winter skiing and skating on the lake, but wishes they could slow their pace; she would like to amble, take in the wonder. The Chief points to the sun's track relative to this peak, that headland. He talks about points on the compass – she has never used a compass. He draws his arm in a sweep to show how the autumn sun slides along the top of that sharp ridge on its dip toward winter. The landscape is nothing like the chocolate box beauty of home. It is exactly as Mr Rudi coined it – *a starkness fierce with splendour.*

It saps Wanny of conversation. Keeping an orderly hut, cooking on a second-rate stove, sleeping on a hard, wooden bunk: these things she can do without question. But those are not why she is here. She has to work and manage out here on her own. She half listens, uttering a *yes* or giving a nod to each of the Chief's instructions.

Even growing up on Sommarøy, spending much of her childhood exploring the island alone, there was still an ever-present sense of people: voices over a hill, a woman tilling a paddock, the *donk*, *donk* of a boat engine, the aromatic scent of pipe tobacco. Here in Hornsund, it is she and the tall man ahead, two human heartbeats in a vast, alien terrain.

Wanny looks to the mountains. She turns to an expanse of ocean, giddy with wonderment. A godless land, Mr Rudi named it.

Settle, Ivanna. Do not lose your head.

They follow the coast southward, four or five kilometres of home territory. 'Trapping grounds for fox and bear when the time comes,' he tells her. '*Rype* nest across the scree. The only bird to stay through winter. We bait the fox traps with *rype*.' Where a stream braids through the gravel, they pick their way across raised ribbons of wet ground. They pass marshland and head toward a tarn, the surrounds lush with moss and reed.

A *hoot-hoot*.

'Geese,' the woman says.

'Pink-footed.' He knows each kind by its call. Anders slips the shotgun from his shoulder. 'The far side. There.' He points. 'We wait, see if they come closer. In spring these tarns are thick with birds.'

'Should I get my rifle ready?'

'This time you watch and learn.' At least she doesn't drive him mad with mindless talk.

He kneels, unmoving, his elbow beneath the gun anchored on the soft part of his knee. He keeps his voice to a murmur. A flash of movement, a fracas: Anders watches geese race across the water, a beating of wings. He takes up his gun but already the flock is in the sky, moving away.

He nods. 'There you are.' A small creature padding across the tundra. A fox, pale, its tawny patches almost washed out. It stops abruptly, stares their way.

'How does it know?' the woman says.

'Sixth sense. As it is with all these wild creatures.' He sets down the shotgun. 'A young one, probably just left the den, finding its way on its own. Which means there will be more.'

'You won't shoot it?'

Anders stands. He slings his gun back across his shoulder. 'No one pays for a pelt ruined with shot.'

'I see.'

He feels his temper spike. 'Do you?' A partner who knows nothing. 'What do you say about its colour?'

'The fox is white.'

He issues a sonorous snort. A taste of her own medicine. 'Not even close. The coat is rubbish. We let it settle, wait for it to fully grow its winter pelt.' He taps his nose. 'October twenty-fourth.'

A chill wind blows down the mountain; cloud scuds overhead. Wanny buttons her leather coat, hindered by straps but not daring to stop to rearrange the load. The weight of the shotgun strapped across her shoulder tugs at her rucksack. Any creature worth shooting will be long gone by the time she sorts herself out. They trudge upward, the loose scree streaked white with guano and whiffs of ammonia, yet there are no creatures in sight. They reach larger rocks edged with snow.

For an hour they climb, Wanny taking care over slabs slick with snowmelt, through ankle-deep patches of snow. Warnings she was given back in Tromsø whisper to her now, from infected wounds to a burst appendix, to plunging headlong into a bottomless crevasse. No chance of rescue. No outside help should she break a limb or grow unwell. No one will know if she plummets from a mountain ledge or, most gruesome, is taken by a bear. Even Mr Rudi, normally so jovial. *You go with the understanding that you rely on yourself. Your partner will not be waiting in the wings to save you. You get yourself into trouble, you get yourself out.*

Wanny believed she knew much about survival on her own, but this is different. *Your boys,* said her friend from the farm where her sons are boarded for the year. Bjørvik and Alf were too young to comprehend the loss of their father and yet their lives have been altered. She is all the flesh and blood they have. What mother ushers risk through her own front door, a woman's wild needs ahead of her small ones' welfare? *A woman without a heart.*

Wanny looks ahead to the Chief's lean frame, his long strides, hears snippets of a tune. An odd man, surly in one breath, pensive the next, both sides a contrast to the rakish, pumped-up type he made himself to be in Tromsø. He, not she, is the one marking out his territory.

She chides herself. Be grateful to Anders Sæterdal. Look at the chance he has given you, how badly you longed to be here. Yet it wounds her, this slap of rejection now that they are here.

Be patient, Ivanna. Earn your place.

In every crevice a plant: the scraggly remains of yellow saxifrage, tufts of moss campion, their pink flowers mostly spent but still a splash of cheeriness against the rock. The Chief starts up a steep promontory. The air feels sharp. When he turns to look back from where they've come, Wanny hears his laboured breath. 'Two months of town living is enough to kill a man.'

Onward they go.

This last summer, Wanny collected a woman in her taxi from Tromsø's Grand Hotel. When she asked the destination, the woman threw up her hands. 'I have the afternoon. Take me somewhere out of the way, a place you like to go.'

Wanny had suggested Sommarøy because the woman was wearing a floral summer frock and Sommarøy, by name and nature, was the perfect place for summer. A fishing village that had been coined the Riviera for its white beaches and turquoise water, for its view of the island of Håja's remarkable mountain, a pyramid of rock rising from the ocean, more grand in its design than any castle or cathedral. The woman seemed unconcerned that part of the route would be a pot-holed track. 'If you are game, dear, then so am I.'

Wanny warmed to the woman's spirit. They would have been a similar age, although a different league. The woman was a contrast of pale skin and coiffured hair, elegant in the manner she sat straight-backed, a small handbag at her side. She was travelling alone, itself a curiosity. During the ride they had eased into friendly conversation, the woman complimenting Wanny. Even in Oslo, she said, she had never heard of a woman chauffeur. 'Your husband does not object to an enterprising wife?'

Without thought, 'I am widowed,' Wanny had uttered. All the intervening years and this, still, is how she views herself.

None of the usual platitudes. No commiserations. 'Then I say you are fortunate to do as you please.'

Wanny had concentrated on the road. She had sought out the woman in the rear-view mirror. 'You are widowed?'

'Why do you ask?'

'You travel alone.'

'My husband stays in Oslo.'

Wanny's hands tightened on the wheel. A woman who wanted for nothing, passing judgement on her life. 'Then you are also fortunate. Yes?'

'How so?'

'To be free to travel as you please. Without the bother of a husband.' *Uncalled for, Ivanna.*

'Touché,' the woman said quietly.

The return trip had passed in thoughtful silence. Parked outside the hotel, the woman handed Wanny the fare, a brilliant day's takings, plus an extra note. Wanny thanked her and stepped around to open the door.

'May I say something?' The woman stood beside her on the footpath. 'Perhaps it was different for you. I meant no offence. For me, I never understood that marriage could be so lonely. So . . . ordinary.'

She had met the woman's pensive gaze but could not bring herself to speak.

'You think me churlish,' the woman said. 'All that I have.'

'It is not my place to judge you.' She could not tell her that with Othar there had been only love, their time together charged with promise and purpose. She could not proffer these pure moments of her life without owning who she has become.

Were it a different situation, had they been of equal standing, Wanny would have held that woman in her arms, not to offer solace but to honour her admission, an unnamed woman in a smart summer frock, more valorous and honourable than she.

Wanny adjusts her rucksack, pulls taut her rifle strap. She registers a dull throb deep inside her bones, an inexplicable ache she has carried through a good part of her life.

From where she and the Chief rest at the saddle of the mountain, Wanny looks down to the coastal strip, to a series of tarns and a braided stream running out to the coast. She looks north-west to Hyttevika, the site of their meagre dwelling. Their hut is set on a narrow strip of lowland between mountain and sea. From this height, its framework of driftwood planks is as tiny as a matchbox. A belt of pale stone keeps it anchored to the earth. 'A humble abode amid all this grandeur,' she says.

'The main base is the Grand Hotel compared to our pair of satellite huts.'

They stand above the mouth of Hornsund, a broad inroad of water that cuts through the south-west corner of Spitsbergen. Ice dots its breadth. Slicks of muddy glacial melt bleed into the blue, curdling the fjord.

A band of emotions charges through her. A thread of exhilaration, of fear, the sharp realisation of her own inadequacy against this land's might. It has her grappling to gain her bearings.

'Gåshamna.' The Chief points to the southern side of the fjord. 'Look,' he says. 'You see Hanssen there?' Wanny follows to where he points. 'The Italian is wearing his funny hat.'

Wanny peers intently before she catches his expression. It takes her a long moment to realise he is teasing her. She loosens. It feels so very good to laugh. 'How far is it?' she asks him.

'Ten kilometres give or take. Feels twice as long rowing on your own.'

'What brought you here, Chief?'

'To Hornsund?'

'To Spitsbergen. The trapper's life.'

'The Depression, to start, same as every other man needing to find a different means of living. A year or two's trapping, I told my wife. Our children were still small. Come home a rich man.' He turns away from her. She hears discomfort in his voice. 'Turns out the pelts paid a fraction of what they once fetched. So, here I am, still, six years on.'

'Your family do not mind?' Wanny ventures. A question not hers to ask.

He gives a hard laugh. 'These days my daughter and son live with their mother.' He turns to the waters of Hornsund. 'She'd soon tell you this life is for a single man. That her children barely know their father.'

'When they are old enough, could you bring them up here, share it with them?'

He gives a grunt. 'Their mother would have her own views on that idea.'

On the opposite side of the ridge, across to the east, Wanny looks down to a small peninsula, at its heel a tiny stamp of grey in the shape of a shed.

'Once you start up here,' the Chief says, 'it alters you. The work, the life. It becomes something other than the money.' He speaks to the fjord, as if she is forgotten. 'Svalbard suits who I am. The land. The space. No one but myself to answer to.'

Beyond the finger of land an ice tongue pushes out across the water. Inland is a patchwork of crater rims, knife-edge ridges, pointed mountains too numerous to count, each broad valley filled with a river of ice. It is not simply the sight of all this wonder that has her turn to look again; it is the need to place herself solidly within it. People see her as a woman of small stature but out in nature she has always felt tall, made bigger and stronger by breathing in the mountains of home. Yet here she is as small as a saxifrage flower. 'It is a grand design,' she says. Wanny could trick herself into thinking that the length and breadth of Spitsbergen is made of countless islands floating in a frozen sea. 'It makes a mockery of the glaciers at home.' All the stories the trappers tell; none can fully prepare you.

The Chief points to the ice tongue. 'The glacier is Hansbreen.' A thick trunk of ice slicking out across the water; inland, its frozen branches wind around the mountains. 'Down there, this side of the glacier, you see the first satellite hut?'

'The shed?'

'That shed is the hut. Isbjørnhamn. Ice Bear Harbour. The halfway point of our travels. Mostly we use the hut to rest overnight. Isbjørnhamn is the place we leave the rowboat over winter.

'Why not Hyttevika?'

'Come spring, beneath the glacier is the first frozen stretch to break out into open water. First chance to use the boat.' He points east to a mountain rising from the far side of the glacier. 'Fannytoppen. We angle down its slopes to reach the last satellite hut built beneath the cliffs and ledges of Fuglefjell.'

Fuglefjell. Bird Mountain. More names to learn.

'In summer Fuglefjell is the place for birds. Where there are birds there are certain to be foxes. We've had good luck there in the past. Blue foxes and whites.'

Blue? She dare not show her ignorance. 'All of it is your territory?'

'And yours,' he says, kindlier than the man he was this morning. 'Around three miles from Hyttevika to Fuglefjell. As far east as we go. By the time you leave Hornsund next year you'll know the way with your eyes closed.'

He means three Norwegian miles. Thirty kilometres. A sixty-kilometre round trip. 'We'll cross the glacier?'

'Come winter. For now, it's the sea route in the dinghy. I was hoping to secure a motorboat this season. It wasn't to be.'

At last, a task she can do. 'I'd row out to the fishing banks when I was small. I'd rather that than help in the kitchen.'

'Where?' he asks.

Wanny feels a small unwinding. 'Sommarøy, until I left for work. My father fished when I was small.' The first of herself she has wanted to give. 'When he died I helped my mother run the farm.'

'I see,' he says wistfully. 'Very good then. The boat has two sets of oars. You can show me how it's done.'

FOX

the tundra closes down

THE LARGEST KIT halts at the headland, looks back at the den where vixen and dog fox stand watch. The vixen sees her young-ling raise its muzzle and turn its snout. East, it will go. The rising wind carries seed and dust, and when the vixen blinks grit from her eyes the kit is gone.

The first.

The mountain grows less raucous. Chicks fledge and those that drop from the sky are sparse now. Guillemots vacate their ledges and fly out to sea with no urge to return until next season. Pair after pair, kittiwakes abandon their nests. Last to leave the lofty reaches of Fuglefjell are fulmars. They linger on the slopes and circle in the thermals; they fish and feed then rest upon the water, bulking up before their journey south.

Across the slopes the tundra closes down. A metre below, summer and winter, the ground never thaws. Leaves of Arctic willow turn gold and russet; they wither, consumed into the permafrost's water-logged skin. The spent fronds of bell heather, the desiccated stalks of lousewort and knotweed, slowly crumble into powder. Late bloom flowers on northern slopes lose brilliance and fade; seed heads part from their stalks. The vixen sees wisps of Arctic cotton dance through the air, its white fluff catching the back of her mate. But for his tawny underside, dog fox wears a coat of winter white. All but one kit in his image, their young now fully grown.

Only the runt mirrors the vixen, their dark summer coats lost to the moult. The winter fur is not fully silver, not quite the hue of pewter, while the tips, dark as coal dust, add to the pelt's strange metallic glow. Blue, the trappers call their kind, though the colour is nothing like the face of a glacier whose sapphire ice cracks and calves, thunderous, into the fjord. This pelt brings to mind the dusting of moraine that Svalbard's frozen rivers heave on their backs; an assortment of ice, stone and grit that is lustrous in one light while steely as a mountain in another.

The vixen and her youngling wear a jet snout. The eyes, rimmed with black, shine glassy as obsidian. Only when light penetrates their gaze is the amber of the iris apparent. No mistaking lineage: stark white fur brands each of their muzzles and runs as a ridge from snout to crown. Dark fur concentrates around their ears. Each blue fox exudes a precious metal glow. The trappers say one fox in ten litters is born this odd, arresting colour, these blues who fetch the sweetest price.

The runt naps high up on the slopes, her tail curled around her muzzle to shield her from the wind. Her belly, swollen and stretched tight, pulses with bird and entrails, splinters of bone, a bolus of grass, the briny tang of seaweed. A sound. A rhythm. She opens an eye, raises her head.

The vessel rounds into view. Two sets of oars clip the water. An upright creature seated at the back; another, higher, in the front. The boat creaks and grates beneath a hillock of shapes.

The runt stands, puzzled at the arrangement. Wholly alert.

She tips her ears to voices snatched by the wind. Draws in their strange scent.

The trappers heave their oars, waves slopping hard as the laden boat inches into shore.

5

Fuglefjell, September

FUGLEFJELL, BIRD MOUNTAIN: the trappers' local name for towering stone walls and craggy cliffs rising up through pockets of mist. Against its craggy base rest landslides of gravel, outcrops of rock, fallen boulders, terraces of tundra. Wanny realigns her focus to bring this furthest satellite hut into being. A tiny hut whose fore edge sits proud of the ground, dainty and inviting with its sweep of native grass, long and lush around the bleached rib whalebone propped against its pocket-sized portico. The back half of the hut is sunk deep, weighted down by the mountain's boot of rubble.

The Chief, desperate to step ashore, rushes to the boulders at the far end of the beach. If she were a fellow, he'd have no need for privacy. She had denied her thirst during the five-hour rowing trip. Her throat feels parched yet the sting of her bladder presses upon her. She paces up the gravel beach, the boat's anchor in her grip. She stamps it firm amongst the loose cobbles that form this roughened beach – greys and rusts and sea-worn rounds as pale as ivory.

Along the brow of the beach, a wound ball of dried kelp, hummocks of seaweed whose briny stink she draws deep into her lungs, as pungent as spice. She paces in the opposite direction to the

Chief, slows where trickles of water burble up through the gravel to wet the stone. Water warm to her fingers. Fresh. A spring. A faint smell of sulphur. The pads of her palms, the crook of each thumb, are red raw from working oars too large a girth. Her thoughts turn to the dogs, Mira and the two Alsatians, thirty kilometres away at Hyttevika, left chained to a long line at the main base hut. The Chief had filled their drinking trough with slabs of ice dripping from melt, their only sustenance a hunk of meat thrown their way on leaving. His dogs were born up here, used to gorging during feast-time to withstand the famine. Her poor Mira learned just in time to claim her portion of food, issuing a snarl, teeth bared, before the Alsatians snatched her meal away.

Wanny hears the cry of birds high up on the mountainside, somewhere hidden in the mist, though the Chief tells her the guillemots and kittiwakes have all but flown for the winter. Out in the fjord, beyond reef and hidden rocks where waves surge and break, flocks of dovekies settle – birds so numerous, so tiny, they move across the fjord as a shadow cast by dappled cloud. Ice. So much ice the glare of it pains her eyes. At the head of the bay two glaciers splinter with sunlight. The fjord shimmers and sparkles with bergs and drifting floes. The Chief had grumbled about the time it took to detour around a floe or pick their way between the smaller bits, but Wanny pinched herself. To be here, amongst all this wonder.

She finds a high rock and squats behind it, eyes to the ocean, her back to a warm *foehn* wind that runs down the mountain and skips across the fjord, teasing open stretches of that great broad waterway into rushing waves. Wanny's head throbs, thick with dehydration. A telltale cramp grips deep within her abdomen. The last thing she needs. She inspects the wadding that lines her underwear. The discomfort is nothing. Her concern is the first heavy days, the need to check and change, and how will it play out with slopes to climb and hours of work to be done? She watches a pair of oystercatchers totter down to the waterline. They fossick amongst weed, their orange bills fluorescent against their shimmering black.

Where will she rinse and dry these offending markers of womanhood? Even the most strident naysayer in Tromsø hadn't dared raise this delicate topic when naming her unfit for the Arctic.

She buttons her woollen trousers, tucks down her shirt-tails, damp with sweat. She pulls her braces back on her shoulders. *You get on with it, Ivanna. You manage best you can.*

❄

Fox spoor: tracks every place Anders looks, scattered around the hut, fresh scats along the shoreline, evidence of the many fox that patrol these slopes. Lean years might see all the young pushed out early to fend for themselves. The old Hornsund trappers speak of seasons of plenty, gilded years when a single family with a dozen kits patrol these slopes, amongst them the blues. If food is plentiful the young may stay on through winter. Let this be a year of plenty.

His fox traps from last season are much as he left them, each makeshift wooden frame stowed beneath a weight of stones. Several slats have sprung a nail and loosened from their frames. Stray stones have been shoved by wind and are now resting in a dip, metres away. A day or two to put this score of traps in order, evenings to fashion trigger locks and whittle bait sticks.

In several more weeks, this eastern end of Hornsund will begin its freeze: a crust of ice impossible to navigate by boat, vulnerable to wind and tide, a death sentence to cross unless you are as dainty as a fox, or a bear designed for frigid water. Their winter route will be on skis across the blue ice of Hansbreen, the three dogs pulling the sled across the frozen river as far east as Fannytoppen. From there, whatever is needed at this furthest hut they must carry on their backs down the mountain. Their first need, he has told the woman, is a stock of seal for dog food and bear bait, the best cuts set aside for their own meals. Two dozen *snadd* – the small, ringed seals – or, if luck is with them, a handful of *storkobber*, the large, bearded seals.

The cloud cover is low but the wind has dropped away. Water smoothing out to glass. Out beyond these skerries, both ringed and bearded seals haul up on icefloes, or cruise near the bergs. Anders angles his way down the slope to the hut. They need to be out there hunting while the weather lasts.

Inside, the walls and roof drip with steam. A new pot of water sits bubbling on the stove. He has told the woman that firewood at this inner end of the fjord is in limited supply. She turns from her stance at the table, her forearms wet and silked with soap, the washbasin shielded from his view. Anders feels his chest tighten. Hasn't he aired the mattresses, wiped down every damned surface to rid the place of mould? 'What the devil are you doing?'

She startles. 'My laundry is all.'

'Laundry?' The utterance of the word, here in this setting, makes him grin. Anders loosens. He laughs. 'We haven't been here two days.' A trapper could count on one hand the hours he devotes to *laundry*. 'It is a well-known fact that dirty clothes are warmer than clean.'

Her brow furrows. Within that look a silent plea. He tries to fathom the puzzle. She waits, tight-lipped, blinking at his clue-lessness. She gives a huff. 'I have my monthly.' She turns to the window. 'It is said,' she mutters.

Fool that he is. He gestures to the fjord. 'There are seals about. I am wanting to head out. You need to stay and rest?'

She softens, tips her gaze toward him. 'I need only a few minutes to finish.'

'I see,' he says. Does he? In all their wedded years he and Othelie never shared such conversation. Only a silent understanding the week she turned away from him, the same each month as if this were a shameful thing. If Anders were a better, bolder man he would have told Othelie, would tell this woman, that her cycle is as natural as the seasons. Ask any fox or bear, any deer, any warm-blooded creature he can name. 'Shall I get the boat ready?' he says.

'I will be there in a moment.'

He ducks through the door but slows at a memory of his wife's cloths pegged from view between the linens. He turns back, newly buoyant. 'I will string a line up outside. Things dry fast in the north.'

A glimmer of a smile. She turns back to her basin. 'Thank you, Chief.'

The double-barrelled shotgun, slugs, harpoon, rod and line, a stack of hessian sacks, a flensing knife with a deadly blade too large for any sheath.

Neither of them dares utter a word or clear their throat or make a human sound. Wanny works the oars, taking care with their angle, mindful not to splash the water with the blades. Stroke upon sound-less stroke. The Chief sits alert at the stern, both barrels loaded, the shotgun on his knee resting on the gunwale. He signals with his hands: ease up. Wanny swings the oars into the boat, gingerly sets down each blade upon the middle thwart. Momentum carries the boat forward.

Seals, bigger than any she has known, slumber on an icefloe. 'Storkobber,' he mouths the word. Bearded seal. Will they smell a human presence, dive to safety?

She takes up the field glasses, though the creatures are near enough for her to see the snouts stained copper, the long, curled whiskers. They bring to mind two old Norse gentlemen dozing with their news sheets at the Grand Hotel.

The Chief takes up his gun. Without a sound he moves his hip to rest against the edge of his seat, one foot chocked against the side ribbing, his other knee set firm upon the folded sacks. The rifle glides to his cheek; his eye lines the sights. Wanny blocks her ears. The shot booms out across the fjord, blasts away tranquillity. The world seems to throb. She sees the seal slump, dead before it has woken. The other is already galloping to the ice edge, hauling headlong over the edge to dive. A second *crack*. A spray of bloody gristle. The flesh of the tail flipper shreds to pieces as the seal disappears, its wounded wake a rippling of red.

They heave the boat's bow onto the floe, throw out the anchor, the ice given traction by its coating of snow. The slaughtered seal, eyes glazed, sorrowful in death, bleeds a scarlet halo. 'Best you watch and learn. You feel a movement in the ice, hear a crack' – he stamps his boot heel into snow – 'you save the boat. Understand?'

'Yes.'

He takes up his flensing knife. The blade pierces skin and sprays blood across Wanny's trousers. He plunges the knife deep. She watches it run from chest to anus, the innards sending a reek through the air. He cuts away each flipper and slings them toward the boat. 'Save them for stew.' The blade slices beneath the skin and peels away an inch-thick layer of blubber. He chops it into pieces and has her cart them to the boat. They feel warm and greasy, the smell as fetid as cod on the turn. Within minutes the seal's body is quartered into slabs so rich with blood they dye the flesh burgundy.

She remembers the villagers of Sommarøy celebrating a drowned minke whale coddled in a lashing of net. The day it took her father and neighbouring boats to tow the minke home and free the tangle. Its meat was as dark as *storkobber*, the flavour more intense than any ocean salmon baked for Sunday lunch, a texture more delicate than the sheep her mother slaughtered at *Juletid*. A meal so extraordinary to a child, so beyond her scope of experience, that she barely trusts the memory of it.

Wanny senses the rise and fall beneath her feet. They are on a floating piece of ice. Is this what he means by movement? She clambers in the boat, their lifeline to the shore. The hut is gone from sight. The ocean current has sailed them deep into Burgerbukta, the western branch of the fjord with twin glaciers pushed apart by an island peak. The movement settles and she climbs back out, turning a circle to take in her surrounds. Icebergs. Glaciers. Does Sæterdal even see how extraordinary it is? How lucky he is to be here? Wanny could be wandering through the pages of her boys' childhood picture book with its fantastical paintings of icebergs and polar bears.

Throughout the rowing journey she had marvelled at bergs larger than their boat, moulded into shapes that she likened to dragons and giant swans, a turreted castle, each spire an artful defiance to gravity. The Chief pointed to former waterlines angled high across these bergs; lines, he said, that told their own history. They had seen such a story play out. The crack of a rifle, Wanny first thought. No, it was a slab of ice plummeting to the water. *Look*, the Chief had said and she had watched transfixed as the berg slowly leaned, teetering to and fro. *There it goes*, she'd cried, the entire iceberg upending, hauling its submerged underside up amid a gushing waterfall. The old waterline was metres in the air, their boat lifting and falling in the berg's wake.

The Chief calls her over now to cart blubber and flesh and stack it into hessian sacks laid out on the dinghy floor. The filled bags feel lumpy and warm. The bilge water curdles rainbow with seal oil, milking to pink.

Anders finishes. He kneels on the carcase of the seal, blood past his elbows, a smear across his brow. He takes stock of the flaying, the fully exposed vertebrae. Beside him the severed head stares wide-eyed at its butcher, its long stately whiskers strangely tragic. The woman's hands are slick with blood and he thinks of her morning laundry. Her trousers soaked in blood. Every footprint in the snow stamped scarlet. A wry nod to them all.

After the warmth of seal flesh, he feels the shock of plunging his hands into frigid water. He washes his skin free of blood and slime, mindful of the time he lost a flensing knife to slippery fingers. He grips the knife and dips handle and blade in the water. He rakes it back and forward to rid it of muck. He takes clean snow and scrubs his forearms and elbows. 'There.' He stands. As clean as he can hope for.

The woman sits at the bow, keeping the boat nudged against the icefloe while he reloads his gun. 'Chief,' she whispers to him. He sees the dark head off the back of the boat, sees it slide back below the water. Curled whiskers. A doglike snout. Another *storkobber*. Anders quietly steps into the boat, places the harpoon within his reach, the end of its rope affixed to the ring at the bow. 'Keep watching,' he whispers. 'It has to surface for air.' The seal will stay up for only the time it takes to draw a breath. One chance to knock it in the head if he can do so without killing it. 'We need it to stay afloat. Long enough to fix the harpoon. Push the rope firm into the notch,' he tells her. 'Don't let it tangle around you.'

A head. He shoots. A mist of blood. 'Row to it!' He scrambles for the rod. 'Row for your life.' Anders heaves the harpoon. It arrows through air to pierce the seal, the barb fixed deep into its giant flank. 'It will run,' he cries. 'Be ready.' The seal dives. 'If it goes beneath an icefloe you cut the rope.' The seal pulls with such power that the dinghy speeds like a motorboat. Anders holds on, a grip on the gun, the woman kneeled at the bow, eyes ahead, her sheath knife ready at the rope.

Perhaps the seal is blinded by the shot, for it rushes full speed not below but up onto an icefloe. 'Hang on!' Anders cries, the boat mounting the ice and skiing in an arc across it. They bounce back into open water. A momentary calm, the rope slack before it yanks tight again. The pace slows. The seal rises to the surface, blood streaming down its back, the rope wound around its girth. Anders hears its heaving breath, the throaty rattle. 'He gave us one hell of a ride,' he whoops, clambering to the front. Anders takes aim with his rifle.

'Let the suffering be done,' he hears the woman mutter.

The boat low in the water, both sets of oars labouring shoreward. They sit amongst sacks of seal meat, ankle deep in bloodied water, the second *storkobber* dragging as a sea anchor, a strap cut into the skin of its neck and tethered to the boat to haul it back to Fuglefjell. *The Villa*, their country home, the Chief calls this easternmost hut.

The petite hut comprises a few lengths of driftwood, a flimsy wrap of tar paper to keep out wind and snow. The living space is so small that if one of them is cooking the other one must sit at the tiny table, take to their bunk or move to the porch. Wanny fries seal steaks on a stove that looks fit for a doll's house. She sits low on a stool and turns the meat, spoons blood gravy over the potatoes. Her back aches. Her hands are blistered. The hut soon heats with the warmth of the stove. She cannot remember such weariness since her boys were tots; baby Alf in her arms, saturated with fever, Bjørvik howling in his cot, herself newly widowed.

Wanny collects a cord of wood from the portico. The Chief tells her that at this hut, the farthest from their main base, driftwood seldom washes in, though she struggles to believe it, at least if the roof-high stack in the portico is anything to go by. Wood collection seems something of a devotion to the Chief, who scours the shoreline morning and night, hours each day given to chopping and sharpening his axe and chopping some more, the porticos of all three huts stacked high with hewn lengths.

Here at Fuglefjell, nail heads studded across the walls and ceiling each hold a stub of bark. The Chief tells her that birch bark, brought from home and used as an insulating liner in the huts, has been ripped away to fuel the stove. He never speaks harshly of his comrades; states simply that those from past seasons will have been unlucky in their search for driftwood. These trappers, she guesses, are like any other, some more or less industrious than others, some without the forward planning of the Chief to set sufficient wood aside in readiness for next season. Wanny begins to understand the benefit in maintaining the same leasehold from one year to the next; the Chief looks upon these well-stocked huts as if they were his home.

They feast on seal, washed down with mugs of coffee. 'I will do the dishes in the morning,' the Chief says. Wanny wonders if he is waiting for her to object, she being the woman. No. They are not man and wife, far from it. They are working partners, expected to each do their fair share of inside and outside tasks. 'Then I will take one last look outside,' she says, fighting to stay awake but not wanting to miss a moment of this place.

'You do not need my permission,' he says, free of gruffness.

Wanny stands on the shore turning circles. She is inconsequential within these mammoth surrounds, a tiny speck of human life. On the southern side of the fjord, a trio of glaciers blazes pink in the evening light. Immediately below the hut, their own small bay lies calm, while out beyond the skerries the deeper water, black as tar from the shadow of the mountain, ruffles with breeze. She toilets at the shore then ambles uphill to a rise behind their tiny dwelling. She cranes her neck and shoulders, and stretches her back to view Fuglefjell's highest ledges and crags. The top of the mountain looks to pierce the sky. Partway up she spies a commotion of agitated birds. They shriek and shuffle on their ledge, several taking to the sky. Beneath them, on a narrow strip of turf, Wanny catches the cause of their distress. A small fox paces, its coat so dark that its form only comes into being when it moves against a pale rock. Wanny glances up, distracted by the fulmars wheeling around the mountain top. When she looks back, the fox has gone, melded into dusk.

'You saw it?'

She startles at the Chief behind her. 'The brown fox?'

'A blue,' he tells her. 'One of our prize animals. Making the most of the mountain while there are birds still to hunt.'

Wanny crawls up to her bunk, finally surrendering to fatigue. She is growing used to the close air within these wooded walls, the continual semi-darkness that the paraffin lamp fails to brighten, a match required to find a hairpin fallen to the floor. Yet inside this tiny dwelling, tucked beneath this matriarch of mountain, she cannot recall such a ridiculous feeling of security. She feels like a child, too tired to sleep, her mind still ticking from the intensity of the day. She props her pillow against the wall and takes up her journal, lacking the energy to write. 'I wonder how our dogs are faring,' she says. Mira is her main concern.

'They will manage well enough.'

'They will be hungry.'

'They are working dogs, including yours. A few days of going without won't do them harm.'

From her top bunk she can see no more of the Chief than his shoes and socks poking out below. The crisscross of lines that hang beneath the roof are crammed with wet work clothes, with woollen socks and woollen underwear that smell of sodden sheep, and with the Chief's handkerchiefs he rinses in the ocean and scrubs against the stones.

'Chief,' she calls down.

'What now?'

'Why are huts set in stone and gravel?' It is not so much the question she needs answering as a sudden hunger for conversation.

'All huts?'

'This hut. The Villa.'

Wanny pictures the Chief gazing out the window, in another world. 'That is how it has to be.'

'How so?'

'The winter storms that roar down Fuglefjell's mountain. Without the wall of stone, this hut would sweep away.'

Her dry clothes are stowed on the inside of her bunk; on the narrow shelf she keeps her hairbrush and pins, a jar of lanolin, a pack of tooth powder. On his, a framed photograph of his children. Wanny's boys are held between the pages of her journal. She studies those tender faces, picturing how they might have spent their day. Alf's last year at school, Bjørvik, his big brother, turned fourteen, almost a man, a paid helper at her friend's farm where Wanny has them boarded for the year. Weariness turns a person tearful. Wanny reflects on the frantic fortnight she spent making arrangements for this year, the Chief innocent to her family's existence and the uprooting of their lives. Hard enough that her sons would be without their mother. Never would she separate her boys from one another, and she knew that Alf, especially, would need a woman's tender touch.

She hears the Chief change into his sleeping shirt, kick off his clogs. A creaking of boards as he settles in his bunk. 'Chief,' she whispers down.

'This is he.'

'Were you happy with the day?' She waits for him to answer. To tell her she did well. He is the kind to dwell on things.

'Two *storkobber*. Steaks for dinner. No complaints from the ground floor.'

Is he happy with *her*, she wishes to know.

'You?' he says. 'What does your journal have to say about the day?'

She hasn't yet written a word. She is still making sense of the day, its heady mix of thrill and terror, blood and gore. 'It wonders if perhaps there was a little too much excitement for its first day of hunting.'

'Tell it that all parties worked as they should. That it ended safe and well.'

A release of her breath. She is not one to call on prayer when things are low, but if there is a God she promises Him she will make it up to her boys. She slides her journal beneath her pillow, turns to the wall, her sleeping bag warm around her shoulders.

FOX

a land turned white

THE RUNT WAITS for the man to leave the hut, to join him on his morning walk along the shoreline.

She stays high, trots well ahead to lead the way. She halts when the man halts, springs to action when he moves.

He climbs the saddle to pass the point. The man slows at a tall wooden structure which emits a scent, faint and aged. It howls and shrieks when the wind grows strong, squeals in pitches painful to a fox's ear. Its post stands tall, knotted in the way of logs that bump the shore, its base lavished with fox spray. The runt watches and waits. The man tips his gaze to the great height of the structure, its angled crossbars too high for even a man to leave his mark.

On they go.

The runt scampers between rocks, prances over moss beds, leaving an imprint of her paws. She angles down toward the cobbled shore and settles for the morning ritual. The man squats, his rump to the ocean, chin rested on his hands. The fox adds the man's defecation to her memory map.

He rises and dresses; she readies herself to leave. For no conscious reason she takes fright and races away, helter-skelter over rocks.

She flies across the slope until the moment, her body panting, bristling from exertion, the man feels far away.

The hunters labour up the slopes. The man attends to his traps, repairs loose slats, his toil hammering a sharp beat across the mountainside.

The woman gathers stones, steps slowly and deliberately as she hauls the largest up the slope. The runt hears the effort in her breath. From time to time the hunters halt, steaming liquid poured from a thermos, the tantalising smell of bread and meat they carry in their rucksacks. They rise together, gather their belongings, move farther along.

She hears their talk. The different timbre of their sounds.

She baffles at scraps of food the man drops across the slopes and scatters near the traps: blubber and meat ready to snatch and steal away, other pieces harder to free, caught beneath stones. Each day, the aroma beneath those immovable stones grows strong; the runt craving the food she is denied.

❄

The runt creeps past the hut and rubs against the boat pulled up on shore. For minutes she sits on the beach, watching, listening.

Then she is on the boat's bow, as wound as a spring. All fours on a meagre V of wood, perched there as a figurehead. The runt turns her ear, listens to the rhythmic beat of hammering, listens hard for other fox.

She skulks down into the boat, tantalised. She laps at seawater pooled beneath the seat, baulking at its saltiness, driven for more by the tinny sweetness of the blood. She licks at planks of wood. She noses at leathered specks of seal trapped beneath the running boards. She paws. She bites at the edges of the boards, her teeth puncturing wood. She gnaws to reach the tiny scraps of seal meat, her snout curled back into folds, the white of her teeth, the pink of her gums fully exposed. A sound. A scent. She halts. Danger. Rises to the seat. A pale fox, nosing this way. A brother.

He has her scent. He speeds toward her. The runt leaps and lands awkwardly on gravel. She falters. She is quick, but her brother is strong-limbed and in moments has her down. His teeth pierce her back; she hears her own yip as he tears her skin to pull his weight upon her. It is dominance he wants, for she will not come into heat until the spring. The runt grows fierce. She pushes back to knock him off his paws, she toppling with him, the pair tumbling down the beach in a plait of fox.

She turns to free herself; she lashes with claws and teeth, tufts of silver and white fur taking to the air. She tries to run, hears gravel crunch beneath her claws, but the dog fox has her newly held, his jaw fixed fast on the butt of her tail. The runt writhes. She twists with all her might. She lunges at his snout, her incisor digging hard into his eye. His cry of pain. He loosens his hold. She grips his ear in a frenzy, feels it shred as the young dog yanks free. Away he races, a split ear, his ruined eye a bowl of blood.

The runt watches, pants, slow to make sense of it. He has gone. He is larger. She has won. She is wounded. She is away, up the slope, darting through the hunters in a dash of supremacy.

Both of them startle. 'It is you.' The woman laughs.

'Liten Blå,' says the man. *Little Blue.*

The young fox clambers to the highest point she knows below the cliffs. She drops through a crevice of rock to a cramped enclosure. A refuge to ease her trembling body, to tend her wounds, a sleeping den. She is punctured and torn. Her pink tongue laps at air.

❄

Windows covered, studded with nails. The front door barred. The beach below the hut lies empty.

Snow falls in flurries, lands on the runt's eyelashes, tickles her nose. Snow settles on grass around the hut and fills the runnel where the boat has been dragged down to the water. Snow peppers each hummock of seaweed. A land turned white.

The runt moves gingerly, her ribs and hindquarter tender, the wounds on her back and tail festering with pus. She hasn't eaten for days.

She treads a path to the saddle of the point and slows at the wooden structure to nose around the base. Traces of the man upon a faded trace of men from bygone times, layers storied in the wood. She sprays across the post. Fox scent, new on old.

She wanders down to the cobbled shore where the man often rests on his haunches at the water's edge. The shoreline stands empty but for a fresh gathering of seaweed, chunks of ice stranded with the tide, their edges softened with snow. The runt chews on baubles and stems of seaweed. She licks snow. She moves up toward the rocks in a flurry of wind and snowdrift that has her blink and shake her head. She stops. Tilts her snout. A scent so faint, so far away, she would have missed it without the breeze to carry it.

Driven by hunger, she retraces her steps, makes her way far along the shoreline, beyond the edge of known land. She scrambles over steep rocks slick with algae, follows the scalloping of headlands, the narrowing of points. She halts at a cove, fixes her eyes on its small gravel beach.

The inlet of the cove is flanked with walls daubed with rust, each a dripping slab of rock. The runt is at the far side of the mountain, east into the opening of a fjord that leads to distant glaciers. Here, water no longer burbles in narrow rivulets but slides as sheets down faces of rock. Beneath overhanging ledges grow carpets of moss, gardens lush and green with soft-leafed fern. On the small gravel beach, pushed up by the tide, slumps a mountain of meat. An odour so mesmerising she forgets her wounds.

She makes her way through flurries of snow to the carcase, days old, where a troupe of glaucous gulls squabble and shriek, where adults and fledglings pick at the *storkobber*'s eyes. A bird dances from foot to foot with its bill inside the nostril of the seal. Gulls yank the loosened nails of flippers.

These gulls are bold and strong but slower to take flight than a kittiwake. The runt rushes at the gulls as her mother would do to snag a bird slow to scatter. Fledgling gulls take to the air in a slap of wings. Adult gulls step back beyond the reach of this fierce young hunter.

The runt pierces the sealskin with needle-sharp teeth. She rubs her muzzle across the oozing tear, seal fat glistening her snout. She gobbles through blubber, hankering for the prized meat below.

She eats her fill of flesh until she gags. She steps away to defecate then saunters back. She sidles against the *storkobber*'s head to sniff its snout. She pulls back at the touch of its coarse whiskers, wiry and limp.

The fox climbs upon the *storkobber*'s back, surveys the mass dusted with snow. She paces the length, halts at the rump, blinks snow from her lashes to study her domain. A shredded sweep of tail flippers. Severed stumps of flesh gravelled with silver shot.

Upon the seal's rump she settles, a small blue fox with her back to the wind, a thick brush curled around her head.

6

Hyttevika, October

ONLY WHEN THE Chief leaves the hut, spurred into action by driftwood newly washed in with the tide, does Wanny turn her thoughts to acts of madness. Only once the table is wiped clean, the kitchen knives sharpened on the grindstone, her rifle cleaned and oiled and stowed inside its woollen sock, a flank of seal simmering in broth turned inky from its blood; only when her hands are washed and dry will she kneel at the foot of the bunks and reach for the parcel beneath.

The wrapping is no longer new but as pliable as bread dough. She frees the string, smooths out the folds. She lifts the bundle from within – each time the weight of it astonishes her – and carries it as gently as a sleeping child to lay upon the bunk. The wolf of the *pelskåpe* still holds its wild scent. She strokes the fur, thinking it a wonder that a creature of the forest – a coat that shielded it from cold – now serves as *her* coat. She shakes her head at the lunacy. If her father were alive, he would pull her pigtail, *The trolls, Ivanna, have stolen your senses*. Not once in her childhood would a Sommarøy fisherman, any shrewd farmwife, consider such extravagance without the means to pay for it.

They haven't yet set the traps though she catches sight of fox daily now, their coats turning pale, trotting across the landscape, slowing to snuffle out titbits the Chief scatters around the hut. He is adamant that those traps will not be set until the hallowed date.

Wanny turns from the bunks to the hut's large open room where they cook and eat and wash, where she darns the heels of socks already worn from the distances they trek. Flaying knives are jammed between the rounds of the driftwood wall. They stow their rifles on the walls above the bunks. The great tunnel of provisions stored in the enclosed portico never appears to reduce, box after box stacked floor to roof and the thing she searches for invariably down there at the bottom. Everything they eat and use, the tools they hunt with, all of it on credit. She ought to fret more, but here, a winter away from the mess she left behind, life feels free of complication, abundant in its fundamental way of eking out a living.

The *pelskåpe* has no collar, as though the maker ran short of fur. The lining is neither silk nor satin, just the cotton plaid of any working coat. Why can't she bring herself to wear the wretched thing?

Wanny carries it to the small mirror on the wall, holds the amber fur against her throat. *You look ridiculous.*

Does she? Her hair is split and dulled of shine. It tangles so easily she must braid it as she did when she was a child. Her nose feels perpetually red. Her cheeks are blotched from icy wind in spite of cream, her forehead peeling, as if her skin, the very layers of herself, are being sloughed away. *Who are you, Ivanna?* Can she even recognise the woman she left behind in Tromsø?

A yelp, all three dogs mad with excitement. For weeks the Chief has been training Karo and Storm, his two young dogs initially pulling a driftwood pole as they learned to move apace, all the while following his commands. He is so proud of their progress that he constantly sings their praises.

You will find Mira quite capable, she had ventured.

You think she will heed anyone's word but your own?

She is quick to learn if you show her what you want. Praise her as you do the others. A plea as easily given on her own behalf. *Mira and I have been practising your commands.*

Have you now.

Today is the first time he has included her dog. It fills Wanny's heart to see Mira on the trace; Karo in front, Storm behind, Mira trotting easily at the rear to match the brothers' pace. The runners of the sledge glide over the snow bank and spark rocks as the Chief races them to the hut. Quickly, Wanny folds the coat and returns it to its wrapping, slides it deep beneath the bunk.

The Chief sees her at the door. He gives a theatrical bow and sweeps his arm toward the sledge as if presenting the most extravagant of riches.

'Camphor wood,' he calls. 'Burns hot as Old Nick. Save it for the bread baking.'

A bounty. She pulls to the ground slender logs belying their weight. The Chief turns the sledge around, rallies the dogs. 'And more!' His voice gleeful. Off they race. A different man. A happy man.

Wanny drags the camphor to the block for chopping. She slows. An image bites her skin. Their first seal hunt, pink froth spewing from the *storkobber*'s mouth and nostrils. It was not only the seal's suffering that had her grimace and turn away. It was the acid reminder of Othar, panting for air, his face clown-like, as if the mahogany patches that daubed his cheeks were scooped from a pot of rouge. Feet black as frostbite. Wanny can no longer conjure an image of the proud, strong man she'd married. Cannot rid her head of the ugly English verse the children skipped to on the street.

I had a little bird

Its name was Enza

I opened the window

And in-flu-enza

The old and infirm and her own babies spared, while the town's men, those at their prime, drowned as their lungs filled and frothed.

Wanny sets about her work, in her mind the image of her youngest swaddled in his dying father's arms. Back then, she could sense the dread in the way people held themselves when they left their homes. The fear of who was next. The tightened rush to walk the street. How was it she was spared?

Othar. If you were here to share this place. The long and weary ache of it.

Outside, the lee wall of the hut now houses a stack of firewood as high as her shoulder. Some of the logs arrive at the shore so bleached and light in weight they could be pumice; others so laden with seawater that they struggle to heft them above the tide line, even with the dogs.

Driftwood. Felled trunks that roll with ocean currents and spin with countless tides. She knows nothing of the world. Nothing of her purpose in it. Only that salt from the wood is surely rusting out the stove which, in her book, rates as their most vital possession. What choice do they have? Only Tromsø's wealthy, or trappers to the north whose huts lie within reach of Advent Bay, can claim the luxury of Spitsbergen coal. The coal that burns the hottest.

The days now are icy, too cold for bare hands. The light grows dim, snow and mountains bathed pink by afternoon. She and the Chief take turns to stoke the firebox through the night, their growing stack of wood plenty good enough to warm the hut.

Anders systematically works each of the *selvskudds*, affixing new boards to the cases to keep them tight from snow. According to the woman, these self-shooting traps set across the headlands bring to mind a parlour of newly carpentered coffins, each resting atop its own workhorse. At the closed end of the case, Anders pegs the hatch that gives access to the sawn-off Remington. When the time is ripe for polar bear, he will lace a cord to the shotgun trigger, thread it around a bobbin of nails and along the length of case to the open end. He will tie the far end of the cord to a hunk of seal meat or blubber and place it in from the opening of the case. A good tug on the bait from a hungry bear, a cartridge primed with shot, a nod from Lady Luck, and Mister Bear plugs himself square in the head.

The woman does not hold his appreciation for ingenuity. *The* selvskudds *were an invention of Norwegian trappers right here in Svalbard*, he told her; still she looked at them askance.

How can there be sport for hunter or bear in such an uneven battle?

Even-handedness? She is an odd one. *Our goal here is bearskin. Is it not?* She had no comeback for that.

The *selvskudds* weigh as much as a man, but winter winds will knock a man down. In dimming light, Anders anchors the legs of each trap with stones, then shovels snow on top to freeze and bind them.

It is unlikely to have a bear come south so early in the season, but unlikely *is not* impossible, he harps at the woman. *Take your rifle, even to toilet.* Every headland they cross, every mound of snow, could rise in the shape of a bear. The end of the shoreline, the brow of a hill. *Be ready.* Anders worries. If she freezes with fear, if she shoots and misses and he is not around, a bear is faster, more powerful than any man. There is no saying it softly. She and he are meat.

He whistles to his dogs, far ahead. 'Home now.' He sees them launch across the landscape. A dark blur of Alsatian.

They look to him, panting and expectant. 'What you say?' he says to Storm, patting the dog's belly. 'What you say?' He scratches Karo's rump. Even the woman's dog lines up for a pat.

They probably say they have never eaten as well. They probably say that the offcuts of fried seal the woman throws their way when she thinks he isn't looking, the scrapings of gravy and porridge, are what fully counts in a working dog's day.

If the woman keeps herself alive, if she fails to shoot a single bear or flay a fox, will he still deem it poor judgement to have brought her along? She doesn't shirk hard work, though she will never be his equal in strength. She melts more pots of water than any trapper he has known. She keeps the hut good and clean. In his years of trapping he has never eaten so well. A newly embroidered cloth has appeared on the table. *To make me feel at home.* She asks to sew curtains for the window, *For added cheeriness,* she says, showing him the length of fabric she brought along. Hut life feels less . . . elemental.

She wants to be part of it all, having him show her new skills, watching carefully as he harnesses the dogs to pull the sled, changes the runners, splices a broken rope, demonstrates how a lineman's loop works to hold the load secure. In the evening she reads aloud from the aged newspapers stacked in the porch. Sometimes he talks as he would to a man. She has read of the Russians buying the Barentsburg coalmine in Spitsbergen's north. She tells him they are keeping the name of the settlement to honour the Dutch explorer. *What will it mean for Norway?* she then asks. She mourns their polar heroes, Amundsen disappearing in his plane over the ice in search of the Italian dirigible. Nansen now passed away. Her Mr Rudi has no greater admirer. Anders smiles, though he feels himself flinch to hear her speak as if Rudi were a demigod. Twenty-five years a trapper. This, his fourth Greenland winter. She relays Rudi's encounters with Greenland wolves and polar bears, with a hundred-strong troupe of Arctic hares bounding across the tundra like kangaroos, as if she had been there beside him. She knows more about Tromsø's trappers than Anders can keep inside his head. She is utterly entranced with the world of trapping. At the same time, Anders harbours an uneasy suspicion that she would as happily carry out the work without the killing. More so. In her eyes, the reward seems to be in simply being here. How can such a woman learn to be a proper trapper?

He hears the flock before he sees them, the unmistakable beating of their wings, five eiders low in the sky, their sound filling the air as they pass overhead. They are away, but no, they peel downward past the hut, wings aloft as they skid from his sight across the water.

When he reaches the hut, the woman is waiting with the boat at the waterline. Somehow, she has pulled it down the wooden ramp alone. 'I hoped you'd hear them,' she says, her rifle strapped across her shoulder. She passes him his shotgun.

They row in a slow, wide arc to reach the outside of the group, mindful not to scare the birds. The light is dim. The first stars in the sky. October is late for land birds. 'Likely be the last of them,' he says. They keep the eiders between boat and land, slowly, quietly, easing the boat shoreward to lessen the gap.

She keeps her voice low. 'Why don't they fly?'

'They don't like to take off close to shore.'

He raises the shotgun to his cheek. Squints. A blast. Two eiders bob lifeless on the water. Three birds scatter across the water and take to the wing. Anders trains the shotgun at the sky, empties the second barrel.

'You missed!' the woman cries in a voice that has him seethe.

'You shoot them then!' but his words are lost to her rifle. A bird drops from the sky.

❄

A world turned blue. Three dogs happy to be left to sleep beside the stove. Nine in the morning and no hint of the sun, the half-moon tipping the mountains, all their many terraces a pastel sea of snow.

She and Sæterdal trudge through ankle-deep snow, fortified by their morning measure of cod liver oil. 'Soon for the skis,' she says to the Chief. They march across the landscape with rifles on their backs, the air so sharp with cold that Wanny's cap is pulled tight, the fur lining of the flaps soft against her ears. Her chin bumps the toggle of her thickest pullover.

'Soon to be *mørketid*,' says he, his breath a puff of vapour. 'As much a blue time as a dark time up this way.'

'The same as home, then,' she says. In Tromsø, the polar night extends through winter's two deepest months. The season when she thrives. On days when the snow is too deep to drive her taxi upon the roads, she and the boys strap on skis. The swish of snow beneath their skis, their huffing of breath the only human sound as they glide through the quiet of mountain and nature trails. Even in Tromsø's darkest month, the sun skirts just below the horizon, enough to see by. A world turned blue. 'There is nothing better,' she says to the Chief, 'than a winter sky dancing with the lights.'

'Candles and lamp lights,' he says dreamily, 'in all the windows of the houses.'

'Everything *koselig*.' She meets his glassy gaze.

'We are making each other homesick.'

Across the scree slope they search for *rype*, the plumage of the grouse-like ptarmigan birds all but turned from speckled brown to winter white. The last snowfall has transformed the entire slope into a blanket of white, only small stands of tundra and rounds of stones apparent amid a tapestry of bird and fox tracks.

'*Rype* are not hard to shoot,' says the Chief. 'Finding them amongst the snow, making sense of where the tracks lead, is the devil's work.'

Spikes of meadow and hair grass rise above the white, their leaves obscured by snow. During the winter, he tells her, the *rype* will scratch through the snow for the leaves. The Chief favours these south-facing slopes covered with Alpine bistort, the plants' flowers long gone, their leaves withered and spent, their stalks clustered with pockets of minute seeds, black and sweet as *valmuefrø*, a favourite for the ptarmigan.

They step around an outcrop of rock to tracks crisscrossed through the snow, to an explosion of the *kee-ah, kee-ah* of startled *rype*. In moments the birds lay silent and still.

'One good-sized ptarmigan should bait eight traps,' the Chief says, 'though once you've eaten roasted ptarmigan, you will not want to share the choice cuts with foxes.'

'Why not seal? You've been scattering it about for weeks.'

'Seal?' the Chief scoffs. 'Seal is an appetiser. A shout to the world that we are open for business. I have never met a self-respecting fox who will fall for seal in a trap over *rype*. Mikkel Rev, Mister Fox, he knows the good stuff.' He taps his nose. 'It's all fine dining in Hornsund.'

By the time the moon creeps behind the mountains and the long blue dawn brightens into day, they carry five ptarmigan apiece, strung from their shoulders in a boa of feathers, the birds' feet tied with cord.

Fox traps dot the landscape. Some are raised on their trigger lock beneath a weight of stones, though none yet are baited. The Chief places small scraps of seal loose on the ground beneath the slatted wood. 'We let the fox grow used to the trap.' He sets down the birds to demonstrate the workings. 'Mikkel Rev sniffs around, enjoys a treat of seal. Eventually he forgets his own fear.'

He shows her how the ptarmigan is speared to a bait stick. They have spent nights whittling and chipping dozens of spare sticks and trigger locks. 'The baited end of the stick rests on the ground here inside, right at the back of the trap. The leading edge makes up one of the three trigger posts, you see?' They interlock and prop up the fore edge of the trap. 'Just high enough for Mister Fox to crawl in and take the bait.' The Chief pulls at the bait, tries to loosen it from the stick. 'Stand back,' he cries then kicks the trigger lock apart. The entire trap collapses to the ground. 'One dearly departed fox. Thirty kilograms of stone to seal the deal. The pelt remains in perfect condition.'

'Elegant simplicity,' Wanny says. Rather this, an instant death, than a blast in the face from the gruesome *selvskudd*.

The Chief looks pleased.

'October twenty-fourth,' she says as they gather up their birds and continue on. 'Tomorrow is the big day.'

'Tonight we eat *rype*.'

FOX

withered heads of bistort

THE RUNT PATROLS the base of the bird cliffs. She rubs against the rock face where tundra still clings to autumn, the perimeter snow-free, tainted and acrid from dried guano.

She pads through plants of alpine bistort, grasses with dried seed heads that tickle her nose, small stands of purple and tufted saxifrage, their blooms long spent. A sound. The fox halts mid step, front paw held. She cocks an ear to the calls, *kee-ah*, *kee-ah*. In return a call that is higher, sharper to her ears. The runt slinks down low, haunches taut. Gravel, the sharp edge of rock, a crush of saxifrage grazes her belly. A stealth hunter bides her time.

A movement. She bristles, slowly lifts her head to gain clear view. Ground birds. A ptarmigan hen, three fully grown chicks. The hen is winter white; the chicks, her equal in size, are dappled with markings of brown and grey, white feathers coating legs and feet. The young give out a short, sharp *kee-kee*. The hen pulls at the withered heads of bistort, their slender pods crackling open with seed, the chicks pecking madly at the ground.

The runt shifts on her haunches. She could spring forward, seize the nearest chick, snap its neck in a single crunch. Her pink tongue laps at the prospect of warm meat. She wants them all.

She remains low and out of view, slinks farther out so she is directly downwind and downslope of the birds. She surveys the contours of rock, trying to make sense of the family's random course, waiting for a moment where they might close in against the cliff face, when she can rush at the birds and corral them.

The runt waits, sharp eddies of air blasting gravel and grit, her nostrils lined with rock dust white with guano.

The young follow the mother hen. They move in the fox's direction. They are near. They slow to fossick amongst the saxifrage. They are close. The first is nearly above the runt. She wrestles with patience, bristles with the need to wait. She raises her hind quarters. She tingles, readies to pounce. From behind her a bolt of movement, a rush of air, a sharp familial smell as dog fox, her father, rushes by her left, knocking her aside, her mother tearing past her other shoulder. The ptarmigan chicks do not scatter. They are unmoving as if frozen to the ground before this pair of seasoned hunters who tear the life from the first chick, seizing the second. The runt, assaulted into action, rushes toward the hen tottering down the slope to gain momentum, wings aloft in a mad show of flapping.

The runt may be fast but the vixen is a seasoned hunter. She sees the runt take after the hen, sees it seize a wing tip. This is *their* catch. The vixen leaves her mate to finish off the chicks. She races downhill. She shunts the runt off balance as she pounces on the beleaguered hen. She pins the ptarmigan, locks her jaw around its skull, holds fast until life loosens and cracks free, the bird still.

The family of ptarmigan is taken. Dog fox halts from tearing at the chicks. He stands tall and snarls at the runt. The vixen readies to set upon her youngling.

The runt turns tail. She bolts to safety, her singular prize a white wing feather snagged in her teeth.

7

Hyttevika, early November

EVEN WITH ITS ungainly lean, the cross left by the Russian Pomors, north of the main base hut, stands audacious in height, the driftwood weathered and aged. The cross feels wiry to the touch with its coarse skin of lichen growing thickest at the base, giving it an altogether hairy-legged appearance. Wanny and the Chief halt beneath the cross to go their separate ways, all but the last few fox traps checked and accounted for. The Chief's two noisy dogs hold little reverence for this sacred site, these century-old crosses, their peaked tops fashioned in the way of a channel's navigation marker to lead the way, paying honour to the God that once watched over old Russian hunting grounds, both here at Hyttevika and east at Fuglefjell. The dogs cock their leg in sequence against the wood, as eager to leave their canine mark as they are to be harnessed to a sled laden with tools and timbers, shotgun cartridges, a load reeking with slabs of seal.

The Chief pulls off surplus sticks and hands them to Wanny, their sharpened tips ready to be baited. He will travel south, back toward the main hut, staying close to the coastline where the *selvskudds* stand grim as reapers within sight and sniffing distance of the ocean. Each contraption ready to be threaded with seal, each sawn-off Remington to be loaded and cocked.

'No self-respecting bear will come ashore yet,' the Chief says knowingly. 'Not until the pack ice forms a solid cover.' Sea ice or no sea ice, nothing will dissuade his belief that the start of November is the right and proper time to arm these ghastly traps.

'No self-respecting bear,' she says, 'would choose to end his days by shooting himself in the face.'

'You think it any different to the fox traps?' he says. 'Those bait sticks are just as deadly a trigger, the weight of fallen stones as instant as a rifle blast. Likely these people's ingenuity we have to thank.' He nods to the Pomor cross. The Chief moves away, the sled runners grating across rock until they ease into a lead of snow. 'Elegant simplicity,' he calls back at her, then bellows at his dogs to get a move along.

'Stay here, now. We have traps to bait.' Wanny pats Mira who whimpers and looks to the sledging party with a furrowed brow. Wanny ties the bait sticks to her rucksack. Ten days since the hallowed date when they set these traps across the home territory; since then a good many hours travelling out and back each day to check that bait and triggers remain intact, that the traps have not stuffed themselves with snow. Still no sign of Mister Fox. For a practical man, Anders Sæterdal is an enigma, faithful to super-stition, sworn to his belief in some mystical calendar of fortune. The Chief argues that if worshipping creature spirits and the protection of supernatural forces worked for the Russian Pomors a century ago – then placing faith in a touch of magic and a dash of Lady Luck should be good enough for them now.

'You have to trust in something,' she speaks his words aloud. *How else can you find your way?*

Can she put her faith in anything again? After Othar she turned her back on the savage hand of God, the empty placations of her church, determining never again to follow so blindly. If this is a godless place, as Mr Rudi has it, what is left to believe in and worship but the will of the land itself?

Wanny registers the span of day by the feeble pulse of light. The sun is now too pale and distant to lift itself to sight, these last weeks sheened with soft jewelled light, a midday dawn which by mid-afternoon deepens into dusk. Day, night – both ends of day turned creatures of deceit, for now, when the moon is risen and full, they rely as much on its light to give the land its form.

Perhaps it is the thought of the Pomor cross, its people who looked to the occult and believed in creature magic, that delivers a portent silence. Perhaps it is the eerie calmness of the day that invites a shroud of vulnerability. She feels it almost every day out here, a taut thread of fear that charges her senses, keeps her on edge. She is adept with a rifle yet she feels wide open. She carries a foreboding that isn't solely the prospect of an unseen bear, a predator that would take her in an instant if she were too slow to act or if her rifle failed. The land commands its own reverence. She feels the power in its harshness. Its unforgiving strength. In hand with this disquiet is how alive it makes her feel, how taken she is with its raw, rugged magnificence. This daily chore of trekking twenty kilometres to attend to fox traps stands as its own act of boldness; this vital sense of purpose her reward. Wanny slows, overheated. She looks around. The air is so still that the only sounds are those of their steps and Mira's panting, the air clammy and unseasonably warmer than it has been for weeks.

Wanny sinks to her knees in wet snow while Mira bounds through it like a porpoising seal. It is a between time, with too much open rock to travel by skis, too many tracts of snow to keep a good pace in boots. 'Come, Mira,' she calls, thankful for her dog's company as they head up the slope.

At the crest, Mira halts and issues a soft rumbling growl. Wanny's skin prickles. Ahead of them, a fallen trap, a small mound of white. A fox? She looks around, the prospect of a bear intruding on her thoughts. She nears the trap to see the full scope of carnage. A white fox, its head crushed beneath the frame's weight of stones. She feels a momentary rush of thrill but the limp body laying loose of the trap is wrong, strips of skin torn loose, flesh gnawed from its bones. Teeth marks, she looks closely, from a creature that can only be another fox. 'Oh, Mira,' she says. 'The waste.'

Wanny sets aside the stones, lifts the wooden frame and reaches for the scruff of the fox's neck. She lifts it between her fingers as she might a mewling kitten. The impossible softness of the fur. A pelt of silken air. She is struck by the tiny weight of the creature, as light as a small cat; the plushness of its winter coat doubling its size. No flecks of summer brown, the fur pure white but for dried streaks of blood. Desecrated. The pelt ruined. Should she take it with her to the hut? She examines the brush, still intact, still good. She pictures it made into a collar or cuffs, nature's slaughter transformed.

Wanny takes her knife to cut across the base of the tail. She stops. If she leaves the carcase, another marauding fox could be spurred on to savage the next. She resets the trap then takes rope from her pack. She ties the creature's paws, a bundle of fox draped from her rucksack. On they go to bait the final traps.

The light falls away as she and Mira turn southward toward the Hyttevika hut. She slows as she passes by the Pomor cross, wonders at its arrangement of crossbars, two metres in length. Strewn about the base are the remains of timbers the length of a door that once sat atop the cross as a peaked roof, their edges ornate. How did its people raise a structure of such weight and height? A wisp of mist glides low, momentarily obscuring the peak of the cross. Above, a crescent moon.

Wanny walks on, avoiding the deepest snow patches. At the next rise she looks down the valley to realign her bearings. She searches for the large scree slope. Nothing. She looks for the tarn where they first saw a fox stalking geese. She searches for its pale frozen surface, its ice rivulets that have part thawed with this spell of warmth. She sees nothing. She scans the horizon for the backdrop of mountains, for terraces lined with snow. There is nothing. Not a landmark. She searches south for the hut, still far away, willing its border of pale stones into view. She searches to the west and spies a pall of white where she believes ocean and pack ice should be. Ahead of her, Mira's shape softens to a blur. Fog. She is surrounded by it. Held within its clammy grip. Even as she stands here, the air thickens to gauze. Her skin feels damp. Her gut tightens. The Chief talks of summer fogs rolling in thick and white after days of calm and warmth. But summer is gone. Now is the onset of winter.

She must continue in the same direction. She must not veer off course. Though she cannot see the marks of land, she must stay true to their order mapped in her mind, physical features as good as any well-formed track, thanks to Sæterdal's insistence that she learn her way. Mira nudges her side. She hears her dog whimper. 'Come on, girl. Home we go.' She continues on, imagining the point in the distance she needs to reach. Minutes pass. Wanny's foot catches a rock buried by snow. She stumbles hard, jars her wrists to break the fall. The rifle shunts forward between her shoulder blades and she cringes, half expecting the safety catch to knock and the weapon to fire. The steel barrel rests cold against her cheek. The fox slumps against her neck, its claws prickling her skin as if readying to pounce. Wanny gets herself up, regains her composure, sorts her rifle and pack, the fox dead and where it ought to be against her thigh. Mira sits alert, her ears pricked, nose to the air.

They march on, a knot growing in Wanny's gut, slowly losing pace as the undulations, the shape of rock, the sparsity of tundra, everything around her, grows small and unfamiliar. She feels suddenly, stupidly unsure of the gradient, losing sense of where the ground rises and where it levels out. The world is askew. She grows cautious, taking plodding steps, shuffling, seeing herself in years to come, old and less sure of her step. Mira senses her uncertainty and whines, reluctant to follow. 'Mira,' she says sternly, waiting for her dog to catch up.

Wanny takes a slow circle, searching for some cue to direction. A fox would be unperturbed. A fox would map its route with its nose. From what distance does a bear track the scent of prey? The *selvskudds* are set fifty metres from the waterline with the thinking that any bear that crosses the pack ice to shore will sniff the bait of rotting seal. Would Mira warn her if a bear were near? Did the Pomors look to spirit creatures to find their way? Or did they simply *know*, attuned to the land in a way she is not? Not yet. She pulls herself together.

If she veers right, heads more or less west, she will reach the coastline. A given. From there she will walk two, three kilometres south, she will keep the ocean on her right until she reaches the hut. What if she should miss the hut? What if Anders himself is lost? The Chief will not be lost. He may not be home to light the lanterns. How easy it would be to walk on by. A half hour since she left the cross. She will keep track of her watch to measure the distance. She will know she is near when she reaches the driftwood boat ramp that runs up from the shoreline. A ramp empty of its landmark boat. On their return from Fuglefjell, they brought the boat ashore at the halfway hut where the glacier tongue calves into the sound, breaking up the sea ice in early spring. She had her doubts the heavy beast could be moved without the dogs. *Trust me*, the Chief had said. *It will go like a dance.* A block and tackle set up to inch it from the water, slender driftwood logs laid out on the shore over which they rolled the boat with manageable effort and surprising ease. Using a plank as a lever, together they propped the boat on its side then eased it belly down to meet the cobbled ground. Tied it fast for winter.

Wanny turns to her right and Mira darts ahead as if she has drawn new life. As if her dog agrees that this most certainly is the way. Together they plod along, thirty, forty minutes, no shoreline in sight. Mira continually angles away, inland it seems to Wanny, who each time stops to call her back. She listens for the ocean, though on such a still evening the water will surely be at rest beneath a fresh seal of ice. She listens for the yelp of Sæterdal's dogs. For the Chief himself who may have turned back to find her. Any sound will do. Mira tires of indecision. She heads inland with intent, turns only to look back when Wanny calls – that furrowed brow. Away she trots. Should Wanny follow? Relinquish control? Her thought turns to Martin at home, a widower as much in need of homely company as he was of a housekeeper, a paid appointment at a time when she was destitute, widowed with two small boys. She did not discourage his advances, shy and dithering as they were, nor overlook his gentle kindness with her boys. An offer of marriage. A contract of companionable necessity to serve them both.

Wanny turns to follow her dog. What choice did she have?

Anders waits. He stands at the door of the hut. He calls. Air as thick as the inside of a cauliflower. He reasons that if she fails to find her way, Mira will lead them home. His own dogs speared for the hut the minute he gave the word. He'll organise the makings for dinner and if there's still no sign he will harness the boys and head out to look. Anders itches to make himself useful. Keep himself busy. He will heat a tin of soup in readiness, bolster it with rice. He searches through the boxes in the cold porch, unpacks a tin, thinks he hears a sound and opens the door. He waits, listens, the can in one hand as he issues a long mournful call that sets his two dogs into a howling discord.

Anders cranks the stove with wood, bangs the can's frozen contents into a battered pot, lifts away the inner ring of the stovetop. Rice. Which box? He rates himself a satisfactory cook, can turn a cut of meat, turnip and potato into a tasty stew, though this season his skills have barely had a workout. An arrangement to suit both parties, he trusts, for the woman's cooking is superior, with one exception. *It is a very long time since I've needed to bake bread*, she had said by way of apology as she'd set the steaming brick down upon the table. One piece of the dreadful stuff, a crust of charcoal concealing a core of dough, had set his stomach churning, along with his resolve to resurrect his bread baking.

It hadn't helped, he admitted, and nor did it need reminding, that Anders himself had neglected to purchase a new supply of baker's yeast. In desperation he had resorted to chiselling a sorry-looking specimen, in residence since seasons past, from the outside of a tin, determined to resuscitate whatever it proved to be with the help of water, warmth and daily words of tenderness. Anders claimed with some authority that if the scraping were in fact dormant yeast then all it needed was reawakening, absorbing wild spores from the air, precisely as they did it in the old days.

Wanny had looked askance at his ritual of taking the brew to bed and keeping it warm inside his reindeer bag until, more proudly than he could say, he had presented his triumph, shared its zesty tang and pointed out the living bubbles. The culture now sits pride of place above the stove, expanding with warmth, replenished after each baking day with rye and warm water. He has dried a quantity to set aside in the event of an emergency, but the precious jar of culture will travel on foot with them across the glacier to Fuglefjell.

Bread and coffee are the staff of life, and at least in the baking department, Anders views himself as something of a saviour.

His dogs start up a fearful racket. 'Are they home?' he asks the soup. Anders pulls a tea towel from the line to wipe his hands. He pulls on his coat and carries the lantern out through the cold porch. A golden halo amid the fog. He releases the dogs from their chain and away they bound. He searches through the pall. 'Are you out there?' he calls. Far away, Mira's bark.

'Wanny,' Anders shouts.

He hears a feeble cry. 'We are here.'

'It is late,' he calls back.

'The fog.'

'You found your way.'

'Mira. She led the way.'

Those rascals have the magic. What he would give to have their canine intuition.

The form of the woman emerges through the gloom, a trio of dogs in close pursuit.

'Well,' he says to the bundle of fox draped from her pack. 'I see you've brought the luck.'

'Oh, Anders,' she cries. 'It isn't as it seems.'

'This way.' He holds out the lantern. 'You are home now.'

FOX

maddening with want

DAYS NARROW INTO dawn and dusk, the interval punctuated by a fleeting strip of light. The outlines of hills and mountains are given form by a sky layered with pastel pinks and blues, a wash of mauve. As quickly as the strip of light rises into being, the runt's world gives way to darkness. Stars glitter. The moon waxes, its half-fullness casting broken shadows across the ice of the fjord. The runt sits beneath the Pomor cross, her neck craned toward the curve of the moon. She hears dog fox call from outside his den, a guttural sound escalating to a bark. A shudder seizes the runt's body. She shakes her forepaws. A silver night so still that, from far across the fjord, she hears a return of shrieking barks from other older foxes.

The runt shifts focus to the trappers' hut below, empty now for weeks. Beyond its front door, a small new house stands perched on legs, its open end pointed to the ocean. The rotting lump of seal held within its walls grows more tantalising by the day, an aroma perfuming the air of Fuglefjell. Daily, the lure of its fetid scent draws the runt down from the slopes to shore, her belly maddening with want. No matter how high she leaps, the prize stays beyond her reach. The runt paces in manic circles, pausing only to chew splinters of wood from the legs.

A snow ramp now presses against the hut's eastern wall, patterned with her paw prints from numerous explorations. The runt claims as her own this trappers' roof, the headland she sits upon, and other high and precarious lookouts. This is *her* land. She surveys the landscape before her. Tundra appears, vanishes, reappears, its withered plant life buried by each fresh fall of snow that each new squalling storm clears away. Gone from the cobbled beach is the briny tang of seaweed, concealed now beneath frozen runnels and frills of sea ice jammed against the shoreline. Water from the spring trickles warm and clear.

The mountain behind the hut remains empty and silent. No shrieks from guillemots and kittiwakes. No food issued from the sky. Involuntarily the runt's pink tongue unfurls to lick her muzzle.

Out across the fjord, the slapping of water gives way to sea ice yawing and creaking as it expands and retracts. Bergs grind and grate against frozen collars of sea ice. They overturn, collapse through sea ice and send out a wave of frigid water. With each new week the sea ice grows thicker, strong enough to resist gales, to withstand the push and pull of ocean. The frozen fjord is plenty strong enough to hold her weight. Regularly now, she ventures out to explore and forage. The runt will pattern her travels alongside a tide crack, will pad along its length to a breathing hole kept open by seals who scrape back the ice with their teeth. The runt will wait and watch for the recurrence of a fish which flung itself from that hole and slid across the ice. With a quivering rush the runt had sprung into the air and brought down her weight, pummelling the fish's head with her paws. The creature had slithered, refusing to still. In desperation the runt had torn at its gills, snagging her nose on its backbone of spines. Once the creature had fallen dead, its body swaddled with slime, the runt had dragged it ashore by the stump of its tail, a creature her equal in weight.

Along the tide cracks, the runt hears a trilling beneath her paws, a strange unnerving song from the underside of ice which causes her to bolt, her escape stymied when she skates full circle across a snow-free slick of ice.

The frozen fjord invites new arrivals, mostly young foxes ousted from their family dens. Whites, a smattering of blues, are enticed from miles away by the reek of the long-dead bearded seal. They wait for the runt to eat; they take their place in her domain. The carcase of the seal is now a macabre thing with its eye socket stare, blubber and flesh hollowed out beneath slabs of wizened skin. A length of vertebrae and framework of ribs sit proud and exposed, harbouring yellowed strands of ligament and tatters of tendon. The cage of bone holds the seal's liver, uneaten and toxic. Shrivelled loops of bowel, putrid and blackened, cushion the seal's hind quarters.

The wooden cross squeals in the wind. The runt curls her brush and turns her sight upward. She blinks at the sky's silver eyes. On a clear night, foxes prance across mountain tops and leap across the sky, their tails splashing the world vivid and vibrant with colour. The shifting light scintillates so brightly with greens and pinks that the runt's eyes glint as coloured glass, her silvery coat shimmering an unearthly hue.

The runt refuses to leave this place in the way of her siblings. One of the newcomers, this season's young from a litter across the fjord, joins her when she allows, the friend quick to retreat when the runt bares her teeth. The runt is smaller than her follower, yet attitude determines their hierarchy.

The runt has a sleeping nook, a den for one within a tight crevice of rocks. She travels tens of kilometres for food, caches her supply in crevices high along the slopes, far to the west where rubble beneath her paws smooths into the ice of Hansbreen. Above the trappers' hut at Fuglefjell her parents guard their den, patrol their winter larder. Should a fox venture near, dog fox bares his teeth – one broken, several missing – coarse grey hairs visible around his muzzle. The vixen, younger than her mate, watches, limbs taut, observing the runt, weighing up their hold on their domain.

The runt stands tall beneath the Pomor cross, ears pricked. She catches a movement down upon the ice, a shape, a creature of enormous proportion, larger than a reindeer, greater than a man, its bulk luminescing a shimmer of green beneath the northern lights. A tremor charges across the runt's back. The bear appears to amble, belying its pace across the ice. A gait of heavy limbs, broad paddles for paws, a vast girth of belly. The bear raises its snout, sniffs toward the shore. In it angles.

8

Fuglefjell, late November

MOONLIGHT USHERS THE route to Fuglefjell. The Chief times their Hansbreen ice crossing to be brighter still when they return, the moon waxing near to full. Up ahead he skis across glacial ice at a pace, barely slowing to raise his stock to indicate a change in course that Wanny and the dogs should follow with the sled. They angle inland, up a gradient to where bumps and ridges smooth away, to ice that stretches fine and unbroken for as far as Wanny can see. Behind them, back toward the ocean, the glacier stands jagged and torn with crevasses, a vast cloth of uneven embroidery. She sits at the rear of the sledge cushioned with hessian sacks, their three dogs pulling an easy load in a harmony of happy panting. Tails upright, Karo in the lead, Storm next, her Mira at the rear. Whichever way the Chief heads, these three dogs follow, though now and again – through some tacit canine agreement – they deviate to skirt around uneven snow. The Chief never denies the dogs their knowing. He says those rascals can sense a crevasse concealed beneath a snow bridge. Do they feel a hollow crunch beneath their paws? A change in pitch beyond the reach of a human ear? This glacier is familiar territory to the Chief yet he is more cautious than she has seen before. Periodically he halts to take the compass from his pocket, switches on the flashlight to check their heading. The toughest stretch is still to come, the icy slopes of Fannytoppen, the mountain's silhouette looming on the far side of the glacier.

'The tulips of spring, they bloom for me,' Wanny sings the song spooling in her head since she heard it on the hut's wind-up gramophone. Ahead of her the Chief slows. She sees him turn back at her choice of song. A grin? A grimace. On he goes. She laughs. The absurdity of tulips while travelling across a glacier, the air minus thirty with the first flurry of breeze, clouds skating across the moon and dappling the ice. Just them and the dogs. Not another living soul.

Partway down the mountainside they tether their skis and the sledge to a large rock, the dogs newly boisterous at being unharnessed. Karo and Storm slide down the icy slope, Mira follows, the three dogs tumbling and rolling, paws scrabbling at air before a stretch of snow drags them to a stop. They shake themselves off then charge back up the hill with enough verve to bowl a person off their feet.

'The mountain looks passable.' The Chief buckles tight his crampons. 'A freeze after a spell of rain, the entire slope turns to a slick of ice. Even with an ice axe you struggle to gain a purchase.' Directly below them, the scree slope finishes at the cliff line, from there, a fifty-metre plunge to frozen ocean.

Wanny pours warm coffee from the thermos, the largest cup for Sæterdal who has worked up a fearsome thirst. She transfers a pannikin of seal stew to her rucksack, ready to heat on their arrival. She binds her own crampons fast around her boots.

Gingerly they make their way across rock and ice, mindful of each step, of digging their spikes hard into ice. Their course across loose scree sends rocks tumbling down the slope to a chasm of nothingness. On this open slope the darkness swaddles. And yet she finds herself looking out for bears, her imagination sensing a white flash of movement in the corner of her eye that has her reach for her rifle strap – nothing more than a flurry of snow. She follows the Chief as they travel beyond the cliffs to Fuglefjell, to a bird's-eye view of the Villa, their pint-sized hut nestled into rock beneath the moonlight.

'The *selvskudd*.' The Chief gestures. 'Any action?'

Wanny had helped assemble the self-shooting trap on their previous visit, insurance against a hungry bear smashing the hut wall to get to the larder of frozen seal inside the portico. She focuses the field glasses, searches left to right. 'I cannot see it at all.'

'The hut must be blocking your view.'

'I can't tell.'

'Someone down there needs to light the lantern.'

Late November, the eastern end of Hornsund's fjord sealed with ice. Where are all the bears? A wearying surge of thrill and dread rises with each new prospect of a bear, then disappointment at each non-event. Her apprehension is not something to easily share with the Chief. It is enough that he teases her, in one breath advising that, when the moment comes, she must aim for the bear's shoulder or chest, in the next asking her mockingly how she intends to stop her rifle shaking. His masked jeering surfaces from time to time, as if deep down he hopes that she will falter. Wanny will not let it irk her. In her mind she has trained a hundred times for the moment she meets her first bear. She cannot lose her composure. She will not. Wanny thinks to the hunting tales she coaxed from trappers while taxiing them through town. More than one, loosened by beer, spoke of losing his senses, standing paralysed at an unexpected encounter with a bear. Mr Rudi, a trapper esteemed by every other for the bears he has encountered, said that no one should feel shamed by their feelings in the face of a bear. That she is a woman makes no difference: Wanny needs to show *herself* that she is capable, especially in the face of fear.

The dogs race ahead to the hut. But then Karo slows. The three dogs halt. They issue a guttural growl. The Chief slides his rifle from his back, unlocks the safety. 'Your rifle,' he says. 'Keep a sharp lookout.'

The *selvskudd* is smashed into a tumble of wood, the seal bait gone. The Chief kneels down beside paw prints larger than his boot, broad pads edged with claw marks. 'Old prints. One week or more.'

'A bear?' she states the obvious.

'Most certainly a bear.' The Remington rests metres away, strewn amongst the shattered wood. The Chief gathers it up, inspects the barrel. 'It happens.' He empties the shotgun of its cartridge. 'Guns jam.' He turns his attention to the hut. 'We can be thankful the bear didn't punch down the door before it went upon its way.'

They unbar the window shutters, still on edge as they walk down to the shoreline to collect ice jammed along the waterline, taking care to pick clear ice calved from the glacier. She has learned the difference between fresh water ice and its saltwater lookalike. She still smiles at the pucker across Sæterdal's face, a mouthful of salty coffee spat into his mug.

Wanny barely gets the stove alight to melt a pot of ice before the wind rises to a shrill, snow collecting at the corners of the two small windows.

'I'd say we're in for it.' The Chief swaps damp socks for dry, pulls on an old set of clogs he has left here at the farthest hut. The dogs, relegated first to the portico and then outside the hut for their foul air and lack of available floor space, are compensated with hunks of frozen seal that they chomp in seconds before bedding down in snow. Mira now holds her own beside the two Alsatians.

A blizzard from the west keeps Wanny and the Chief hostage indoors. Night and day, sheets of ice break from the fjord and strike the land with an immense roar that jolts Wanny from sleep and puts a temporary pause to the Chief's snoring. Grit and small stones whipped up by the blizzard shower the glass panes on the western wall with such ferocity that Wanny and the Chief pull on anoraks to crawl outside to close the shutter. The wind blasts as they round the corner in the dark on hands and knees, feel their way past the ice box. They blindly dig down into a cornice of hard snow to free the window shutter and set it back in place.

Inside the Villa, they sit on the hut's two square stools with mugs of coffee, the table no bigger than four handkerchiefs joined as a square. Hut-bound by a blizzard, the Chief is uncharacteristically chatty.

'Above me I could hear the poles creaking from the bear's weight. Each time it took a step I expected the roof to cave in on top of me.'

'You stayed there inside?'

The Chief scoffs. 'It turned into a game of waiting. For both of us. In the end I opened the door, rifle ready. Better to be outside, on even terms, than a prisoner in my own hut.'

'You took the bear on the roof?'

'I stood in the doorway and cursed it, loud as I could. Next thing it leaps from the roof to the ground and rushes me. I plugged it square in the snout. A second round to be sure.'

The Chief pours more coffee, hot and strong, the pot on the stove large enough to see them through a day. 'It is not until afterward,' he says, 'that you think what would happen if your rifle jammed.' He hands a fresh mug to Wanny. 'Not all hunters care for their rifle the way you do. Clean and oiled and dry.'

A small compliment that has her glow. 'You think here at Fuglefjell is our best chance for blue fox?'

'Enough to warrant the effort of travelling sixty kilometres out and back every few weeks.' He takes a noisy slurp. 'That is *hot*,' he says. 'A good place for white fox as well. The whites are our bread and butter. Blues are the cream on the milk.'

'I will not believe there is anything in the world finer than a white fox pelt.'

He shrugs. 'The well-heeled argue otherwise. They want what is hardest to obtain. The rarer, the more exotic, the greater the demand. Commerce has always been that way. Take Spitsbergen coal,' he says. 'Rich folk on the mainland fork out the extra, those miners at Advent Bay risking their bacon to earn ten or fifteen kroner a day. Not me,' he says. 'I'd rather battle a bear than be lying in a coffin-sized hole under frozen ground, hammering at rock night and day.'

'How much for a blue fox?'

'In prime condition?' The Chief gives a whistle. 'Eight hundred, one thousand kroner. At least, they used to fetch that much.'

'Hmm.' Wanny strums her mug, the coffee scalding. 'Watch out, Little Blue.'

❄

Finally, the wind abates. Day eases apart to a low-slung moon casting daggered shadows, a throw of deep blue light, a fleeting hint of gold on the opposite shore. Hillocks of snow outside the hut door wriggle into life, three dogs shaking off their snow blankets, icicles stuck to their mat of hind hair.

The blizzard has transformed the shoreline into a rampart of ice blown in from the fjord, layer upon layer rafted up, in places metres high. Farther out on the fjord, even in dim light, leads of inky water contrast against stark pans of ice. Wanny and the Chief may as easily be standing on the moon as here at the end station on the earthly shores of Hornsund. On the lee side of the hut a ramp of snow gravelled with grit and stone reaches the roof, upon it a fresh set of fox prints up and down.

'He must have been on our roof this very morning.' The Chief rubs his hands. 'It is a good omen. Our first house fox, right above our heads, while you three,' he turns to the dogs, 'were too buried in your snow beds to even notice.'

The Chief chops a frozen flank of seal into four. One each for the hungry dogs; the fourth he dices small, and flings upon the roof beyond the reach of the dogs.

'We won't set traps too near the hut. For now, we want the rascal alive. If it's a young fox it is likely to attract others to our neighbourhood, especially when there's free food on offer.'

The Chief takes the dogs to search for driftwood, then up onto the slopes to hunt for ptarmigan. Wanny packs her rucksack to tend the fox traps. She finds the small shovel in the portico to dig snow from the traps. She latches the hut door behind her and straps her rifle across her shoulder. Perhaps the echo of the Chief's bear on the hut roof has her glance up. She startles. Sitting daintily, casually licking its muzzle, sits a small silver fox.

'Well, hello,' she says softly. The small fox has a familiar pattern of fur on its snout and ears. 'Is that you, Little Blue?' In every other way it looks entirely different, transformed from its summer to its winter coat. 'Just look at you in all your finery.' The fox holds her gaze as if just the lilt of her voice is a curiosity. 'You've found yourself a treat up there.'

The fox rises. It patters down the snow slope from the roof in a motion as fluid as a fish. Then it halts, two metres away. It looks to Wanny, raises its snout, tips its head to the side in a questioning gesture. *What is it?* Wanny wonders. The fox turns and tears away, fast as lightning, up into the slopes where a score of traps lay waiting to be baited. 'Keep your wits about you.' Wanny sets off in the same direction.

Do not grow soft, Ivanna. Eight hundred, one thousand kroner.

Three of the nearest traps are fallen with fox, two are perfect white specimens; the third, the largest, one eye blind, one ear torn and ragged. The softness of each pelt. The thrill of it. If those at home could see her now. Her aging husband named her naïve for believing she could do this. Words to punch a person down like bread dough, knock them into shape. She pictures Martin alone in the house, wilting without her there.

By afternoon her back and arms ache from baiting sticks, from lifting each frame, setting each trigger lock, gingerly piling a weight of stone upon each trap while waiting for the whole assembly to collapse.

Wanny carries the bundle of white fox down the hill to the Villa, her eyes adjusting to the dark. Perhaps Little Blue is somewhere out there now.

She hangs the trio of fox, a silky cloud of white against her cheek, inside the portico ready for flensing. She lights the paraffin lantern and hangs it in the window above the table, the room a golden glow. She relights the stove. The firebox is so small it can only smoulder for a few hours. She pours herself the dregs of coffee grown stale in its pot since morning, barely tepid and sludgy with grounds. Imagine serving up this brew at the Grand.

She gets on with the makings for supper, potatoes kept from freezing in a towel in her sleeping bag, thick slabs of bacon, corn-flour and meat powder for the gravy, the heel of the Chief's bread to soak the juices. She has much to report: a morning visitor up there on the roof, three fine white foxes hanging in the portico. She listens to the spit and crackle of the stove, the rising warmth of the hut. Wanny reaches for the cutting board. She sits at the tiny table, the weight off her feet. She takes up her knife, the window glass so pitted and scratched that the world of Fuglefjell would be obscured even if it were light enough outside to see. She peels and quarters potatoes, puts them in a battered pot. The feeling of warmth radiating from the stove. Simple joys, a trapper once described it. 'Yes,' she murmurs to the window.

❄

'I flense the first one,' Anders tells her. 'You watch and learn, then you must do the next.'

The woman shakes her head. 'I couldn't stand to damage it.'

'I will talk you through it. You watch for now.' He guesses she will be as quick to learn this as with every other task he has shown her.

Anders has his favourite knife ready on the table, small and deadly sharp, a pair of pliers and a larger fleshing knife. From a nail on the wall he hangs the fox by its leg. Carefully he slices the skin from the back of the opposite heel, runs a line up the back of the leg all the way to the vent. He rehangs the fox by the worked leg and does the same with the other. He draws a circle with his knife to cut the vent free.

'Fox are thin skinned,' he tells the woman. 'A touch of fat early in the season, but all in all they have scant to keep them warm.'

'They need their winter coat,' she says.

He gives a wry smirk. 'Not this fellow.' He holds the fox in his hands, lays it on its back upon the tiny table. 'First, the tail.' Blade edge up, Anders cuts a line through the fur partway down from the stem of the tail. 'Just far enough along to grip the head of the tail bone with your hand. You see?' With the skin in one hand and tail bone in the other, he pulls the length of tail free in a single sweep. 'The same as pulling a knife from its scabbard. Then we make a neat cut right down the centre line so the tail can open and dry.'

'It gives off a fearful stench,' the woman says.

'We could wait until it is frozen, but this way we don't need to open out the guts.' The rank insides would give anyone cause for complaint. 'Once you get to this point,' he tells her, 'it takes very little force to ease off the rest of the skin. After one or two you'll get a feel for it.' She covers her nose with her handkerchief. He looks to her and grins. 'Are you managing?'

Behind her handkerchief mask she nods vigorously. Her eyes are the green of the lights.

Slowly and carefully Anders pulls down the skin in small measured tugs, pausing to scrape back the webbing of membrane strung between skin and flesh. 'Take care with your knife as you do this, careful not to pierce the skin.' He reaches the juncture of the arms and pulls one arm through, then the other. 'Claws and all,' he says. He continues dragging off the skin until he reaches the crushed curve of skull.

'It is like pulling off a sweater,' she says.

'The same.'

Gradually he works the skin from each ear with his fingers, small pieces of cartilage, still attached. Anders takes his pliers to isolate each ear bud, a sharp knife to work them free, using his fingers to pull the ear skin through, scrape away the last of the cartilage then push the ear flap back to skin-side out. He uses his knife to tease the skin from the rims around the eyes, then tugs the pelt over the top of the crown and down over the fox's snout. The lips and snout peel off with it.

What is left of the fox sits on the table between them. 'A creature without its coat is a sorry-looking specimen.'

'Meat,' he says in reply. 'Though not for human consumption. Even a dog will turn up its nose at a feed of fox. Some are riddled with worms and parasites.'

She brightens the lamp in a hum of paraffin. Anders turns the tube of skin to inspect it. 'Wanny, we want to preserve this middle section – this reddish skin here around the saddle. But these small globules of fat, here under the arms, here around the hind area, we scrape away without breaking the skin.' He takes his larger fleshing knife and works it down the length of the skin. 'You see how I do it? Different to a bearskin where you must apply a great deal of pressure.' He turns the pelt to scrape the next section.

'Is it a good grade?' she asks.

He nods. 'First class. The fur is fine and is snow white all the way to the skin. As good as it comes.'

Smiling eyes. He returns his focus to the fox. 'A young one,' he says.

'The size?'

'All Svalbard foxes are small beside their mainland cousins. Because of the harshness, finding enough food to survive. You tip your cap to a Svalbard fox simply for getting through a winter.'

Anders takes the carcase and opens the jaw to show her the teeth. 'Two perfect white rows. There's always the exception, but most of the time the teeth give you some idea of the age. By three years of age a fox is likely to have lost or broken some of its teeth. By four it's nearing the end of its hunting days. Some old fox have no teeth left at all. The same applies to the condition of the skin. An older fox who has lived a hard life, has had its share of scrapes, the skin will be punctured with tears and holes. Damaged pelts are classed such that they pay a fraction of the price. The trouble is,' he says, 'we can't know the condition until we skin them. We take what we get.'

She looks suddenly full of herself.

'What?' he says.

'I had a visitor this morning.'

She is pretty when she smiles. 'Did you now?'

'Upon our very roof.'

'Next you will tell me it was a bear.'

'A fox,' she says. 'Little Blue. At least it looked like Little Blue. Its pelt has changed to the most astonishing silvery steely grey – I can't begin to describe it.'

Did he not say so? 'Very good,' he says. He feels a boyish surge of pride, a flood of warmth in how *taken* she is by it all. It wakens something in him, reels him back to his first season up here, everything new and big. Only a fellow trapper comprehends exactly how it makes you feel. 'That rascal fox found the snacks then. He'll be back for more. You can count on it.'

'Maybe he is a she.'

'Time will tell.' Anders scrapes fat from the base of the tail, lightly scrapes each foot. Small globules oil the wooden table. 'Normally we stretch the fox over a wide board, skin-side out, pull it down tight and tack it in place to dry for a day. Then turn it outside in – the fur-side out – and hang it outdoors on a line to finish drying. These three we'll bag with salt, keep them damp and soft, take them back to the main base to finish off.' He takes a rag from the nail on the door to wipe his hands. 'You are ready?'

'You think I should?'

'Wanny, you must,' he says matter-of-factly, 'if you plan to call yourself a trapper.'

They trade places, he having to move back against the bunk, she sidling past him to reach the opposite side. She retrieves a second fox from the portico and takes her place at the table. She works well, as nimble with a knife as with her needle and embroidery. 'You can see the need for a sharp blade,' he says. From time to time he takes the knife from her hand to demonstrate the best technique. 'That is better,' he says, the feel of her hand warm as he guides it beneath his. 'Now you have it.' He sits back on the stool. Tomorrow morning, he calculates, one last check of the traps, tidy things up. No *selvskudd* to arm, thanks to Mister Bear, and not enough suitable timber here at the Villa to build another in its place. They will head back across the glacier to Hyttevika beneath a near full moon. 'What do you say we try for one more trip out here before Christmas? Any longer and the traps are likely to be scavenged.'

She scrapes back membrane, pulls through each small arm. She pulls the last piece of skin over the snout and stands back. 'How does it look?'

'Scrape away the fat,' he says. 'Use the fleshing knife and then we'll have a look.'

He guides her hand, his on hers, to emphasise the angle of the blade, the lightness of pressure. He feels her pull away. 'I have it now.'

Anders sits back, distracted, an unwanted feeling pulsing inside him. *Do not turn witless, Sæterdal.*

She works slowly and carefully. Rather that than some he's seen tear a skin in haste. She turns the pelt toward the lamplight, holds it to him to inspect. 'Is it as it should be?'

Small hands, her fingernails glossed from flensing. 'Not a blemish. You have done quite well.'

'My first,' she says, holding the softness of it against her cheek. 'Thank you, Chief.'

'For what?'

'For trusting me.'

In a giddy surge he reaches across the table and sets her hand in his, muddled between wanting to shake her hand and clasp it. He is taken aback when she pulls it free.

She busies herself with the knives. He gathers up the carcases, flustered. 'You need a great deal more strength to flense a bear,' says he. 'Have you thought about how you'll manage?'

'I am quite strong,' she says defiantly. 'I have flensed sheep and cow. I will learn if you will teach me.'

Darkness. Wind ramping up from the west, all but a haze from the moon apparent, its beam concealed by thick cloud. He and Wanny round the slopes of Fannytoppen, a long and arduous return on foot to their main base at Hyttevika. The blizzard from days ago has lined each undulation with snow, while along the rises the snow has blown clean, leaving sleek runnels of ice. They dig their crampons in hard and move westward toward the boulder where skis and sledge are tethered. Anders takes the lead, Wanny behind, dogs whimpering as they pick their way around sharp stones and slippery ice. Anders takes a long stride across the ice. He lands hard, his foot turned awkwardly. He slips, slides, tries to right himself by running toward a strip of snow but the ice beneath his boot will have none of it. On his arse sliding over ice spiked with rock. He gets spun around and careens downhill, shoulder first. He gains speed, desperately trying to get himself turned back as he shears down the slope. Below him are the cliffs. He is partway on his back, clawing at ice to gain a purchase. A violent halt. Jolted and choked in the process of stopping. He pants like a dog, too winded to know how badly he is hurt, if bones are broken. He lies rigid and still, his heart pounding in his chest, his breath heaving with pain.

From somewhere above he hears the woman's voice, hazy as a dream.

His legs are loose, his arms free, yet his head he can raise only an inch from the ground. What holds him? He prickles. A broken neck? On either side of him a swathe of shiny ice that brings to mind the satin lining of a coffin. Somewhere below him a precipice.

'Chief,' he hears her cry.

'I have stopped,' he calls in short bursts, his breathing laboured. 'You are not to move from that spot.' The order he musters sounds nothing like his normal voice.

'Anders, are you hurt?' she cries from above. 'Are you safe?'

'There is no danger,' he says. 'I need to lie and rest a while.' He tries to move. A shudder of pain. He hears himself groan.

A crunch of footsteps. 'Do not come any further,' he commands. The footsteps grow closer.

'Chief,' she cries, her silhouette an arm's length away, 'take my arm. Slide your way toward me.'

'I am happy here,' he says.

'Sæterdal!' she snaps. 'Don't be a bloody fool. You are hooked on a stone. Take my arm,' she hisses. 'You are still on slippery ice. Here.' She stretches her arm, takes his in her grip. 'I have a good footing.'

He cannot say who is pulling who, only that the tightness at his head tugs at his throat, resisting release. He hears a rip of fabric. He is free. He slides toward her, gets a single foothold in the snow beside her knee, enough to lever himself away from the slick of ice.

She helps him up to sitting, his back and side racked with pain.

She gestures to where he had lain, to an inch of pointed stone poking up through the ice. 'The hood of your anorak was snagged. That stone is all that stopped you.'

They sit two metres above the drop. He registers the culprit, a loose crampon, twisted to the side of his boot.

Wanny adjusts his crampon and tightens the strap around his boot. 'Are you able to stand? Climb the slope? I will help you.'

'I am perfectly capable,' he says, getting to his knees, shaky on his feet, accepting her shoulder as they plod up the slope.

They reach the sled. She harnesses the dogs without getting in a tangle. Even they, for once, are compliant. 'You are hurt, Anders. You need to rest. Let's have you navigate our course from the sled. I will ski ahead to lead the dogs. You call right, left. Yes?'

Anders nods. 'Perhaps that will work.' Perhaps he has earned himself a small rest.

FOX

onto the frozen fjord

FOOD GROWS SCARCE. The runt inspects the perimeter of empty hut, pausing at each scent to distinguish human from dog from fox. She longs for meat. She climbs to the roof of the hut to search for titbits of seal she might have missed. She sniffs the chimney pipe, ice cold against her snout; she greases it with her muzzle to conjure the heady flavours that rise from the hut when the trappers are within.

Down the snow ramp she goes, her paws swallowed by a fresh topping of soft snow.

There is *something*. A stench of unreachable seal, the prospect so tantalising that, not for the first time, the runt paws at the hut's portico, chews at tar paper, tears at edges of the wood. She burrows down through new snow, her efforts to find a way into the hut once more thwarted by the subterranean seal of frozen earth.

The runt takes to the slopes near her parents' den. She waits for her father to appear. She follows at a distance as he trolls the snowy slopes beneath the bird cliffs, disappearing through a cluster of boulders. She stays downwind, moves further up the slope to where she watches him dig down through snow until all but the white tip of his tail and hind paws are visible. Dog fox reverses up from his tunnel in a mad wriggle, a kittiwake locked in his jaw.

He sits with the desiccative bird held between his forelimbs, his gapped teeth tearing frozen breast from bone. By the time dog fox has moved away, all that remains of the bird are its wings, a scattering of splintered bone, specks of gristle. The runt crunches them down.

Her first companion is no more, too slow for the wooden jaws and its tumble of rocks. The runt had watched the hunter extract it from the trap, the fox laid out on the snow beside two others, one of them her brother, the skulls misshapen into different creatures. A reek of fresh meat had wafted through the air.

A new pair, both young whites, join the runt. It is a tenuous friendship for she will fight for first rights to food.

Hunger drives the trio out onto the frozen fjord in biting wind that parts their coats in ripples of cold. They patrol a tide crack. They linger at a seal hole, the three peering intently for an offering to rise from that frigid bowl of ocean. The runt begins to shiver. The three trace fresh tracks across the ice where other foxes roam. They return to land for protection from the wind, their hunger harder than before.

The runt sleeps. She wakes with a plan. Westward she travels, alone, around the big mountain, guided by the scent from the hunters and their dogs. At the edge of land, the hunters' trail forms ragged lines and patterns across the glacier's broad river of ice. The runt ventures forward. She stops, checks back, searches ahead then eases into a trot, scaling the rising gradient to where snow peters out to a saddle of ice slick. Unless she punctures the ice with the points of her claws, she will slide backward. She slows. She finally stops, unhappy with her footing and the vast breadth of terrain. The glacier is devoid of scent, empty of promise. She turns back. She partially skates, partially paces down the incline until she re-joins her outbound tracks through snow. Onward she bounds, back toward the mountainside.

On the shoreline near the hut sits a headland crowned with an elongated mound of stone. Coarse lichen coats the outer stones, interrupted where the arrangement has been disturbed. The runt has seen the trappers wander here, seen them kneel to peer inside before replenishing the seal of stones. The runt sits here now, a single large stone shattered and rolled loose, too small a gap to wedge her shoulders through. The cavity within is a den of sorts, lined with lengths of bone. The runt pushes her snout in through the gap, her tongue tip meeting the skull, aged and chalky with salt. She takes short sniffs, draws in the faint scent of a long-ago man, the odour of his musty coverings.

The runt and her companions wander the slopes above the trappers' hut, inspecting each gaping wooden jaw. The runt sits, salivating, fixed on the sweetness of the flesh speared within. Meat that is hers for the taking. If she could slink down low. If she could slide in on her belly, steal that meat before the jaws crack down.

9

Hyttevika, Christmas

WANNY WAKES IN her bunk. Directly above her head is the sweet young face of Sonja Henie, Norway's very own 'Pavlova of the ice', who glides effortlessly across the ceiling boards on figure skates. Swimmers and wrestlers, skiers and boxers, their limbs and middles creased, also tumble about above her to their heart's content. The Chief approves of her innovation: the pages of *Sporting Man* newly covering ceiling boards ingrained with two decades of smoke and damp.

She remembers the ice bear of her dream, is seized with the urge to share it before the image escapes her memory. The Chief is up already, moving gingerly from his fall down the mountainside, his face strained, refusing her plea to rest. No. He stands rigid, his back to the stove, kneading his bread dough at the table, inspecting his beloved jar of living yeast.

Wanny leans out from her bunk, strands of her hair as limp as old rope.

'*God morgen*,' she says. '*God Jul*.' Her first at Hyttevika.

'A happy Christmas to you,' he says curtly.

'Is your back bad?'

'I am perfectly well.'

'You do not look it.'

A dismissive grunt. They have not been at ease since Fuglefjell, he seemingly as confounded as her when his hand reached for hers, he offended by the rebuttal. She would have dismissed the moment as a misstep were it not for the mountain. Anders supine on the ice slope, struggling to free himself from the single stone that held him, no notion that freedom would sail him over the cliff. Wanny had taken control. The Chief had no choice but to place his faith in her, his partner, dependent on her help. Wanny had grown bigger in the moment. She had looked down on Sæterdal, his face in anguish, and offered reassurance. She had seen fear quieten into trust. Then or maybe after, she no longer has it straight in her mind, he was hauled across to safety, both of them silent with relief. She had placed his hand in hers and he had not pulled away. With that gesture had come a bodily shift. A reminder of a long-forgotten feeling. Wanny watches the Chief from her bunk. She takes a stuttered breath. *Have it all return to normal.*

'Sæterdal,' she says brightly.

'This is he.'

'I dreamt of a bear.' Wanny describes the vivid image of the bear's heel guards. 'The exact same kind you have on your boots.'

The Chief looks thoughtful. 'Then it is a good omen,' says he. 'Because I, too, dreamt of bears.' He divides the dough into twelve small loaves.

By late morning the Hyttevika hut steams like a washhouse, windows beaded with condensation, the air thick with rising bread dough, washed clothes on their third day of drying strung from one edge of the room to the other. Wanny has put out clean hand towels. A multicoloured cloth newly pinned beneath the window. She has a cheery cloth ready to cover the table once the baking is done. The Chief has chopped extra wood, stacked indoors where they can find a space. She has washed down walls and floor, the hut festive for *Jul*.

She spoons the *formkake* into its tin and slides it in the oven, the last scrapings from the margarine tin set aside for *hjortekakk*, deer antler cookies. She starts on the *fattigmann*, poor man's cookies, the dough needing to rest before rolling it out. All improvised creations that may not be as good without fresh eggs, but every tray that goes into Hyttevika's oven is as keenly anticipated by humans and dogs as it would be by Tromsø's finest households.

The heat! Minus thirty outside and sweltering in here. Wanny peels off a layer, reties her apron. She finds the opener and punctures a new can of Viking, the condensed milk as liquid as summer with the heat of the room. She stands before the mixing bowl, adding cinnamon, a pinch from a tin of cardamom unearthed from the cold porch from Lord knows how many seasons ago, the label long gone. She presses against the table as she folds milk into the mixture, her hip bones knocking the table edge. She has lost some weight. Again, she is without her monthlies. She is thirty-nine. Not old enough, surely, for the change. It has to be the hours outside, the distances they travel. She mixes in a half mug of sugar. Utters a laugh. Perhaps a woman put to work in Svalbard is no different to a house cow that loses its milk when put to the plough. She feels well and healthy and that is what counts. Life is measurably easier without the nuisance days.

The Chief strides in from outside, his movement easier, his demeanour brighter than the man he was this morning. 'All set,' he says of his triumph. 'A trial run before we leave for Fuglefjell.'

He takes her out to the Signal, the new name for their multi-purpose flagpole. He shines the torchlight upon the wooden pole set thirty metres beyond the back wall of the hut. 'When the occupants of Hyttevika both dream of a bear, it must not be ignored.' A slab of seal hangs at half-mast like a crumpled pennant, tied to a cord that winds its way through a pulley at the top of the pole, all the way back to the lesser-used door of the hut. The Chief secures the loose end of cord around a wooden stopper, wedged into a carved hole in the door.

'A cork in a bottle,' she says. The stopper is sufficiently tapered to poke several inches through into the inside of the hut. Over the inner end he drapes a string of old milk cans. He yanks on the cord to demonstrate the effect of a bear taking the bait. A clang of metal to wake the dead.

'When the racket starts up.' He takes aim with an imaginary rifle.

'Won't the bear take fright?'

He thinks on that. 'Bears are skilful hunters. They weigh the risks before committing to action. With a tasty hunk of seal in his chops, he won't be in a hurry to surrender his meal.'

The Chief calls her over to the shooting hatch on the hut's back wall. Carefully he slides it open, the hatch wide enough for the person inside the hut to rest the stock of a barrel, to angle their rifle this way or that, a direct line of fire to the Signal. 'This is a different matter,' he says. 'The hatch must not bang. Not a scrape or squeak. At this point of the game, silence is golden.' He cups a hand to his ear. 'Once Mrs Woldstad hears the cans clatter, she rests down her coffee and newspaper and takes up her rifle. Carefully, slowly.' He opens the hatch. 'Pow! Mister Bear drops conveniently beside the hut.'

'So then I shall be spending the rest of winter with my feet up? Can it really be that easy?'

'Nothing lost by trying,' he says. 'Your Mr Rudi caught a bear or two this way, he told me, from this very hut.'

Sæterdal never misses the chance to tease her. 'He is not *my* Mr Rudi.'

He clasps his hands to his chest with a sigh. 'That old boy's name is hallowed. No other hunter compares.'

She laughs. 'And you, Mr Sæterdal, talk like a green-eyed husband.'

The Chief smirks. Wanny returns to the stove. She feeds small pieces into the fuel box. This shift. The easy banter. How simple it would be. 'I have a husband,' she blurts.

The Chief draws a sharp breath. He crosses over to stand beside her. 'You are widowed.'

'Yes. That too.'

He pulls a stool close to the stove. 'Speak,' he says sharply.

She takes a breath. Where to start? 'My husband, my first husband, he was taken by the influenza. Martin is my second husband. He is many years older. He is – he was, at least, he used to be – a baker.' As if that babble explains how she came to be his wife. How colourless the years. Wanny flounders for words to have Sæterdal comprehend her position. She will not diminish herself by pretending that her reluctance toward him is one of wifely honour. Her dues in that regard are fully paid. In Martin she was granted a kind and willing man with no shared interests, no shred of common ground other than the church they shared and the streets they walked. She looked upon him fondly, indentured, resigned to a future both solitary and dull. A partnership adorned with a simple gold band and the taking of his name. The obligatory submission to marital presumptions. 'It has taken me all this time,' Wanny starts. She stops. Takes a deep breath. 'To re-right myself,' she finally splutters.

The Chief looks at her in puzzlement.

'To stand alone,' she states. She will not lose herself again.

Anders threads his fingers. He straightens pain from his back. Her prattle is lost on him. He feels a cold flare of anger. 'You didn't think to tell me earlier? When you asked to come? That I had the right to know?'

She looks as meek as a lost child. 'You spoke about *my reputation* as a widow. Being married: would that not have made it worse?'

He shakes his head, the air sucked clean out of him. 'I don't know. Only that I should like to have been told.' He stands fixed, waiting to be flung from this eerie calm he feels. 'What does this – what is his name?'

She opens the stove door. Lifts out a baking tin. 'Martin Woldstad.' She stabs the steaming cake with a knife. 'Why is there not a cake skewer in this place?'

'What does he have to say about his wife,' Anders says, 'his property, coming up here, spending the year with me?'

She clangs the stove door, steel on steel, her face flushed red. 'A wife, Sæterdal, in name alone. I am no man's property.' She takes an audible breath. 'What I do is my own concern,' she says. 'Nor would he likely have me back.'

His skin prickles. 'You left your marriage for me?'

'Not at all! Not for you. I came here . . . for this.' She seems to scramble for words. 'Not just this,' she finishes, expecting him to make sense of her disjointed babble.

Anders looks out the window to the noonday gloom, a quarter moon waiting to rise. He looks back to her, her skin gilded by the lantern. A new thought riddles his mind. 'Anything else I should know? That you failed to mention?'

He hears her sigh. 'There is something more.'

'Save us,' he mutters.

'I have two sons. They are not Martin's,' she rushes. 'Othar, my first husband. They were babes when he died.'

'They are children?'

'Bjørvik is fourteen. He is practically a man. Alf is twelve. They are good boys.'

'And where are they while you are here?'

'They are together,' she says defensively. 'Bjørvik has started working. They are boarded with a friend. She is practically an aunt. They are well cared for. I would not have left them otherwise.'

He speaks slowly for effect. 'My children are at home with their mother.' His gaze does not waver. Judge. Jury. Executioner.

The scowl of disdain she gives him. As if he is the accused waiting in the dock. 'What am I to say to that, Sæterdal?' her voice rising. 'Feel ashamed that that is how it ought to be? That a man shall know a freedom that a woman never can?' He meets the steely look.

He has no answer. 'You lied to me,' he reminds her. That is the heart of it.

'I did not *lie*.'

'By omission you did, Mrs Woldstad.' Sting her with the name.

She sighs, deflated. 'I am sorry. Truly, Anders. I so much want to be here. To prove myself to you. You know I am grateful to be given this chance.'

Anders tries to understand. 'Why now? Why tell me now?'

She fidgets with her apron, on the verge of saying something. What is she resisting? Is it only he that feels this push and pull between them? In everything they do, in how they spend each day and night. He studies her stricken face, searching for a truth.

'My boys,' she finally says. 'I miss them but can never speak of them. And you,' she says. 'You have a right to know my circumstances.'

There you have it, Sæterdal: no thought or feeling beyond that expected of a working partner. He scoffs at her pandering. 'A right to know now it is too late. You must have thought me a simpleton, so easy to lead on.'

'That isn't so,' she says. 'That isn't it at all.'

He cannot believe a word she says. He stands and arches his back to stretch, grimaces with pain. He lifts his rifle from its holder on the wall; every muscle in his body hurts from his fall.

'Is it bad?' she asks.

He refuses to show her his wounds. 'I need to get on. Check the *selvskudds*. Start putting things together for Fuglefjell. Bad enough that we missed the last moon. Any fox will be savaged to pieces by the time we get out there.'

She gives an exasperated cry. 'You were injured. You needed extra days to rest.'

'I decide what is right for me. I am no concern of yours.'

He collects a handful of rifle shells, pulls on his thick wool sweater. He lifts his coat from the back of the door. Hat and gloves. The door to the cold porch creaks with a blast of frigid air.

He turns back to face her. 'A baker, you say.'

Yes, she nods.

'He might have taught you how to bake a decent loaf of bread.'

White fox pelts stretch from their line, drying in the frigid cold. Last year, with Levin Winter as his partner, they totalled a record forty-five, amongst them some blues. Four saleable pelts is all he and the woman have to their name so far, their first fox too badly mauled to count, and only one extra white since the three brought back from Fuglefjell. To add to his distress, not one of these barrels is filled with a bearskin. They are well behind. It is entirely the woman's fault. He should have heeded his instincts.

He unleashes the dogs from their chain, Mira refusing to be left behind. He gives a piercing whistle when his two romp away to darkness. 'Here!' he shouts them back. Storm, the straggler, gets the touch of a boot against his rump.

He forges out into the polar night, his dogs close, the crescent moon of meagre help. Before he reaches the first *selvskudd*, the sky brightens of its own accord, a slow realisation to Anders who is lost in darkened thoughts. He stops to look to the heavens above. He turns his ear. The old Sámi hunters say you can hear the lights.

Greens, whites, a ribbon of pink, streaks of wispy cloud that deepen into folds. He fancies the old legend of an Arctic fox leaping through the sky, sparking the lights as its tail brushes mountaintops. He turns, his neck craned, feels himself grow dizzy. A sky dancing with colour and movement. He is not a holy man, but this, he thinks, is as close as a soul can come to godliness. He stands transfixed. The woman never tires of the lights. She will stay outside in bitter cold, marvelling at it all until he calls her back inside.

Fool, Sæterdal. He marches on.

Why be bothered? A woman's husband and children are of scant concern to him. At the end of a year they will shake hands and go their separate ways, same as he and Winter, same as any pair of trappers. So long as she pulls her weight while she works the year with him.

The first *selvskudd* stands baited and untouched. He paces around, the snow a glow of green beneath the lights. Nothing but fox prints.

From high in the mountains a fox calls. The sound eerie, womanly.

He walks beneath the coloured sky. The knot inside him slowly frees itself loose. This place calms him. Always has, this raw terrain a world apart from the soft green slopes of home. He is a different man here – he feels the difference – a man he prefers to who he is in town. In Tromsø he has always felt on show, measured by the yardsticks of those around him. The rough way he dresses, the loose way he speaks, a joviality he exploits for the laughs it wins before laughter itself grows weary. They know him as a talker, while up here, checking traps, the *selvskudds*, he and his dogs, even out here with the woman, the place does all the speaking.

It is their life inside the hut that unsettles him. A domesticity that lures him back into a softer world. Bodily thoughts that turn him inside out. Svalbard is no place for a woman.

He tenses, picks up his pace. Deceit is what riles him.

Would you have taken her, Sæterdal, had you known her encumbrance?
My word he would not.

He feels his breath labour as he climbs the hill to the next
selvskudd. He suspects a cracked rib from his mishap down the
mountainside, in which case there is nothing to be done, no cure
but time. Pointless to complain or dwell on the discomfort. He
relives the prospect of plunging to his death had he been on the
mountain alone. Everything upended, his life entrusted to a woman.
A strength that had humbled him.

The second *selvskudd* is as the first. Several rocks stacked on
top to weight it down have tumbled. He slides off his rucksack,
reaches for his rifle to rest it on his pack. He halts. The lightness
to his back. He startles. He has no rifle. He turns. It will be back
at the first *selvskudd*. No. He would not lay a rifle down in snow.
His skin prickles. The hut. He has left it propped in the cold
porch. Only a novice, a town man, would forget his rifle. It is her
fault for discombobulating him. He looks around. Out here with
no defence. In the dark. A hunter reduced to easy prey.

He feels panicked. He thinks to retrieve the sawn-off Remington
from the *selvskudd*. To do so he must disassemble the wooden box,
undo the fiddly arrangement of screws. He could be halfway home
in the time it would take. All for a single shell at meagre range.
The snow dances with the reflection of the lights. *Sæterdal. Stop.
Stop and think.* He has the dogs. They would alert him. He only
needs give the order for Karo and Storm to attack. Young dogs
they may be, but ready to fight, fuelled with the memory of their
mother cut down by the swipe of a bear paw. Mira, the woman's
dog, he cannot be sure of.

Anders feels his chest thud as he marches back toward the hut.
Each deep breath a nod to his injuries. He crosses the rise to a
pinpoint of yellow light – far in the distance, the lantern hanging
in the window. The hut decked out for Christmas. *At least be civil*

to her, man. Just get through the year. He slows, looks about through the dark. He calls his dogs, slows his pace.

The larger of two wash tubs hangs high on the porch wall, a tub the size to bathe a child. Wanny sweeps out the flakes of rust, carries it into the main room and sets it down beside the stove. She checks that she can fit in the thing. Her sides scrape the tin. It will have to do. *Clear your head, Ivanna. Clean your body and put on fresh clothes.*

The Chief's disdain. She has apologised. It is done now. This is Christmas Eve. She empties a kettle of scalding water, another from the large copper basin. Steam rises from the tub. She refills kettle and copper and sets them back on the stove. She adds ice to the tub, testing with her hand until the heat lowers to bearable. She undresses, takes flannel and soap, tentatively lowers herself into the water. She sits with her knees to her chest. The water barely reaches her navel and covers only the top of her thighs. She drapes her legs over the edge of the tub, her feet resting on the floor. At least her upper body is wet and pink from heat. She savours the feeling of being cradled by warmth.

Martin's bathroom with its deep clawfoot bath was the single space she sequestered as her own. The room held just enough space for an inside water closet, installed, at her husband's insistence, for her comfort. During her soak in the tub, no one demanded anything of her. A place free of encroachment. Within that hug of warmth, her body, her imaginings, her softened skin, once more became her own. A quarter hour to fill that ample tub, the bathroom door and window kept shut to hold the heat, the steam in the room as thick as a sauna. A tall copper water heater stood beside the bath atop its own wood burner, stoked night and day with wood that Martin chopped. Not once did he begrudge that excess. As if he understood her need for solitude.

Wanny pours an enamel mug of bathwater over her hair, not caring that water splashes to the floor and spits against the stove. She lathers her hair, scrubbing her scalp, combing out the tangles with her fingers. Warm water slides down her back and chest as she rinses the suds. She soaps the flannel and cleans her arms and hands, her armpits and breasts, the parts of her back she can reach. She cleans her belly, legs, her calloused knees, her intimate parts. She has lost a good deal more weight. She has never been as fit. She wedges one foot at a time inside the bath and cleans between each toe.

She closes her eyes, soaks for a time. The hut warm, the water soothing, the smell of baking lingers. Martin's clothes, his hair, his skin infused with the reek of dough. *Churlish, Ivanna. Who are you to hand down judgement?*

The water cools. She stands in the tub, calf deep in water, dripping before the stove.

A yelp. The dogs. She grabs her towel and wraps it around her body. The porch door. A rush of cold. The Chief. She steps from the tub. 'I wasn't expecting you so soon.'

'You need not worry.' He looks exhausted. He doesn't have the decency to turn away. 'I have seen more than my share of women's bodies. Yours is nothing exceptional.'

She hates him. 'Small wonder you have ended up on your own,' she snaps.

He doesn't answer. He doesn't seem to look *at* her; it's as if his gaze is *through* her, as if she is as insubstantial as a piece of gauze. Wanny takes a breath. *Settle. Get a hold of your temper.* She steps toward her bunk.

'I will use the bathwater if you are finished,' says he. 'I promised myself a bath for Christmas.'

'There is more hot water on the stove.'

'Of course there is,' he mocks. 'I have nothing better to do than chop and cart firewood all day long.'

Wanny draws in on herself but in this hut there is no escape. She dresses at her bunk, towels her hair and combs it through. She removes dried clothes to fit her wet towel on the line. They occupy the same room, the same floor space, they breathe the same air, two strangers in a dance of aversion.

The Chief undresses before her as if he were entirely on his own in this hut. He tops up the bathwater with the kettle, at ease with his nakedness. He lowers himself down to kneel in the tub, drawing breath at the heat. Wanny looks upon his back. His shoulder blades, ribs, knots of spine grazed and red raw, his back purpled and yellow. 'The state of your back,' she says.

He does not turn. 'Not as resplendent as the rest of me?'

'You look to be pummelled with a meat mallet.'

He laughs. A real laugh. Wanny loosens. 'There are some who might enjoy that,' he says.

I am here to help you, she wants to tell him. Not to battle with you. Not to be a hindrance. 'Let me rub in some salve when you finish.'

'Perhaps,' he says. 'I will see what is left once I wash off the dirt.'

Not a no. It is something.

Evening. They set the table for Christmas Eve dinner. Music from the wind-up gramophone lifts the mood. They sit down to rissoles, potatoes, green peas. The stilted conversation turns to one of bears. Bear steaks. Bearskins. The legend that a bear will visit a hunter on Christmas Eve, will knock loudly on the door then spirit itself away. They finish in silence with stewed fruit, a tin of cream. He thanks her for the meal. Somewhere in that gesture is reconciliation.

While Wanny washes dishes, the Chief deliberates over the box of disc recordings, a collection so small he must know them all by heart. 'This one.' He cleans the disc with his handkerchief and sets it in on the turntable. He winds the motor, lowers the stylus, the needle crackling into song. '*Glade Jul*', 'Silent Night', which makes Wanny slow. She breathes, her thoughts turned to home. Two boys without their mother. Before leaving Tromsø she had wrapped their Christmas gifts with paper from the cupboard, given the parcels to her friend to save. Alf will have opened her card first before turning to the ice skates he has been hankering after all year. If her calculations are right the skates will still be a size too big but hardly worn and too good to pass up. With them a new pair of socks to help with the fit, the thickest wool Wanny had on hand, which she raced to knit. Her youngest will savour her letter until he is alone. She pictures him in bed, that gentle face softened by candlelight, absorbing her words. Bjørvik will have set his card aside, eager to unwrap his pocket watch. A gift for a working man. Do they know how much she loves them? What she would give to have them here beside her?

The Chief must think of his own son and daughter. The cost of what it takes to be here. As if by mutual understanding, neither of them speaks of home. This is not a place to welcome sad thoughts or talk of past hardship. He makes coffee. They eat cakes and toast with Curaçao. 'It is quite a feast,' she says, pulling herself out of melancholy.

Wanny's offering sits in a wrap of newspaper. She chews over the very act of giving it to him. What he will say to something flippant, intended to deliver a smile? It suddenly seems all wrong. But she brings the parcel to the table. 'For tradition. I am sorry it is not something better.'

She watches him tear the wrapping open. He beams like a child at the contents, a return to his old, steady self. He stands tall to hold up the hand-stitched shirt she has spent nights back-stitching beneath the lamp light, wishing for her sewing machine.

'It is a fine shirt.' He holds it to the light.

'The fabric is all I had on hand.'

'Yes. It is quite vivid.' He looks genuinely pleased. 'I will be the pinnacle of fashion back in Tromsø.' He draws the shirt to his nose. Closes his eyes. 'The fabric smells of home,' he says. He lays it on his bunk. 'I have something for you. The wrapping is the same.' He grows shy when he hands her a parcel tied with string, voluminous, as light as air. Carefully she loosens the bow. The paper falls away. Inside a white fox skin, their first from Fuglefjell, the finest they have caught.

She feels her breath catch. Her eyes well with his generosity. 'It is too much,' she says. She does not deserve this.

'You are quite right. I shall take it back.'

'No!' she cries. He issues a lopsided smile. She turns the fox in her hands. Holds it to her cheek. She cannot stop stroking it. 'I will hang it on the wall beside my bunk. Touch it each night, look at it each morning when I wake.'

'You have earned it,' he says.

She pours coffee. She breathes in the swell of his words. She is no different from Mira who has never responded well to hard words, a dog who thrives on praise. The Chief reads aloud, not from the well-worn stack of newspapers they keep in the cold porch; tonight it is a book from the shelf, the story of Norwegian hunters working in north-east Greenland. She pictures Mr Rudi as she listens to the hardships the hunters endure in that vast terrain. 'It makes life at Hornsund seem,' Wanny searches for the word, 'humdrum.'

'Hardly,' the Chief argues. 'Their life is not so different from our own. It is how they tell it that makes it seem exceptional.' He raps the cover of the book. 'Is there a word in here of washing dishes, chopping firewood, treadling the grindstone with a stack of dull knives? Is there anything of darning socks or changing the runners on the sledge? There is next to nothing of the ordinary chores that fill a hunter's day. Their world is all thrills and spills. It is what the writers do to make their books.'

The hour is late when she tidies things away. Christmas Eve in Hornsund is over. 'The bear did not knock,' she calls across the room. The Chief, fully clothed and flat out in his bunk, snores softly. His shirt made from old door curtains rests at his side. 'One day,' she tells herself. One day the bear will knock. Wanny stokes the stove. Sets the kettle aside. She extinguishes the lantern, climbs into her bunk. She lies awake in the dark listening to a rising wind, warm inside her reindeer bag.

FOX

---

ice owl

A CLATTER OF rock ricochets off Fuglefjell's wall of mountain. Another white fox fallen to the traps. The vixen scans the winter landscape. She watches the runt, registers the contrast in her coat to the two young white foxes that follow her. The three close in on the fallen trap.

They nose the carcase, the body of the fox still warm. A black snout pushes in beneath the butt of tail. Another snout sniffs at the head, clear liquid oozing from an ear. The runt raises her muzzle to the air. She meets her mother's gaze across a rise of rock and snow.

The whites burrow through fur to incise the skin and tear it back. They pull strands of meat from the thigh. The runt climbs onto the fallen trap, the crushed skull propping up the forefront of wood. Lightly she treads across the top of the framework, drops a paw through the slats. She scratches at the bait stick until the pointed tip skews into reach, a ptarmigan head exposed between the slats. The runt pushes her muzzle between the slats, pulls at the frozen meat until it breaks from the stick. She carries it away, sits amongst rocks to crunch it down, morsel by tantalising morsel. She closes her eyes to sensory rapture.

The two whites gorge on the dead fox, undeterred by the bitter tang of flesh. Finally, the runt joins in, her senses momentarily assaulted by the acrid sharpness after the sweetness of ptarmigan. She pulls at flesh and sinew, eats without taste to fill a starving belly. She tugs at the fox's front paw with her teeth, determined to win a battle that takes all her strength until she feels skin tear, cartilage and bone parting from the body. She carries away the fur-lined paw to bury in snow.

The three young foxes are ousted by vixen and dog fox who close in with a snarl, the vixen baring her teeth. The pair of older fox commandeer the carcase, working together to strip away the pelt, denude the fox of flesh.

An ice owl perches high on the cliffs, a bird white as snow, its strong limbs clad in feathered trousers. A formidable hunter biding its time.

❄

The whites come and go, they defecate scats peppered with bone and fox fur amid a putrid release of gas. The tightness of their bellies is both a comfort and the source of pain. They slumber with their brushes curled around their snouts for warmth, their breath entrapped and fetid.

The runt roams the slopes. She halts at a line of traps. She stays amongst them for a day, pacing, looking longingly to the ptarmigan head held within. She lightly climbs onto a trap, its jaws packed with snow, gauging any movement underfoot. She pads over the weight of stones. She peers down through the slats to sniff at the meat, hidden in the snow. Her companions join her for a time. They wander. They return, hungering for food. They register the runt's boldness when she sits before the trap and slinks down low. The small fox folds down her ears, slides her head beneath the fore frame, the clearance reducing the further in she eases. She noses her way through snow. Blindly, she reaches for the ptarmigan, cautious not to bump the central post. She cranes her neck, tries to make herself longer, pushes at snow with her tongue. She cannot reach that meat speared to a stick.

She wriggles back out. Sneezes. Shakes off snow.

She ponders the jaws of the trap.

Waits another day.

The whites stand to attention when the runt makes her move. She hunkers down low to slide in beneath the wooden jaw. She is small. Her rear paws lever her in, her head and shoulders almost within reach of her prize. Her heart races. She brings her teeth to the bait and gives a sideways tug, a piece of the meat parting from the stick. She retreats, the bait held fast in her jaw. She is clear. She is out. She looks at the frame, its stones, the jaw gaping and unmoved. She sits, breathless with escape, ptarmigan thawing in her mouth.

She places the ptarmigan between her paws to eat, snarls at the whites when they move in. She holds court before her audience, feasting on her prize.

The runt's puzzlement shifts to supremacy. She grows reckless with success. She returns to the trap craving the remainder of the ptarmigan that sits somewhere in snow at the back of the trap. When one of the whites attempts to follow her in, she turns and snaps, nipping the white hard on the snout. *Her* meat.

She takes time to slink down low, gauging the distance from the crown of her skull to the underside of jaw. She sidles in, pushes forward. She burrows her snout through snow, far enough in to stretch to reach the meat. The frame above grazes her head. She snatches the ptarmigan breast in fright, retreats at speed, unsure if she has it in her grip.

The runt sits beside the trap, victorious. She tears at flesh, salivates. There is nothing in a fox's world sweeter than the breast meat of a ptarmigan.

The two whites circle as she eats; they stare longingly into the emptied trap. They lick their muzzles with the promise of cast-off meat. Forlornly they watch as the runt gulps it down, each onlooker hoping for an offering. She finishes it all, paces away to urinate, leaving her friends to lick the snow, her drool infused with bird.

The runt saunters to the adjacent trap, but the whites are spurred into action. They bare their teeth lest she beats them to another feed. Reluctantly, the runt retreats to watch.

In unison the young white foxes ease down low as they have seen it done. They move in beneath the fore frame of the trap, one either side of the central post, their crowns brushing the wooden jaw.

Further in they go. The bolder white fox edges close enough to reach the bait, its companion stung with the prospect of missing out. The slower fox rises to lunge, both animals bearing down on the frozen meat, yanking bait and stick.

A click of wood. The trigger lock frees.

A rumble of stone.

10

Fuglefjell, January 1933

ANDERS SEETHES. 'This is precisely as I feared,' he says to the woman beside him, who he partially blames, for what he cannot summons at this particular moment. He is irate. The remains of the mauled fox are unrecognisable but for a disembodied head pinned beneath the frame. 'We cannot leave it this long again. We are keeping Fuglefjell's foxes plump for winter while we miss out on an income.'

'I am sorry,' she says.

'You have no need to be sorry,' he snaps. 'It was not you who ate the fox.' Out of sorts with everything and everyone, though up here everyone is only one, beside himself. He clears the trap. 'We are a long way behind where we ought to be. This time last year –' he starts, but the stony set to her face brings his sermon to a close.

Together they rebait and reset the trap, piling it with heavy rocks. On they go to the next.

'Look who is here,' says the woman. Little Blue above them in the snow. 'Are you the culprit?' she sings to the fox.

'You can be certain of that.' Anders huffs. 'You and your cannibal friends.' Little Blue stands with a tilt to its head as if trying hard to comprehend Anders's words. The fox trots alongside, just metres away.

'You are a pretty little thing,' says the woman.

'Who will one day feel the prettiness of a trap.'

'Perhaps not. It has seen what happens to its brethren.'

It is true that some fox will not go near a fall trap. Anders considers the alternative, the swan neck scissors, not his favourite form of trap as it would sever a hand or cripple a foot as easily as clamp itself around a fox's neck. A necessarily evil if numbers stay low. He contemplates sledding the steel trap out here from Hyttevika. Never mind having to lug the beast on his back halfway around the mountain.

Next time. Once his back is fully healed.

Minute by minute, day by lengthening day, Anders senses the wan strip of midday dawn pulling away from its dusk companion. Soon it will find its own place in the morning hours. A new year. They have passed the winter solstice. The cycle of seasons is never more evident than when their winter work relies more on light from the moon. There are times when they manage with no moon at all – the work must go on – his feel for the landscape drawing on senses other than vision.

The middle month of winter. He is struck with how the woman has acclimatised. These last weeks he has held firm to gruffness, a hardness no other trapper would stand for. *Let it go, Sæterdal.* Wind and bitter cold, the days at their darkest, not once out here has she shirked her tasks. 'Six weeks until the sun returns,' he says. He points to the silhouette of mountains across the fjord. He resists the momentary impulse to place his hand on her shoulder as he would another man. 'Through that valley we will see it first appear.'

'Nineteen thirty-three,' she annunciates each word as if testing out the sound of them. 'If time would only slow.'

The year he turns forty. No. He recalculates. Thirty-nine. He brightens. A year's reprieve. 'For time to slow you would have to put up with this ornery old trapper for even longer.'

'That is so.' He turns to gauge if she is serious. 'And you with me, Chief. A married woman.'

The first mention on the subject. He permits himself the glimmer of a smile. 'You are a disgrace all round,' he says. 'Beyond help.'

Little Blue tires of the banter. The small fox bounds ahead, anticipating their direction. The creature looks back to check that they are following, as if eager to show them the way.

'The foxes of Hornsund will soon be on the move. Through January, with luck, we will see them all across the landscape, travelling about to find a mate.'

'You hear that?' the woman calls to the fox. 'Will you and your mate be giving us a fine family of blue fox?'

'Not if the traps have their way first.' If it does survive, the little devil could be up the other end of Spitsbergen by next season.

The shore below the hut is a barrier of ice, pieces rammed up where the frozen fjord has buckled and stretched. The eastern end of Hornsund's waterway is sleek and solid from one shore to the other, just crying out for bears.

'Chief, look,' Wanny cries.

A fallen trap. 'That is more like it,' he says. A trap with not one but two white foxes. Neither ruined. Anders feels his spirits buoy. They free the dead foxes. He checks their teeth. 'Youngsters, both of them. In prime condition.' He ties their back paws.

The adjacent trap is stuffed with snow disturbed from digging. Together they lift away rocks and set the trap aside. Wanny pulls away the trigger lock to sweep the snow clear. 'Look here.' She holds the empty bait stick. 'I must have missed baiting it.'

'You did not forget,' he says. 'The trap is jammed open with snow. Mikkel Rev was granted a lucky escape, a prize treat in the process.'

❇

When Wanny opens the Villa's door in the morning, Little Blue sits waiting. If the dogs were here, if the Chief were about, this small creature would not be as bold. The small blue fox seems to understand who is the gentle touch. 'Wait here,' she says and returns inside to pick two pieces from the stockfish soaking for their evening dinner.

She offers a piece to Little Blue. Cautiously the fox approaches, sniffing its way toward her. The creature is so tame it almost takes the fish from her hand. Normally it races away with its food but here it is before her, eating daintily, licking its muzzle, its eyes shifting between her and the extra piece of fish set down upon the bench. Wanny checks her loaded rifle, loops it over her shoulder, squares of newspaper folded in her pocket for morning ablutions. Whether it be their diet of seal or the prospect of exposing bare skin to the cold, her body willingly obliges. There is no dillydallying at Hornsund.

A sharp ruffle of air moves above her in the darkness. A flutter from something big and close. Wanny cowers. A large white owl materialises inches from her face. It plunges down to steal the stockfish from the bench. The fox bolts. A threshing of wings. The thief vanishes as quickly as it appeared; Arctic creatures dissolving into darkness. Wanny catches her breath. Where did it come from? She looks around, checks that the hut door is secure. She makes her way out through the darkness.

❇

Ptarmigan at Fuglefjell have grown scant. On the trek home to the main base, they halt before crossing the glacier, leaving the dogs to bark and whine at being tethered to the sledge. This is the first time Wanny has scaled the upper reaches of Fannytoppen, taking care of her step, the half-moon slow to break the shield of mountain. According to the Chief's sense of time, it is early morning. The middle of the night by Wanny's measure. Night and day are gradations of the same. They leave flurries of breeze that kick up the snow. They walk between protected clefts of rock, alert at each turn for a sleeping bear. A bear would surely wake to their scent, to the sound of their breath rasping with brittle air, to the squeak and crunch of snow crust beneath their boots. They follow a meander of bird tracks, a minefield of excavation where *rype* have dug down through snow to reach buried plants. 'At least we know they are about,' the Chief says.

Wanny slows at a pattern in the snow that catches her eye, a series of small undulations. Something burrowed beneath the snow? She waits, watches, stamps her feet, startled when four ptarmigan explode into life amid a shower of snow. These defenceless birds stand rigid before her shotgun as if resigned to their fate. A one-sided hunt to scoop them up this way.

They cache the four birds in a pile and continue their climb, the moon sliding over twin knolls which mark the summit, the snow turning crystalline in its light, daggered with shadow. Ahead of her, the Chief is a silhouette beneath the moon's eerie glow.

When they turn to retrace the route, they have two extra ptarmigan apiece. 'Eight in total,' she exclaims. 'Our best to date.'

'Still not a patch on last winter's count,' says he.

'You.' She gives him a good sideways shove, forgetting his injuries from his slide down the mountain.

'What did I do to deserve that?'

'Sæterdal, if I brought home thirty blue foxes, you would still find a reason to whimper. Can you not be satisfied with what we have? With where we are? Look at this mighty place!'

He waggles his head. 'Bring me ten fine blues and I will waltz you around the hut.'

She has to forgive all his curses when they return to their cache of birds strewn through the snow. The breast of one is stripped from the bone, another carried off and dumped in the distance, a third spirited away before their eyes, held in the jaws of a rascal thief, its silhouette silvered by the moon. 'There's your blue,' she cries. The small fox bolts away, the bird in its jaw equal its size, the Chief making chase. Wanny breaks into a giggle. The Chief looks back at her as if she is taken with madness. She doubles over with laughter at his ungainly pursuit, up to his knees in soft snow, outmatched and outmanoeuvred by a small, agile fox.

The glacier is a vast snowy plain, all glitter and sparkle beneath a star-spangled sky. They make their way across its back, east to west, homeward to Hyttevika. The dogs trot along keenly to keep up with Sæterdal who, despite his painful back, sets out on skis as a man on his way to fetch the midwife.

On the western side of the glacier the ice runs downhill and peters out above Isbjørnhamn. From there the snow slope angles down to the tiny halfway hut. Wanny can make out the tracks of the sled from their outward journey. They stop at the high point for mugs of coffee, a sandwich each, debating whether they will stop at the hut to rest or continue the five hours more to Hyttevika. The labour of unpacking and repacking the sledge. Wanny looks back at the glacier tongue so brilliant with reflection that it scintillates its own constellation. The hood of the Chief's anorak is rimmed with ice from his breath. Hers feels to be the same.

'I am happy to go on if you are,' she says. These days she walks two Norwegian miles around the traps, no more weary at the end of a day than when she set out.

'Five minutes,' he says. 'Then keep on.'

To the south, across the great frozen fjord of Hornsund, the Chief spies a flicker of light, so small and dim Wanny has to squint to see it. Their neighbours' hut at Gåshamna – Hanssen and the Italian – the sight of which infuses Wanny with a warmth that has her forget the frigid air. The Chief feels it too. 'They are up early,' he banters. 'Hanssen will be cooking their breakfast. Will it be porridge or pancakes this morning?'

'They are celebrating the turning of the year with waffles and tinned cream.'

'A jar of lingonberry jam saved for the occasion.'

A good part of their conversation revolves around food. She used to marvel at the volume her boys could consume. If they could see their mother now.

The Chief tears off a hunk of sandwich. 'They'll soon be out to check their traps,' he quips, his mouth full. 'The Italian will have the hang of it by now.'

'No inkling of we two ice owls up here surveying the frozen domain.' She gulps down her coffee. 'Perhaps their foxes have trotted across to our side.'

'Better that than the other way around.' He stows thermos and mugs, checks the tie-downs on the sledge. He praises the dogs for their good work. Wanny feels a rush of warmth at Mira lining up before the Chief for her share of attention. He gives each a scratch beneath the chin. 'Last big push,' he tells the dogs. 'Home we go.'

The Chief eases downhill on skis. Dogs and sledge move at a steady pace, tracing their old tracks. The slope eases out and they pick up speed over fresh snow, covering the first mile back to Hyttevika. Ahead, the Chief halts. 'Stop,' he calls back, a sharpness to his tone. 'Drop,' he orders the dogs. He makes his way back to the sledge, points down to the snow.

Tracks, pads broader than the span of her hand, each toeprint strangely human-like, fused with an imprint of claws. 'A bear,' she says solemnly.

'Yes, indeed,' says the Chief. 'And it has been here quite recently.' He follows the course of the tracks. 'We must have passed him.'

'What do we do?'

'We retrace our steps, follow his tracks. See if we can catch him.'

'The dogs?'

'I'll set off first. You follow with the dogs and sledge, quickly and quietly as you can. Keep a distance back. Have your rifle ready. If you see the bear within range, you shoot. You remember what I told you?'

'Shoulder or chest.' She struggles to keep her voice steady. Her heart races, a shiver through her body. Every story she's been told. This is the moment.

'If the bear runs, you let the dogs loose. Understand?'

She does.

He starts off on skis. He halts, grins back at her. 'Are you afraid?'

'Of course not,' she lies. 'Perhaps a whisker.'

'A whisker is expected,' he says. 'One more thing.'

'What is it?' What a time to be smirking.

'Try not to shoot me in the process.'

'I will do my best.'

Following the bear track through soft stretches of snow is clear enough, but with each hard crust it becomes near impossible without full moonlight. Wanny has not before noticed how much noise a sledge makes: the grating of the runners on hard crust, the crunch on pieces of ice, the scrape of stones sounding out like doomsday trombones.

Sæterdal glides on ahead, she trying to maintain a good distance, at the same time searching about, her heart in her throat, a thousand thoughts swirling through her mind. Who will see it first? Will they see the bear at all? Wanny grips her rifle, five cartridges in the magazine, one in the barrel. Release the catch and fire.

Up every rise, over every mound of snow, she expects the bear to appear, to leap out and confront her face to face. By now they must have travelled a full kilometre. Ahead of her Sæterdal searches about, a grip on his rifle. The thought of him ahead bolsters her courage.

In the corner of her sight stands a line of rocks, a buttery mound. Not the cool white of snow. A fox? Ptarmigan? Surely dirty snow. She has lost all sense of scale. She pulls the sledge to a slow. She keeps her eyes trained on the spot. There it is. A yellowish mass that slowly slides out from behind a rock. She does not trust her eyes. It has to be a bear. A head. A black snout. The thing turns, stops, slowly ambles her way. Wanny blinks. She shakes off the spell holding her in place. 'Drop!' she hisses at the dogs, their ears pricked, a ridge of hair raised down their backs. Karo's entire body tenses, ready to attack. Storm whimpers. Mira gives a deep, guttural growl.

The bear stops, raises its head. It sniffs the air, a snout that fixes on her direction. The size of the thing. The girth of its belly. A wall of shoulders and limbs. Wanny kneels behind the sledge, pushes back her hood, props her rifle firm on her rucksack. The sledge is no defence at all but offers something solid and comforting between her and the bear. A low grumble from the Alsatians. 'Hush,' she orders and for once Sæterdal's dogs heed her command. She digs her knees and boots in snow, the safety off, the stock of the rifle firm against her cheek. She lines up the sights, the post centred in the V of the notch. She shifts her focus to the shoulder of the bear, one-hundred metres away. She waits, her finger crooked lightly against the trigger. She does not shake. The bear moves.

It strides out toward her. The rifle cracks, the kick of the stock a jolt against her shoulder.

She slides the bolt. Aligns the sights. Again.

The bear stops mid stride. The moment hangs suspended. The bear's head hangs to one side, a shoulder drops. In a dream-like motion, a moving picture playing out the death throes of a warrior, the animal slumps to the ground.

The shots still ring through her ear closest to the stock. She stands. Draws breath. A dog barks. She wants to laugh. She wants to shout, *The bear is dead! The bear is dead!*

The dogs bark and squabble, yank at their harnesses. She sets them free. She runs over hard crust toward the bear. She falls to her knees in soft snow, tumbling in the process. She rights herself. An iron claw digs hard into her shoulder. She turns to Sæterdal, the Chief breathing heavily, his eyes an inch from hers. 'Haven't I told you!' he yells. 'You do not go near a bear, even if it looks dead. Have you any idea what it means to have a wounded bear in your face?'

Not even his fury can douse her exhilaration. 'Anders.' She beams. 'The first is killed!' *Hooray for me!* she wants to shout.

He catches his breath. 'Perhaps,' he grumbles. 'But you give it another shot before you go near. Then we shall see.'

She fires. The mountain of muscle remains still. 'All right then,' he says.

The dogs growl as they approach, stiff legged, hair along their spine on end. Tentatively they push at the bear with their snouts until they, too, are convinced the creature is no longer a threat. All three dogs lie down beside it.

'Look,' she whispers. 'The bear has heel guards exactly as my dream. They are the same.' Wanny kneels in the snow, marvelling at the might of such a being, the plushness of its coat, the gauntlets of fur covering each paw. She removes her glove, brushes the back of her hand against the round of the belly, still warm to the touch. She feels a strange, unnerving reverence. She looks upon the bear with a momentary rush of pride. She draws back. The life of this creature extinguished in an instant. She looks beyond to a shimmering darkness, a night-filled wilderness. A sharp intake of melancholy she cannot fathom or explain.

The Chief inspects the shot wounds, one straight through the shoulder, the other at an angle through shoulder and chest. 'You have done very well.' He studies her, his eyes soft and pensive. 'My word you have.'

Hard-won praise that reduces her to tears.

FOX

ptarmigan territory

FOXES WHEREVER THE runt turns. The landscape is alive with their comings and goings, with well-worn tracks as foxes pad across the slopes, some appearing from far out on the pack ice. The runt, bereft of her two companions fallen to the traps, allows a new pair of males to approach. They nose at her rear and she raises her tail, allowing them to press their snouts against her. She isn't close to reaching oestrus. The first loses interest and moves on. The second retreats when she tires of the game and turns, her teeth bared.

Hunting grows lean, the slopes scoured of ptarmigan by passing foxes. The runt grows bold, caution no match for hunger. She turns on larger foxes. She ignores young foxes that seek to befriend her. She hunts alone, inspecting each ridge for morsels the man sprinkles around the traps, fought over by other hungry fox. She inspects each trap, ready to make a meal of whichever fox has ventured beneath. Every trap lays empty. She sits beside a baited trap for a day and a night, moving only when the trappers venture near.

When the man and his dogs walk along the shore, the runt scampers to the hut, nosing for leftover meat the dogs may have neglected, desperate for any scraps the woman throws her way. The runt's coat is at its plushest. Her belly at its emptiest.

She pads far out across the frozen fjord, trots toward a darkened shape. She slows. It is not the carcase of a seal, nor is it a fish. She sniffs at a pole of wood released by ice and rolled free with the wind. From far out on the fjord, wind and sound sweeping down the mountain, she catches wisps of voice from the man, the thuds from his axe that crack like ice. The small fox turns back to the shore.

She waits out of sight as the trappers shut and bar their hut. Seized with desperation, she bolts ahead of them, races westward around the mountain slope to where they keep their sledge. She climbs over wooden slats, squats to urinate across the soft, curved wood. She chews flavour from the lashings, tugs at a taut length of rope. She jumps upon a storage box lashed to the sled and paws at its lid. She sits atop the box with her back to the wind. Time passes before she hears the dogs. She stands tall as, far in the distance, the trappers emerge into view. Away she races to sit high on a ridge, to listen to the dogs shriek and howl at her scent sprayed across the sledge. She waits for them to be harnessed. She dozes until the sledge sounds with movement and the trappers forge on. Cautiously, the runt makes her way down the talus to trail behind the party, nose low, downwind of their track.

When the trappers halt, the runt halts. She listens to the cadence of their voices, to their dogs whimpering and yowling at being left tethered to a sledge. The trappers climb to a cleft in the mountain that looks down upon the glacier, to dried spikes of tundra exposed by wind. Ptarmigan territory. The runt follows. She sniffs at their imprint. She chooses a lookout on which to settle. She waits. She dozes. She wakes and scans the surrounds. Click. *Boom.* Click. *Boom.*

She remains out of sight when the trappers drop four white birds in a pile, the combs of the birds the red of blood, hers for the taking once the trappers venture away over a rise.

The starving young fox launches herself on the catch. She tears a ptarmigan apart, gulps down breast meat, strips meat from a leg, her gullet choked with food. She stops to sneeze and rid her muzzle of feathers. The runt surveys the remaining three birds. She is charged with new vigour, determined that the whole catch can be hers. She abandons the part-eaten bird and drags another bird free, hauling it far away and setting it down behind a rock. *Boom. Boom.* She scampers back to steal another bird. She has the neck firm in her jaw when she lifts her snout, alert to the waft of human, unsure if the trappers' scent is purely that smeared across her bird, or the trappers themselves returning. She carts the bird as fast as she can carry it then drops it in the snow well short of the first. She races back to collect the final, largest ptarmigan, tugging at its weight, in her frenzy gripping its wing to drag it away. She runs awkwardly, unable to clear it of the ground, the bird bumping and tripping her. She has no time to take a better grip. The runt labours. The trappers' scent grows sharp. She grapples with risk, hungers for reward. She remembers the family of ptarmigan taken from under her nose by her parents. A thud of human footsteps through the snow. She is a lone hunter, a fox without the advantage of a mate. She abandons the final bird and races to the second bird she has dropped in the snow. She halts mid stride. Cocks her ear. She salivates at the catch splayed before her. She blinks in turmoil. She must choose one bird from them all. She bolts without hindrance to the rock, the safety of distance. She seizes the first bird she dumped here. She bounds through a deep stretch of snow, labouring with the drag of weight, her heart pounding against her refusal to slow until she is beyond the trappers' reach.

From a long way back, she hears a startled cry. The small blue fox turns to see the outline of the trappers. She hears the woman's laughter, the familiar curses of the man. The runt leaves the snow for a faster footing over rock. She angles downhill with her prize, slowly easing to a trot.

11

Hyttevika, January

WANNY WORKS BY the stove, hail pelting the roof with a violence that could be iron nails shot from the sky. She cannot hear herself think. The timbers of the hut yaw and creak. She watches the stovepipe, except for the stove their most vital possession, expecting it to loosen and be sucked away into the sky. Twice now they have had to climb up to the roof during a storm and secure it back in place. Her fingertips feel gluey from handling strips of blubber. She lattices the fat across the boned loin to tenderise the bear as it roasts, rolling the joint methodically, tying it off with string. January fifteen. If it were not for the record she keeps in her journal, she would have bypassed the day as just another Sunday bringing winter storms. She has surpassed Othar by thirteen years. *What would you think, Othar, your wife turning forty, here in this place in britches and braces, hands as calloused as a gravedigger's?*

No proper funeral. No dignified goodbye. She is not a woman to live in the past, but the past lives in her, searing images apt to percolate unannounced. The town bereft of coffins; the undertaker, carpenters, the gravediggers all overwhelmed. Everything she was and would become, the brightness of their future, a candle extinguished with Othar's last exhalation. Her own spear of sorrow, the ache in her bones inflamed with solitude, another new widow labelled 'unclean'. Yes, she could reason, yes, she understood, but with it the acrid tang of abandonment: her friends, her neighbours, the priest who married them, no one dare come near. *You were on your own*, she says to that stricken young girl.

What would Othar think of her here?

She sees him smile with wonder.

The hut reeks of bear, sour and rotten. The Chief sits behind her at the table, scraping blubber from skin, the pelt as expansive as carpet. The three dogs keep their eyes trained on Anders then shift to her, anticipating whether cook or flayer will be the first to send a treat their way. A second bear, its face gruesome with shot, consumes the remainder of the floor where it has been thawing for days. The bunks are the only corner of the room free of skin and blubber, dogs and chaos. The one part of the hut to maintain civility. On that they have agreed.

She considered the bear she shot to be large – *her* bear, she thinks of it – a two-year-old male, flayed and butchered out there on the snow. The Chief wore gloves and worked with speed and precision. Ninety minutes to strip the animal of its fleece before the bear froze, he doing the bulk of the work. With gloves, she had no feel for the knife, no control. Without gloves her fingers turned wooden and refused to work.

'A forest flaying is never easy. I will teach you on the next one.' A fine pelt, he named it, all fifty kilograms rolled and heaved onto the sledge, now draped across his knees to work the blubber clean, ready to salt and barrel. The bear's pale pelt seems at odds with its thick jet skin.

If her bear weighed two hundred kilograms, the second bear slumped here at their feet, dead before a *selvskudd*, is easily double the size. How could the frozen hulk be moved from where it lay

stiff on the snow? A task beyond the scope of human strength.
Yet they had managed, with ingenuity, heaving the giant onto the
sledge with ropes and tie-downs, wooden poles as levers, the pulling
power of dogs attuned to the Chief's commands, Mira as hardy
as the other two. With the help of blocks and tackles, together
they had shoved the bear in through the hut's outer door, through
the porch door and to the main room. The pulleys redirected the
immense weight and distributed the strain, the Chief applying
all his body weight to each haul on the rope, the hulk shifting
incrementally across the wooden boards. Wanny had sidled herself
from one side of the bear to the other, climbing over the top of it
to pull and shove each great paw, which weighed as much as she,
manoeuvre its limbs as if it were a mechanical beast, positioning
the head and swivelling the body to angle the bear's great girth
through the door. A vessel eased through the neck of a bottle. An
effort that took most of a day. She has to step over the thing to reach
her bunk, has to search it out with her foot if she gets up through
the night. She circles it each time she tends the stove. She laughs
aloud. 'Perhaps every home should have a four-hundred-kilogram
ice bear taking up its floor.'

The Chief looks up from his work. 'Those who buy these skins
have little notion.'

She rubs at the itch on her cheek with her sleeve. In all her
imaginings she could not have pictured this scene when Othar first
laid a rifle in her hands. *Cheek firm against the stock, Ivanna.* He
was never one to call her Wanny. She had been apprehensive of the
weapon, the damage it could wreak. Now her rifle is a part of her.
She had believed them blessed, she and he, all the years ahead.
Death can break those left behind or instil them with resilience.
She takes an intake of breath. Othar lives within her boys.

'It is my birthday,' she says to Anders above the wind and sleet.

He gives a nod. 'Congratulations. When I finish up, we will polish off an extra piece of cake to celebrate. No. We will have two extra helpings.'

'And that will be the finish of our New Year baking. My mother-in-law used to say that, in a well-ordered house, the Christmas cakes should last until Easter.'

He throws her a smirk. 'Which mother-in-law told you that nonsense?' He takes a slug of coffee and returns to scraping.

What would Othar make of Anders?

He would see him as a decent man. A good man. He would want for her happiness. Then and now.

The stovepipe rattles. 'Anders,' she says.

'Do not fret, woman. If the pipe should blow away, I will send you straight out to bring it back.' He looks up from his work to grin. 'Without delay.'

Wanny huffs. 'If it blows away, we will have a room filled with smoke and a raw bear roast.'

'It is very strange weather for January.'

Their New Year trip to Fuglefjell has been delayed thanks to a second inscrutable week of heavy snow, then showers of rain, then freeze and hail, the only constant a fierceness of wind which jams new rafts of ice and logs of driftwood up along the shoreline. Out in the fjord, bergs locked in the sea ice split and topple, issuing a booming thunder and opening up the ice until the gash refreezes. When snowdrift eases enough to see out the back door, to make headway on skis beyond the Signal, they slip and slither on patches of black ice. Their dogs slide on their haunches in a knot of harnesses, the sledge toppling when it hits the snow. Wanny loses count of the trigger locks she pulls apart, the wooden pieces doused with rain then frozen in place, all along the trap line. She struggles physically and mentally at the thought of twenty traps – the kilograms of stone to be offloaded, each trap cleared of snow before it can be rebaited, the aching effort of gingerly reloading thirty, forty kilograms of stone back onto a frame, praying, *Please, Lord, do not let the blasted thing collapse midway.* The foxes of Hyttevika show an uncanny sense for which traps make easy pickings. For all their effort they have only three new fox to add to the count – the pair from Fuglefjell, another she flayed and stretched last week. Yet the bears come thick and strong, two new carcasses buried in the snow, waiting to be flayed, the *selvskudds* working overtime.

'Why should a bearskin be worth less than a fox? It is many times the size,' Wanny says aloud, frustrated by an answer she already knows. Unless you are a people of the snow – the Greenlanders, the Sámi and such – bear fur is rarely called for as a garment, the pelt of such a hefty weight it is impractical for warmth. A bearskin destined for the homes of Europe and America is purely for show.

The Chief scoffs. 'Next time you are hobnobbing in your taxi, ask your own fair sex why they squander their husband's savings to wear a fox's coat.'

He dismisses women so harshly. 'Perhaps because it is practical,' she retaliates. 'Because fox is warm and light as air to wear. Because it is soft and utterly beautiful.'

'Beautiful, it may be. Nought to do with practicality. There are plenty of other options to keep a person warm. With ladies,' he says, 'it is all about fashion and vanity. The gentle art of persuasion that wives excel at with their husbands' wallets,' he says. 'You can be sure it is not you or me to reap the reward. Fur traders are the ones growing fat on the profits.'

She cannot tell when he is joking. He will taunt her just to get a rise. 'You do women a disservice, Sæterdal,' Wanny says quietly. 'Even those who are wealthy. Do not paint all of us with the same ungainly brushstroke.'

The Chief looks to her. 'You are different,' he says. 'You may well be one of a kind.'

Wanny huffs. 'Backhanded praise.'

'I mean it as a compliment. How many women can call themselves self-made? How many choose to hunt and trap on Svalbard?'

'If that is true it is because too few women have a choice in how they live their life. To become a wife is too often to rely solely on a husband. On the choices *he* makes on her behalf. On *his* goodwill.' She feels a tightness in her voice. 'Do you know how hard it is for a woman to survive on her own? To be a mother on her own?'

The Chief studies her, his eyes turned strangely sad in a way that heightens her own upset. 'Nay impossible,' he speaks in a whisper then returns to his work.

Wanny scrubs her hands in the basin. She dries them on her apron and slides the loin roast onto the shelf of the stove, the heat just right. She pours a mug of coffee. 'Now I am free to help.'

'You relax,' he says. 'I will soon be done with this one.'

The Chief throws a single strip of blubber high in the air which he knows will set the dogs squabbling and jostling. They scramble across the bear. Storm nips at Mira, Mira yelps and turns on Karo who snatches the treat and wolfs it down. 'The Chief is a wicked man,' she tells the two who missed out. She takes up her embroidery cloth, a length of lavender thread for the bluebells.

'It is coming along,' he says.

'To remind us of springtime at home.'

They are a married couple in every way but one.

❄

Anders faces the fjord to urinate, his back to the wind. Each new day a little lighter, brighter, enough to make out horizontal ridges of snow, mountaintops chiselled flat. He buttons his trousers, tucks in his shirt-tails. He turns a slow circle, sweeping for bears. He gets to work, levering blocks of ice at the shoreline to free a large new pole of driftwood. He harnesses the pole to Karo and Storm and leads them up over cobblestones, onto firmer ground where he chocks the pole with stones. 'There you go.' He frees his dogs, who in sequence cock their leg against the pole.

With his broad axe, Anders strikes deep into the wood. He manages to push the pole a half turn and jam in new chocks. He heaves the axe once more until the length of wood splits. The air is minus thirty, brittle with cold, his sweat chilling his skin the moment he stops to catch his breath. It takes all of his determination and a full refrain of curses to roll then lift then heave each length up onto the sledge. He is a human machine. He will not be beaten. Mira arrives, leaping about like a pup in her eagerness to help. She shrieks when she catches her paw beneath a rolled log. 'Get off with you!' Anders roars at her. He ties down the driftwood and secures his axe in its hessian sack.

The brother dogs tussle in a fierce kind of play that any moment will turn into a brawl. He yanks Storm free. 'Sons of Satan!' He untangles their leads and gets them harnessed to the sledge. 'Now you two can earn your keep.' Mira lags, she licks her paw, slow to get herself up and moving. Anders checks her paw, wiggles each toe. She licks his arm as he runs his hand down the leg bones. Not a whimper. 'Nothing broken, girl. Just a bruise.'

They move across the landscape, tracking the coast, the runners of the sled sliding free, all but the largest boulders buried with new snow. He scours the snow for bear tracks. Fox prints. Ptarmigan.

They pass by a *selvskudd*, the bait intact.

From the direction of the hut, the boom of a shotgun. He turns his head. Brings the sledge to a stop. He waits. A follow-up shot will rule out a *selvskudd*. A follow-up shot may mean a bear at the Signal, though the woman knows better than to spray the pelt with shotgun lead. Anders listens. Nought but the sound of wind. The *selvskudd*. 'Do we have ourselves a bear?' he asks his dogs.

Anders removes his rifle from his back, checks that it is fully loaded, the safety on, a cartridge in the chamber.

The creature slumped before the *selvskudd* still holds a hint of warmth. Their largest bear yet. The Alsatians sniff at the ruined skull, they nose through the snow, nuzzling at scraps. Mira shows no interest. She favours her sore paw, circles her tail, finally sets herself down. Anders checks her paw again. She folds back her ears at his touch. 'What ails you, girl?'

Anders curls back the bear's black upper lip to teeth stained yellow, to fearsome incisors, one broken, molars worn down. A grand old boy, five hundred and fifty, six hundred kilograms. Claws longer than Anders's fingers. He combs out a gauntlet of fur that measures more than a ruler length. He kneels before the animal in silence, an honouring to send the stately creature on its way.

Anders pontificates. He cannot keep up with the bears being taken by the *selvskudds*. He wants to flay the creature here and now before it freezes to the ice. The hour is late, the sledge laden with driftwood that has taken him all day to cut and load. Mira. He is one dog down. He sighs. They cannot afford to lose a dog this early in the season, or for it to be the woman's dog. He shovels snow across the bear's carcase where it can stay until tomorrow, when he'll bring out a sack of salt to free it from the ice. A good half-day for the collective might of man, woman and dogs to prise it on the sledge and haul it home. Anders harnesses the boys. He lifts Mira onto a hessian sack to ride upon the sledge, but her ladyship will have none of it. She jumps down and trots happily beside the sledge, speeding up to match the boys the nearer they get to home.

When the hut door opens, Mira halts. Anders cannot make it out. The dog hops on three legs the last metres to the hut, every bit the soldier limping home from war.

The woman. 'Whatever has happened?'

'She is fine. A bruised paw is all.'

'Is all?' Wanny kneels to tend her dog. Mira whimpers at her touch. 'She is far from fine.'

'She's laying it on.'

Wanny glowers at him. 'She is a *dog*. Help me bring her in. Her paw needs bandaging. You two be off,' she says to the Alsatians.

Mira licks Anders's hand. She blinks at him adoringly as she is carried in and set down before the stove. Where she will stay through the night, be given the royal treatment, scratches and attention, the end of the roast and scrapings of gravy. Anders chains the Alsatians outside. He gives each a consolatory pat and ponders life's inequities.

FOX

first to return

VIXEN AND DOG FOX attend to their den at odd intervals – not to breed, for Hornsund is still set too deeply in winter. Their checks are of sovereignty. Alone, or together when their foraging treks align, they position themselves in view of vulpine newcomers. When spring arrives, once coupling begins, they will ward off trespassers intent on claiming the den.

The vixen sits alone to watch the runt pad past the den. Strangers now, competitors, yet each with the familial imprint of the other. The runt could be mimicking her mother's actions, the almost imperceptible movement as the young fox lifts her muzzle to determine the older fox's presence. The runt is audacious, a canny young hunter who assumes this territory as her own. The youngling is now fully grown; another month she may come into heat, though the prospect of kits is slim on the heel of a first Svalbard winter. The vixen is barely larger now, the markings of each coat a mirror of the other. The vixen is more powerful, still. Surely.

The cache of summer food is depleted, the bird cliffs barren of fresh resources until guillemots and kittiwakes, flocks of tiny dovekies, return to Hornsund in the spring. For days, weeks at a time, vixen and dog fox travel alone, nomadic hunters scouring the landscape for ptarmigan, scavenging for carrion. Dog fox favours the sea ice. He tracks out on the trail of bear, his senses attuned to the spoils of a seal hunt. Discarded intestines, pickings from bones, morsels prised from a skull – his paw dainty enough to spoon a seal eye from its socket. He will sniff a bear's fresh excrement, gulp it down if fetid with bonemeal and fat. When the weather turns ferocious, dog fox tracks to a protected ridge of sea ice, a remnant from last season, the snow collected on its downwind side ample for a fox to burrow into, his nostrils open to the air.

The vixen follows her nose around the coastline, trying to conjure into being the memory scent from last winter's reindeer. The doe she at first assumed to be resting. On closer inspection, several nips to the butt and flank to be certain, the beast remained stiff where it had withered and perished. Though little more than skin and bone, the doe had sustained vixen and dog fox through the hardest part of winter.

The vixen moves up the slope, her empty belly yearning. She rounds the mountainside, faded scent from the trappers and their dogs peppered on the talus. She sniffs and leaves her mark. She forges on, westward across the broad glacier, following the sledge tracks. Above her, evening twilight trills with colour from the lights, the backdrop a swathe of stars. The vixen reaches the western edge, the glacial ice gravelled and broken. She turns her attention below, where the silhouette of a hut, small even by a fox's measure, sits proud on a knuckle of land that crooks its finger around the glacier's flank. The vixen settles high amongst ice and rocks, surveying the terrain with her snout and ears. Long gone are the trappers and their dogs. She chews at shards of ice caught in the fur of her footpads. She curls in on herself, closes her eyes and sweeps her brush around her. Slumber is no detriment to keen hearing, to her acute sense of smell. This vixen is primed for ptarmigan.

In the incremental shift from night to morning twilight, the vixen is alert to the cry of fulmars. The first birds to return. The first to usher away the last stretch of winter and screech for the sun's return. The vixen rises and stretches, buoyed by the prospect of spring. She keeps the birds in view. The pair hover high, a distance downwind, their wings aloft. These tube-nosed birds can detect a single bead of oil on water from kilometres away. Can smell a fallen bear, its skinned carcase buried in snow. The birds glide down, melding with the land.

The vixen bounds down the slope, sinking to her shoulders in new snow. Her destination is the coastal plain where the fulmars have gathered. But with the small hut now behind her, wind from its direction delivers a tantalising hint of food. She raises her snout, torn between going forward and veering back to explore. She looks back, turns forward, lifts her muzzle to the sky and closes her eyes as if allowing the air to determine her destiny. She turns tail, decided. She circles back to the tiny trappers' hut.

Buried in snow, a set of rounded iron jaws are splayed out, partially obscured. Ptarmigan. Faint. Hidden somewhere below. Wary of the unfamiliar contraption, the vixen paws at snow. She digs carefully, cautiously, until the bait is exposed. She steps back, assessing the contraption, contemplating the taint of trapper stamped around this place. The vixen sits perfectly still, her concentration on two half-moons of iron which may be waiting for her to blink before they snap into being. She waits, pondering a hunger that resembles starvation, that depletes a fox as suddenly and lethally as it does a reindeer. Half crazed with emptiness, the vixen snatches the ptarmigan head. She pulls back, the prize dangling from her mouth, the iron half-moons silent and still. A lifeline for a vixen who feels the satisfying crack as her jaws clamp down.

Far from sating hunger, thievery spurs the vixen into a ravenous frenzy. She circuits twice around the hut's perimeter, surveying the tattered edges of tar paper, searching for where the stench of mould and rot grows sweetest.

Here.

A metre down, soft snow ends at frozen ground and stone. The vixen digs with everything she's got. She burrows unhindered. She comes up for air, then dives down again to wriggle her way beneath a stretch of makeshift wall, so pliable with damp and decay that it crumbles against her spine. Up she comes with a gasp for air. She is inside the hut. The aroma intoxicating. She is victorious. She noses boxes. Squats to leave her mark. She jumps up on the stovetop, tramples a pack of matches to stretch her full length to the shelf above. She paws at a packet until it topples, its powdered contents coating stovetop and floor. She laps the meaty flavour, craving more.

Her focus returns to the shelf above the stove. Back up she goes. She stretches tall without gaining a hold. Time and again she jumps at the shelf tacked to the wall. She works to propel her body higher, finally catching an edge with her claws. The length of timber tips toward her and topples in a clatter of plates and mugs, cutlery and implements, packets and tins, a glass jar shattered into pieces. She stiffens with alarm, waits, looks about, then turns to bite into the rim of a wooden spoon fallen at her feet, eking out its flavour. She is down on the floor, walking amongst daggers of glass, inspecting the bounty. She fails to stop a can rolling from her clutch each time she tries to puncture its round of metal. In exasperation she turns to an open tin, the first bite of frozen butter pasting her canines, coating her tongue with rancid goodness. She does not fully finish the tin before diverting to fillets of salty stockfish scattered on the floor. They crackle at her bite, the edges ragged and sharp as they pass through the narrow passage of her gullet. The vixen feasts until she gags, her belly stretched with pain. She climbs onto a bunk, ready for sleep, but there is no easy rest within a human den. She rises, grown vulnerable to the alien surrounds. She eats more, intently listening, her body racked with thirst and the urge to be gone.

Her movements are laboured with heaviness, her body tight-bellied. The vixen pushes beneath the hut's rotted wall, out through the tunnel of snow. The air chill and alive.

The vixen dares not slow as she tracks her way back across the glacier, east to her home terrain at Fuglefjell, the atmosphere newly thick with fog. She gathers speed as she weaves down the mountainside, compelled by the abrupt, urgent need to safeguard her den.

She anticipates the trespasser. As she approaches her den, the vixen smells the runt. Through the pall, the runt's head appears from the den's side exit, the silhouette of her body softened by fog as each sights the other. The runt bolts, the vixen in pursuit. Up through the narrow gap of rocks, onto a ledge she bounds, the young fox faster, lighter on her feet, dissolving into fog.

The vixen surveys the surrounds, the wooden cross, the softened outline of the trappers' hut, the cluster of rock defining the den, *her* den, tainted with a thief's intent.

12

Hyttevika, February

THE FIRST BIG snow dump of the year. The cushion of snow comes too late for a sledge badly worn from hauling heavy loads across stone and sand. A morning of repairs before leaving for Isbjørnhamn, an overnight at the halfway hut before crossing the glacier to Fuglefjell. Together Wanny and the Chief upend the sledge and prise worn metal shoes from the runners. 'These had better see us out,' he grumbles as he attaches the last replacements on hand.

A morning to sweep out the hut, wash clothing and tea towels, the two pillowslips she stitched from scraps of hastily packed material, not knowing what she would find within this hut. The line of washing will hang inside to dry stiff as starch. No amount of rinsing makes a difference.

The Chief takes the repaired sledge and dogs for a last run to check the traps. These precious times with the hut to herself. She fills the wash basin with steaming water. A home-sewn flannel, a bar of Lano, a half kettle of water all she needs to feel clean again. She contemplates washing her hair, then decides against it sitting wet and chill around her head. She would chop the lot off if not for protests from the lower bunk.

She takes her coffee outside, the day noticeably less dim, her gloved hands wrapped around the mug. A day of utter silence, a day when the pace of your heartbeat falls somewhere between feeling and sound, her exhalation of breath white through the air.

In the stillness of the moment, she allows herself to be with Othar, the two of them on skates, hand in hand, the winter air a sheen upon her face, the ice of the lake so clear beneath her blades that she can see through to its bed, to perfectly rounded rocks and tendrils of algae teased with the current. She looks down to the movement of small fish. She releases Othar's hand to push on ahead, drawn by a mad urge for speed. Small bonfires line the rim of the lake, their mirror of flame thrown across the ice. Wanny feels to be flying through the sky's swirling scarf of greens, her eyes filled with the fullness of the lights, with Othar, just out of sight, somewhere behind her. The want for nothing more.

From a great distance away a soft sound. Wanny sharpens her ears to the runners of the sledge, the soft thud of paws through the snow. She pictures every fox across the landscape alert to the sound. Once she would not have been attuned to such a thing. Closer now, a rhythm of panting. The Chief hums the tune they play on the gramophone. The party comes into view. He holds up two white foxes, as proud as Bjørvik showing off a hare he'd once trapped at home, little Alf in tow. 'Lookie here,' the Chief shouts.

Each new fox and polar bear they record in the book. Even the dogs look proud.

❋

Another bear felled by a *selvskudd* will have to wait for their return to be flayed. They load provisions into wooden crates, a practised routine – a slab of seal for the dogs, a length of tar paper to patch the Villa where Mister Fox has tried his best to chew through the portico. 'We will see if seals are about. How the ice looks to cross.'

The Chief worries about their diminishing supply of seal. Wanny worries more about the havoc a storm can wreak on sea ice.

They ski unhindered along a coastal plain thick with snow, the dogs romping to keep pace, up to their shoulders in snow.

They stop to survey the big river that runs to the ocean from a tarn at the foot of the mountains. The river's upper layer is solid with ice, a broad gash through the foreshore between the main base and Isbjørnhamn. They cross with the sledge, peering through ice to moving water below, to rounds of pale stone. In springtime, Arctic char move down from the tarn. Springtime is when the thaw floods this river with fury.

They regard Isbjørnhamn as the halfway point even though on foot the tiny satellite hut sits far closer to the Villa, their destination at Fuglefjell, than the main base at Hyttevika. The scissors trap lays skewed at the corner of the halfway hut, fox prints and snow dug away where it has been stripped of bait. 'Another bally Houdini,' the Chief says and curses the no-good trap, a relic he inherited from a bygone trapper, as he kicks the thing to unjam it. Wanny thinks the scissors better suited to medieval torture, the bulbous iron jaws set to clamp the life from its victim. The Chief rests the trap against the sledge. 'Better to try our luck at the Villa than here.' He claims the foxes of Fuglefjell have grown too clever for fall traps.

'Watch out, Little Blue,' she says jovially. But Wanny has learned something unwanted about herself through this winter of travelling to and from Fuglefjell. She has come to feel affection for that small blue fox. She likes that he is there within sight of the hut to greet her. That he magically appears when she is on her own. That he trots along beside her as if they are old pals, setting off to share their day.

She is first to enter the halfway hut. 'What is it?' the Chief says to her gasp of breath.

'See for yourself.' She steps aside. A giant troll may as well have bullied its way through. Beef powder, broken glass, plates, cutlery, the shelf plank pulled from its wall. The unmistakable stench of fox urine. How such a tiny dwelling – no bigger than two large piano cases – can be the centre of utter chaos, leaves her scrambling for words. The Chief holds up a wooden spoon punctured with chew marks. He doesn't need to say it. Fox.

This, Ivanna, is a fox in a human world. Remember this. As untameable as a bear. As driven to survive. 'So,' she sighs.

'So.' The Chief sets to with a pan and brush.

'I can do it.'

'We will do it together.'

Wanny clucks. Two people inside the room can barely move for the other. She presses the flattened matchbox back into shape, removes the inner rings from the stovetop to create a draught. The satisfying strike of a match. The crackle as the scrunch of newspaper flames its way through kindling. She removes the enamel plate used as a lid on a pot of ice. A sniff of the pot's contents lest the fox has added his mark. The Chief puts a consolatory arm around her shoulder. 'You think Mikkel Rev had the good manners to replace the lid on the pot?'

She chortles. 'I know this much,' she says to the one who always reminds her how much chopping is required to melt a pot of ice. 'Hot water is the universal salve for any calamity, major or minor.' From the Chief, a not unfriendly grunt.

The blessing of this small space is not its reek of mould, its narrow bunks and damp mattresses barely long enough for a diminutive woman let alone the Chief's lanky legs, but in how little time and fuel it takes to heat the place and melt a pot of ice. The stove is the heart of every hut. Truly it is. She fills the basin with warm water, swishes the wire caddy until it milks with soap. A rag to wipe down every fox-ridden surface.

The Chief grumbles at the hole in the wall where the fox has dug its way in. 'We don't have enough tar paper to repair both huts.'

'Stick to the plan and save it for the Villa. We can bring more out to this one another day.

'That would be my thought.' He marches out to find a temporary fix to block the hole.

❋

'The difference to the glacier!' she calls to the Chief above the wind as they continue on to Fuglefjell. Below, snow covers the coastal plain, while up here the wind has scoured the glacier clean of its covering. They strap on crampons to gain a purchase on slick ice that in early morning light is an undulating sea, milky blue. Old tracks from the sledge cross fissures through the ice. The tracks cross over one sizable crevasse that has her shudder. 'It felt safer not knowing what was beneath us.'

The dogs baulk at rough leather booties lashed tight around their ankles to give them traction. Wanny tries to cajole Storm into staying still. A clout across the snout from the Chief and all three dogs comply. With Karo in the lead the dogs skirt around crevasses, threatening to overtake the Chief. He can shout and curse them all day long; give them his boot when they misbehave. A few kind words at the end of the working day, a scratch behind the ears, and all is forgotten. The curious way of things.

It is mid-morning, on the eastern edge of the glacier, when they down the last of the coffee and bite into frozen sandwiches. The shadowed slope of Fannytoppen remains inches deep with drifted snow. They pack away crampons, free the dogs of their booties. They carry their skis to start down the slope, dogs following with the sledge.

The snow soon thins out to reveal a slick of ice beneath. In the same instant, they each slip. Wanny gathers speed, skating, knees bent, managing to hold balance. When she comes to a stop, the Chief is stopped above her. 'This mountain,' she cries. 'You think we'd know not to trust it.' The Chief has his back turned to the dogs further up the slope who now rollick downhill as if this were a wild game, the sledge in tow. 'Watch out!' she cries too late. *Oof.* The Chief's thigh takes the brunt of the force, pushing him off his feet. He collapses in the snow, the pain enough that he curls in on himself to nurse his leg.

Wanny shouts so harshly at the dogs' brute clumsiness that all three of them drop to their haunches, fretfully wagging their tails to win back her good graces.

'Anders,' she says. 'Is it bad?'

He grimaces. 'It isn't good.'

He has barely recovered from his last fall. An accident at home in Norway is one thing. Here, on the side of this steep and lonely mountain? Their work, their living, their very lives hinge on being fit and able-bodied. Wanny is strong for her size but not enough to get the Chief, greater in height and weight, all the way down to the Fuglefjell hut. They will have to find another way. Wanny checks his leg, the bones of his ankle. 'Nothing feels broken,' she says. 'I cannot tell with your foot.'

His face is racked with pain. 'If I take off my boot, I'll never get it back on.'

She winds a bandage around the outside of his sock, the ribbing and finish of the wool more evenly crafted than she could ever manage. Who at home knits for the Chief? His homespun woollen socks with the padded heels, his heavy sweater, the shawl neckline edged in *løyesaumen*, colourful embroidery an older woman might choose, secured with a wooden toggle.

She pours coffee from the thermos. He glugs brandy from his hipflask. They rest until the Chief claims the pain has dulled. He sits on the sledge to cross Fannytoppen, the dogs moving more slowly than they care to, she propped alongside the Chief in case the sledge rolls.

Partway down the mountainside, the gradient is too steep to further chance a sledge, too rocky for skis; the singular way to cover the last two kilometres is by foot, crabbing down this accursed slope.

Against the Chief's protests, they leave the scissors trap packed on the tethered sledge, pick only a handful of essentials to add to their rucksacks. Wanny takes the heavy load. Step by painful step, a ski pole as his prop, Wanny helping when he will let her, they ease down the mountainside. The Chief's face glows with perspiration. The temperature is fifteen degrees below.

'Are you all right?' They pause to rest.

He ignores her concern and gestures to the sky. 'You hear?' he says.

Wanny listens. She nods. The cry of birds. The sweetest music after silent months.

'Fulmars,' he says. 'The last birds to leave. The first to return.'

'This place,' she says. 'Is there anywhere as grand?' Usually they would linger at this very spot, he as much as her gazing out across the landscape, registering the shift in light, counting down the days until the sun returns. But now is not the time to marvel at glaciers pouring their weight upon the southern shores of Hornsund, or the stepped ridges of these mountains, each lined with snow that bring to mind a festive cake.

He starts ahead of her. As if tuned to her thoughts he calls back, 'I know you are counting the days. We will be at the Villa for the sun's return.'

Wanny feeds the fire. She upends a frozen block of stew into a pot. The Villa creaks as it heats, the ceiling beaded with condensation. The Chief props in his bunk, slurping coffee laced with a measure from his hipflask to ease the pain.

'Here.' She passes him a draft of laudanum from the hut's small medicine tin. 'You are probably not meant to take it *with* liquor.'

'All the better to sleep.' He takes a glug of each.

Wanny sits on a stool to ease off his boot, an age-old jar of salve thawing by the stove to help massage the injured foot. The wind rises from the north-east.

'We are in for it,' he says.

'The number of times we reach this hut just in time.'

He looks insulted. 'I like to think it comes down to good planning. Consultation with the barometer. A bit of know-how about local weather patterns.'

The *ooh*-ing and *aah*-ing at the pressure of her hands. She stops. 'Am I hurting you?'

'Carry on.'

'I cannot tell if you are in pain or silly with tincture and drink.'

'My foot is craving the attention. The favourite of the household would understand.' Sæterdal hangs his head and puts on a forlorn expression exactly as Mira is apt to do when she feels hard done by. He holds up a limp arm.

Wanny cannot help laughing. 'Then we will take care to bandage your paw. Shush now.'

A snowstorm blasts through the night, and the next day. Being hut-bound comes as a saving, Wanny thinks, the foot massaged and re-strapped, the pain abating. By the third morning the Chief walks tenderly. He dresses to check and reset the traps. A wasted effort to try to talk him out of it.

'One small problem,' he says. 'We have no bait.'

'We still have seal.'

'Seal? The foxes of Hornsund require something superior to seal.' Yet he looks out at the frozen fjord longingly. He speaks of last season when he and Winter sped out on skis to hunt a bearded seal heavy with pup. The effort it took to haul the giant back to land.

The mountain is a chorus, fulmars wheeling in the breeze. Gripping a shotgun with bare hands, aiming for a steady target, would be struggle enough in the wind. A wheeling fulmar when it chances into range? The first shot rings out across the mountain. Another. The air clears of birds with nothing to show for their trouble. The Chief reloads. Again, he misses. 'You give it a try.'

Two cartridges. Two misses. 'It is impossible.'

'Keep trying.'

More reloads. More misses. Wanny's fingers grow numb between rounds, waiting for the fulmars to reappear. She reloads and aims wildly. Two birds fall to the ground. 'Dumb luck,' she says.

The Chief takes the next bird. And the next. Finally, they give into the cold, thawing their hands around thermos coffee, six fulmars laid out on the ground to bait the traps.

'They are bigger than they look in flight.'

'Substantial. The foxes of Hornsund are in your debt.'

Wanny studies the feathered stack. 'It feels unfair,' she says.

'What does?'

'The fulmars. Because of us their homecoming was short-lived.'

The Chief takes his knife. He splits the first bird. She knows that stiffness to his back. He is irritated with her. 'Sentiment is the luxury of town folk,' he says sharply. 'Up here, if you want to call yourself a trapper, needs prevail. If not' – he issues a bullish nod – 'best you stay at home, Wanny.'

She steams at the uncalled-for reprimand. 'Despite what you believe of me, I have no qualms about the nature of our work. If I did I would still be driving my taxi. I understand the need to shoot these birds to bait the traps. I am simply stating the pity of a creature that has flown this vast way that will not have the chance to meet its purpose.' Perhaps it is her throbbing fingers, the frustration of trying to shoot these birds, that makes her so forthright.

'You do not like the *selvskudds*,' he motors on as if her words count for nothing. 'Those you call unfair. You turn up your nose at the scissors. You believe we are engaged in some kind of duel of honour.'

'More or less, we are,' she cries. 'Is it wrong that I do not favour a one-sided battle? That I would rather a creature not suffer needlessly on my behalf because I have not carried out my task as I should? A clean shot. An instant death beneath a weight of stone. Isn't that what we both want? For us and for the creatures.'

He shakes his head. 'We see the world differently.'

'Then we must each learn to accept the other's point of view.' It is the kind of thing she will say to Bjørvik when he gets in a flap. The kind of thing Othar would once have said to the feisty young girl in her.

They sit in silence. Wanny takes up the binoculars. She scans the frozen fjord.

'Anything out there?' he asks her.

'Ice,' she grumps. More than ice. The difference in the light since last trip is striking, the brightness sparking the frozen crust of fjord as rich and lush as Danish silver. Therein a concern. She feels herself burst forth. 'I do not think it wise for us to go out on the fjord to hunt. The ice is too unpredictable.' There. She has said it. The first time she has given voice to their operations. In this regard she has always been the student. She expects to be told she is a worrier. That she knows nothing. Worse, that he sees her as a nag.

Strangely, the Chief does not put her down. 'What of our need for seal?' he asks her.

'We have bear back near the main base,' she says quietly. A skinned bear buried in snow. Likely more by the time they return. A mountain of meat waiting to be flayed. 'More than enough to bring some out here the next time we come.'

She waits for him to say, we do not waste good bear on dogs.

He simply says, 'Your concern is noted.'

Wanny looks to Anders Sæterdal to gauge his tone. He is not dismissing her as stupid or naïve. He returns her gaze with the semblance of a nod. An acknowledgement. The Chief is not an easy man to convince, but something in that gesture tells her he has listened.

❄

On the day the sun returns, they trap three fine white fox, young males, their coats lush and thick. Anders makes that twelve sale-able pelts to date, two others stripped by their cousins. They are under half of where they should be by now. But ten bears, Anders consoles himself, is four more than last season's count, with prime time still ahead of them. The *selvskudds* now do such service that his hands and fingers throb from skinning and scraping pelts. The irony comes in the work it takes, for nowhere near the same return as the skin of a fox.

Numbers fluctuate, Anders reminds himself, place to place, season to season. Back in 1928–29, Schønning Hanssen vowed he'd never spend another winter this north side of Hornsund. No shortage of bears to skin but his winter came and went without a single fox.

The night of the sun's return, Anders rests in his bunk, the candle on his shelf half burned to its holder. He is more than pleased with the day. He is filled with the joy of life. Three fine foxes skinned and hanging in the porch. The wall newly patched. A full belly. A warm hut. The woman at the table writing up the day. All is well with his world. Anders lays down the newspaper he has read a dozen times before. He studies her hands, the lamplight golden in the window, highlighting her face. She looks almost regal, straight-backed on her stool, eyes dreamy, a pencil in hand as she contemplates her writing. 'You are quite pretty,' he says, to which she gives a half smile. 'It is true,' he tells her, thinking beauty has as much to do with who a person is, the presence they hold. His voice catches. 'What does your journal say about the day?'

'It says, *Today, 16th February 1933, we saw sunlight for the first time this year. It was very nice.*'

He nods at the simple pleasure of having shown it off to her. Last year – he cannot remember where he was, here or at Hyttevika – he cannot remember pausing from his work. Not that he and the woman could claim more than the rim of its glow, mountains and glaciers obscuring the southern horizon. Seen or unseen, the sun was there, lifting herself above the horizon, swamping the fjord with pastel light. Its alpenglow briefly tinged the top of Fuglefjell. Anders imagines the fulmars looking out from their lofty nests, eyes glinting with light as the sun came into view.

He had been balanced beside her on a boulder, and for a moment he thought to hold her to the earth for she looked set to step out and glide above the fjord.

He has never known a person to be as moved by nature.

Standing there upon that rock he felt his own emergence, a rebirth into light. The sun his witness.

You are happy? he had asked her.

Whatever spell the new sun's glow had cast was held in the upturn of her face. *Anders.* She had clasped his arm as if to bring herself back. *I cannot find the words.*

Now, seated at the tiny table, she looks to him, watching. 'I forgot to record the time,' she says.

'Eleven thirty-one it rose, according to the almanac. Eleven thirty-three it set again.' Soft light, an amethyst twilight, stretched either side to light their way around the traps. A day to pledge to memory. 'Keep reading,' he says.

'Just as we started home, we saw twelve ptarmigan nearby and brought home the lot. Unheard of luck.' She looks across to him. 'Unlike last time on the mountain.'

'Never underestimate a fox.'

She laughs. 'That canny little thief earned himself his dinner.'

She reads on. *'Lovely ptarmigan soup for dinner and extra bait for the sticks.'* The lamp flickers. A splutter. *'Our dogs sat with their eyes on stalks hoping there would be a little snack for them as well. They get plenty of seal, but ptarmigan is ptarmigan, after all.'* She turns the page. *'Forgotten are all our troubles and struggles, storm, darkness and dangers of all sorts. Time passes quickly and we have plenty still to do.'*

'No end of plenty.' A dying hiss and splutter. The lamplight extinguished. Darkness but for the flicker of the taper at his side and a glow from the stovetop where the rings have warped.

Wanny reaches for matches to relight the lantern. 'They are no use,' he says. 'We are out of paraffin. The spare tin is at Fannytoppen tied to the sledge.'

Her darkened form gives a shrug. 'So ends the reading.'

'Not at all.' He pats his bunk in jest. 'Plenty of light over here I am willing to share.'

He expects to be ignored. She confuses him when she rises from the table with her journal. She looks to make her way to her top bunk but then she is beside him, clogs kicked to the floor. He shifts his body to make room, shares the pillow as if this were their everyday custom. Anders Sæterdal stripped of his senses by a woman in his bed.

She turns her journal to the candlelight. *'Tonight,'* she reads, *'we celebrated with* formkake, *coffee and a wee dram. "Skåles" to the sun. It will not be many more months before a ship anchors outside the islands, before men from the ship row ashore with the post and news of one thing or another to tell. Everything will be news to us, even if it is nearly a year old. The sun brings hope and so much new life, especially to those who have experienced the desolation and loneliness of* mørketiden *without a single breath from the outside world.'*

Loneliness? Desolation? He lifts to his elbow. 'You have been pining?'

Wanny rests the journal on her chest. She looks to him, her eyes soft. 'I am as happy as it is possible to be. Other than dreadfully missing my boys.' She studies his face. 'You, Anders? Are you happy? With me?'

He strokes hair from her cheek. He is quite content. He takes the journal from her hands, leans across her to rest it on the floor. The feel of her fingers touching his face.

FOX

---

the sun tumbles into view

NEVERMORE THE RUNT, the young blue moves across the landscape with the body of a vixen readying to mate. Young suitors track across the slope within her field of scent, their snouts wired to female pheromones. Timing is paramount.

In these ten months the blue has tested the limits of her world, survivor turned warrior, at ease high amongst the bird cliffs, a fox amongst traps. She has chanced death against the mortal hunger of an Arctic winter.

The promise of light floods her world, recalibrates her understanding of the seasons and what they bring. Each day is longer and carries more glint than the day before. More fulmars arrive, preparing their nests high on the mountain. This young vixen has won her place. When it comes to a mate, she has earned the right to be choosy.

She will couple for life with a hunter who stands alongside her, ready to ward off intruders and share in raising her young. Attributes that can only be gauged and trialled through courtship.

Two males contend for her attention, fine young foxes in peak condition, teeth intact, their snow-white pelts healthy and lush. The current favourite bounds toward her.

The pair tumble down the snow in a manner of play the young blue hasn't known since she was a kit. The male gives small affectionate nips around her shoulders and neck. He positions himself alongside her to take the brunt of the weather. He teaches her to purr. He is a promising young suitor, her equal in deliberation. He leaves the territory with a passing female, bigger-boned and in her second year, a vixen already in oestrus and perfectly primed for breeding.

The second suitor is larger in body, at times impetuous. He frolics harder. The young vixen nips the crown of his head, she licks his whiskers and shows off her purr. On a bright clear morning, the March sun tumbles heavy into view over mountains. Daggers of light spark the glaciers as he leads her east around the headland to hunt out on the sea ice. The frozen fjord is bereft of bears, no pickings of seal. They track past the small cove where scoured bones of the bearded seal have been carried out by waves to settle on the seabed, the few bones left on shore strewn by wind.

The pair travel far down the frozen fjord, nearer to the glacier than the young vixen has ventured before. Within the breadth of the fjord, fingers of sea ice raft up against a low hillock of snow, already claimed by her suitor, she can smell by his markings. Distinct from his urine, buried down beneath her paws, the blue vixen draws in a redolence of seal. More. A sour whiff. Milk. They are standing on the roof of a seal lair.

The pair settle on their haunches above the lair, bellies flat on the snow, their concentration on sound, a dull vibration they feel through their bodies, a duet of aromas, and finally, the swish of a seal's body across a frozen floor. Deep below them, water laps against a rim of ice.

The foxes stand, alert, bristling with anticipation. In tandem they angle down through snow, tunnelling at speed. They emerge side by side in a scattering of snow. They are below the subnivean, within a crystal cavern neither fully dark nor light, sized for a ringed seal and her pup. They skirt the breathing hole that links lair to ocean below. They take in the nursery, the glistening bowls of a single pair of eyes. The vixen quivers at the sharp-pitched bleating from a pup so new its coat is matted with fuzz, its snout and whiskers crusted with milk suckled from a mother. This her first absence from her young to forage.

The young hunters slink low.

The pair track back around the headland to the home territory. They swing past the trappers' hut. The young vixen leads her suitor up onto the roof to share in her domain. He licks her muzzle, noses her rear. She is full-bellied, sated; any day she will come into oestrus and remain in heat for several days. Timing is everything. The vixen rolls on her back to tussle and nip. Charged with new vigour she bolts from the roof, her suitor in tow. They race each other up the hill, bounding through snow, springing over rocks. They trot side by side, around and over traps that mark each dip and knoll, across to snow-free scree beneath the overhang of rock. The bird cliffs. Her suitor gazes skyward at the cry of fulmars, his tongue lapping. When kittiwakes and guillemots return, she will take him high up on the cliffs, to all her known ledges.

Her would-be mate is a hunter emboldened with success, temerity his undoing when he chances the jaws of a trap.

Fox tracks meander across the landscape in pairs. The young blue watches couples travel across the sea ice; new pairs trot along the shoreline. She sits alone on the roof of the trappers' hut, watching a male mount a female. The pair remain locked together as the male crooks his hind leg up and over her tail. They face opposite directions, hind to hind, fused as one.

On her first day of oestrus the young blue travels west to the mountain, desperately in search of ptarmigan. She climbs through deep snow against a fierce headwind, reaches bare rock that leads near vertically to a favoured site. Wind fills the air with flurries of snow that line the dip between two knolls, the riot of fresh tracks almost obscured. The young vixen sniffs at remnant pockmarks across the snow where ptarmigan have foraged to eke out bistort. She spies another set of prints, fresh, a fox. An intruder whose scent she fails to pick up against the force of wind. She climbs over rocks and makes her way to the high point of a knoll where the air is clear of flying snow. She searches about, stills at the sight of a fox braced atop the adjacent knoll, his white coat streamlined by the wind. She quizzes at his one amber eye, the other ice blue, an oddness that has the vixen wonder if his sight is blinded. To add to the peculiarity, at the inner corner of each eye his hair is smudged dark like a stain of wet rock. The intruder raises his muzzle to sniff at her, the round of his snout dotted pink from an absence of pigment. The young vixen bares her teeth. She will fight for her right to ptarmigan.

Without the advantage of scent, the crisscrossed tracks through the snow offer no clue to the number of ptarmigan or their direction of travel. The young blue spirals counterclockwise down the knoll, peering into the spindrift, scanning for movement or an aberration of pattern to distinguish feathers from snow.

A flash of red. A cock's comb. She bolts toward the prize, suddenly hindered by a stretch of soft snow that dunks her to her shoulders. At her side, a streak of white. She swerves as the intruder fox barrels across her path and charges ahead.

Around the next turn, forced against a wall of rock, a cluster of three ptarmigan cocks stand paralysed before their slayer, the fox with odd-coloured eyes baring needle white teeth. The vixen takes stock. The white has not darted in to seize his prize, a single hunter assured only of a single bird. He has waited, his position at the outer flank holding the birds at bay. The white's gaze shifts momentarily, a flicker of his ice blue eye to state his intention. The moment of choice. Together they can take all three. Will she then have to fight him for her share? The birds loosen, begin to flap, readying to scatter. The white hovers on his haunches, set to pounce or to divert if that is called for – he will hunt together or alone. The young vixen moves to the opposite flank to enclose the corral.

The two young hunters advance in unison, neither mindful of which fox moves first, only that one must take its cue from the other. A vulpine partnership destined for success. Timing is crucial.

BEAR

---

the quest for seal

A SWELL OF milk spills from the bear's teats, a butterfat trail leaking across the sea ice. The young mother searches warily, sniffs at the air before choosing an icy hummock against which to settle her bulk. She sits upright on a stubbed tail, hind limbs splayed out. Her twin cubs immediately clamber across her belly. A needle of sharp claws as they push themselves up, too large now for her to cradle. Too practised to need guiding to her upper teats. They jostle for space within the span of her chest. They latch on, suckle hard, their warmth pressed upon her chest. Her lungs labour beneath the cubs' shuffling. Soon they settle. A family rhythm. Her breath eases. She closes her eyes to a dream state that floats between sleep and a dull beat of hunger. She will nurse her cubs through this second summer if her fat reserves allow. Beyond the weaning they will stay by her side a full year more to learn to hunt and thrive. Already these twins have the taste for seal.

The cubs finish nursing, reluctant to leave the warmth of her chest. They trot behind their mother along the frozen fjord, a mile out from Gåshamna on Hornsund's southern shore. They stop when she stops, mimicking her actions, heads raised to sniff hard at air. They are attuned to their mother's quest for seal. Onward they go, a caravan across the ice, the twins' fur pale against the buttery hue of their mother. The male cub knows better than to race ahead, but when he plunges into open water to cross a lead, he is close enough behind to send a wash across his mother's rear. He pulls himself up onto ice beside her, shakes and rolls in snow to dry. He is big enough now that his guard hairs have grown in, his skin protected from the icy water. The mother waits for her female cub who lingers behind at the previous ice edge, wanting to be ferried across, kept dry upon her mother's back. The mother issues an almost silent growl. *Come along.*

She is a young mother, six years old, this her first litter. She hungers for seal, the need for replenishment. The mass of weight she gained in readiness for denning, to sustain her through this first full year of nursing, is depleted. She is an adept hunter, but for every ten seals a bear stalks on the ice, nine dive free. She angles in toward a glacier edge where water at the broken edge swirls fast and turbulent, milked with glacial melt, alive with feeding fish. A place where her own mother taught her to scour the sea ice for birthing lairs. She looks around, a cautious hunter, a steadfast mother, attentive to her young, wary of any hungry male bear who would take her cubs. She is the Arctic's apex predator, her sharpest weapon of defence her acute sense of smell. She is also a bear with a heightened sense of caution, ingrained from her younger years.

Snout down, twins in tow, the mother halts mid stance. Her cubs bound toward her, hoping to nurse. Her jaws open to a yawn to issue a command. *Stay back.* The young know the beating they will get for disobedience. They turn and scamper back to a snowy mound to romp and tumble. They jostle and nip at one another, they balance on their bottoms to wrestle and hug. They collapse in a pillow of snow to shake themselves off and romp again.

The mother stands motionless for endless minutes, her ear cocked, her nose drawing in the air, all her senses directed at the ice below. Abruptly, she lifts her tremendous bodyweight and stamps her forelimbs down, smashing the ice beneath her paws. The cubs cease their play, their attention seized by her actions. Her speed belies her bulk. She sinks to hind knees, plunges head and shoulders through the broken rim of ice, only the round of her bottom and pads of her rear paws visible above the icefloe.

She finally reappears, wet to her belly, a seal's hind flipper clamped in her jaws. The cubs bristle as their mother heaves the slippery creature up onto the floe and drags it a safe distance from the edge. The moment she releases her grip the seal gallops toward escape. She blocks its path, her great paw stamped on its back as she buries her canines into each side of its neck.

The cubs race across to join their mother who tears free a strip of sealskin. Despite her hunger, the mother chews delicately, scanning her surrounds, checking on her cubs who bury themselves to their shoulders; their ears, faces, forelimbs and paws a riot of red.

❋

Wind rises. Snow falls. For a week the family ambles in loose zigzags across the breadth of ice, their heads angled down against blasts of spindrift. Sea ice near the glaciers grows unstable with the storm, while out here in the middle of the fjord the mother finds no scent or sight of seal. Several times each day she stops to nurse her young, their appetite insatiable. The twins nap, curled against their mother's belly, warmed by her thinning bulk.

The wind shifts to the north-east, growing fierce until it shrieks down mountainsides and shrills across glaciers. This platform of ice dividing north and south begins to heave, an expanse undulating as a wave. An adult bear will swim unheeded across a vast open waterway, can navigate enormous spans bridged with floes of ice, but should the storm tear this ice apart to ram against itself, she will flounder with these cubs. She leads her young toward Hornsund's northern shore, to the protection of its coastline.

She passes by the hut set back on the plain. A tantalising odour rises as a cloud blown out from shore. Hunger urges her to divert from her course, to venture in and explore. Her cubs catch the scent. They peel away to follow their noses. She brings them to a stop with a growl. They sit restlessly, craning their heads toward shore, looking pleadingly to her. Caution stems this mother's boldness, curbs her urge to hunt. She takes an inordinate time to determine the full sensory palette. Hunters. Dogs. Foxes hanging from a line. A hue of life and death too perilous to chance her cubs.

Onward she marches, still wrestling temptation. Her young are hesitant to follow, edging closer to defiance.

Beyond, to the north, the unmistakable scent of meat. A seal upon the shore.

In she goes.

She lets her young bound ahead of her, thankful not to have them lag across the ice.

Closer into shore they slow to take her lead. Here, the perimeter of ice is broken and jostled, smaller pieces bobbing, larger floes heaving in the swell. The ice proves tiring to traverse with pieces too small to take her weight, larger floes too distant to leap across, too densely packed to swim between. For a morning, she and her cubs take to the water only to haul themselves up to the next floe.

They close in on the headland where the scent is strong. They reach rafts of ice rammed hard and high against the shore. The young mother leaps a body length up onto a broken ledge. She perches to wait for her young to follow. Another leap and the family of three stand upon the land.

Proud on the high point of the headland is a misshapen seal standing tall and alert on angular legs. The young mother looks about warily, surveying the scene, drawing on a memory of her own mother taking meat from such a creature's hold.

The male cub bounds toward the *selvskudd*, overwhelmed by the meat on show, food waiting to be snatched. The mother stops him with her growl. She slaps him with her paw, shunting him off his feet.

Now the lure of seal draws her female cub forward. The young mother issues a sharper growl. Impatient with them both, she takes the female by her neck folds to shake her into compliance. Her male cub, tortured by the scent of seal, chances the distraction as his moment of freedom. He bolts toward the *selvskudd*, his hind legs tall enough to reach up and rest his paws against its edge. His head dives in with open jaws to seize the prize and tear it from its hold. The mother hears the click, a flash of light and a mighty roar, her cub punched backwards to the ground.

The mother halts where she stands. Her female cub darts away in fright.

Cautiously, the mother approaches the *selvskudd*. She sniffs at its case, meat swinging from its jaw. She stands above her motionless cub, its snout powdered black. Its broken bowl of skull. She nudges the fallen cub with her muzzle and paw.

She measures this new state of being, weighs her options. As she did as a cub, her mother still and silent on the ground before her, she snatches the meat free of its hold and pads a distance away. She places down the catch, raises her head, calls her female cub back to share the meal.

Again, the mother stands looking down upon her dead cub. She sniffs at air to scan the overland route that will lead her and her female cub to the north. She rises on hind legs to reach her full towering height, her mighty forepaw armed with a full force of grief as she strikes the *selvskudd* apart. The surviving cub watches as her mother punches the unearthly creature into splinters strewn across the land.

FOX

a bounty of meat

A MALE BEAR and its catch of seal form a pale speck far out across the frozen fjord, nearer to the south side of Hornsund than to this side at Fuglefjell. The bear gorges upon its prey, the bearded seal hefty enough to sustain his needs for weeks. When the bear consumes his fill, the first of many sittings, he wanders to a patch of clean snow to rest, primed to guard his kill should another bear come near.

In the rising wind, the aroma of seal reaches Hornsund's southern shore. A fox ventures out, edging toward the outer limits of the kill, ready to scamper should the bear wake and take exception to a scavenger.

Dog fox trolls the northern edges of the frozen fjord, peering into breathing holes, scavenging for pickings. Flocks of dovekies swarm through the air on their return to Svalbard. The first guillemots of spring swoop overhead, on the lookout for leads of open water. Dog fox studies the far-away aberration on the ice. A movement. He looks back to his shore, to the greater span ahead, but when he picks up a pocket of seal scent, temptation overwhelms distance. He breaks into a trot, his back to a northerly wind that – grown fierce, in concert with an ocean current streaming with the tide – can turn the strongest seal of ice to a frangible skin. One fracture is all it takes.

The iceberg set to topple is not large, but when its side shears away and the mass of it keels, the submerged underbelly lifts and then thunders back down amid a wall of ocean water. The shattering of the sea ice echoes off the mountain where kittiwakes and guillemots have settled in to nest.

The wind shrills. The older vixen moves across the landscape against a blast of headwind. New life grows within her womb. She sits tall beneath the Pomor cross to look out across the ice, to a gash of dark water where pack ice has newly split and teased apart. She moves her weight from paw to paw.

The lead of open water sets the surrounding ice in motion. Farther out, with nothing now to lock the ice in place, new cracks split apart. With the current running strong and the push of the wind, ice edges grate and collide with the same deep thud and boom as storm clouds. As Hornsund's icy platform relinquishes its grip, frozen sheets raft one upon the other. Ice the size of a rowboat, ice shaped as a ship, the force gathering momentum, set to sail down the fjord.

The bear rises when the pad of ice it lies upon splits and separates it from the seal carcase. His hind legs catapult him across the chasm, his front paws catching the edge of the adjacent floe. He propels himself up, ambles to the seal to nose the bloodied mass. Satisfied that nothing is amiss, the bear gives a mighty shake and rolls on the ice, rubbing his back to dry his coat. He contemplates another feed then lies back down to sleep.

The floe is substantial, large enough for two trespassers at its far end to retreat, a white fox from the southern shore, dog fox from the north. Swimmers, no. Their plush coats, scant with fat, offer no protection from this water. For these two beleaguered creatures there is nowhere but here, no option but to remain fixed and alert, hoping for a bridge back to safety. When the wind dies, tomorrow or the next day, the ice will coalesce and the fjord will refreeze. Until then, these two small hunters remain adrift on a crystalline island, a bounty of meat between them and a sleeping bear.

Above them, the cry of Arctic skuas. The pair hover in the wind, peering down at this odd assortment of the living, the slain and the soon-to-perish. The skuas hold their wings aloft to touch down on the floe. The bear momentarily raises its head to give a threatening yawn, its jet tongue sliding from its jaw. The foxes sit motionless. The skuas keep a watchful eye on the bear as they hammer their bills into a bellyful of seal gut, extracting an unwieldy length that requires each bird take an end in its bill, the pair tugging in unison until the entrail breaks in two. The carcase of the seal lies slumped; beneath it a soundless fracture set to cleave the ice.

13

Isbjørnhamn, April

GUILLEMOTS AND DOVEKIES stream into Hornsund. Across the slopes they preach and prattle. According to the woman, the birds' chatter comes as a direct greeting from civilisation, a tangible thread to home where dovekies spend their winter. Anders is surprised by his own feeling of lightness as they row the boat out from Isbjørnhamn on a clear, fine April day. Eighteen degrees below, the storm passed, the water of Hornsund ripples from a zephyr of northerly breeze. Their first time on the water since the onset of winter. 'Doesn't it feel grand?' he says to the back of Wanny's head from where he rows at the bow.

Anders watches Wanny slide her oars and lay them flat across the gunnels. She leans back from her middle thwart and rests her head upon his lap, her eyes closed to the sun. A smile. 'This is the life.' She raises an arm and makes a play of fluttering her hand to issue the boat forward. 'Carry on, Mr Sæterdal.'

'Your ladyship,' says he.

The sound of his oars winding in their rowlocks. Wooden blades tipping and dipping the water. Coronas of bubbles. His lover, a woman trapper, her head resting on his lap, her face flushed with warmth.

By midday the dovekies move in large flocks across the ice, on their way out to open sea to feed. If his partner was not again busy at her oars, she would plug those glaucous gulls that bully their way through the swarm, their bulk knocking out two or three dovekies at a time. By tomorrow morning the tiny birds will be back at their nests, safely tucked away in rocky crevices across the scree slope. Anders accelerates his rowing pace to match his partner's new fervour. They often seem to chat effortlessly in the boat, and he wonders if talk flows more easily in company with industry, or if the shared view of the frozen hinterland inspires lively conversation. A chance to take in the vista, Hansbreen coruscating in midday sun.

'How different it all feels with light,' she says. 'The sun, the birds returned.'

'You wait until next time at Fuglefjell,' he tells her. 'You cannot hear yourself think for the throng of birds. The ledges are crammed with guillemots. Many times more than when you first arrived. Kittiwakes. Fulmars. Dovekies nesting right across the scree slopes.'

'I never stopped to think where the dovekies disappeared to at the end of Tromsø's winter. It seems a miracle that such a tiny bird can fly so far across the stormy seas.' In the next breath, 'Beastly glaucous gulls!' she shouts up to the sky.

Anders resists the temptation to point out her contrary values, that she pities a fulmar shot from the sky while ready to dispatch every glaucous gull within range. Instead he talks about the onset of spring, every Svalbard bird racing against time to breed.

'Love in the air,' Wanny pipes up, convinced that Mira has fallen pregnant. They do not speak aloud of their own nights together. 'You see how easily Mira tires these last weeks,' she says. 'How often she naps. One of your Alsatians,' she throws the accusation back across her shoulder.

The likely culprit *both* his dogs. 'Maybe Mira is laying it on again.' He winds her up. But she may be right. Hard to tell with a dog's winter coat but Mira looks thicker, different somehow, around the girth, and not her usual spry self. 'Early May, I'll bet,' he says. They stake bets on the date she will deliver a litter, the number of pups. 'Name your poison,' says he.

'St Hallvard's.'

'A woman's drink.' When it comes to a decent wager, he is first and foremost a cognac man. They speculate on whether the last big storm of winter has passed, thankful it has opened up this navigable channel, a lead of two kilometres out to the ice. Anders turns to check their course. He shields his eyes to squint. 'Oh, yes, my word,' he cries. Lady Luck is with them all the way. 'See out here.' He has Wanny turn around. 'A pot of gold at the end of the rainbow.'

The woman peers. 'I see it,' she cries. A bearded seal sunning itself on an icefloe.

They swap places, she on the oars at the bow. She rows down-wind of the *storkobber*, holds the oars aloft, both of them still and silent when the seal lifts itself to look around. A seal will believe its nose before its eyes. They wait until it lowers its head, twists to its side, the nails of its flipper more dexterous than any human hand – perfectly designed, Anders thinks, to function as a back scratcher. He glides the Kragen to his cheek. Aims at the head. He meets his target. The huge body jerks and slumps. Wanny pulls hard on the oars in case the seal flings itself into the water. 'Ease up,' he tells her. 'It is quite dead.'

Anders crawls up onto the icefloe. Standing in the sun, the wind easing, he peels off his coat, throws it on a thwart. He pushes up the sleeves of his pullover to save his cuffs. The *storkobber* is a massive creature, six inches of solid blubber perfect for *selvskudd* bait and dog food. The choice meat from the back slides easily from the bone. A juicy strip of steak, ten kilograms or more. He may be a trapper, but he is also an adept butcher with a lethal set of knives.

'This, Mrs Woldstad, is not for any *selvskudd*.' He passes the hefty lump down to the woman who takes it as if it were an infant wet from the bath. 'Chief?' she says. 'Who knitted your sweater?'

'This one?' he inspects it. 'My brother's wife, I expect. She is the premium knitter in the family. Why do you ask?'

She gives a sheepish shrug. 'It is very nicely stitched,' she says and lays the steak in the base of the boat.

Anders works for a concentrated hour to carve off choice cuts, to scrape strips from the ribs. He makes three rough piles: bear bait, dog food, human food. Wanny stacks them on the running boards.

'Remember before Christmas,' he says, 'how tired we were of seal. How we craved the taste of bear.'

'And now we've had more than our fill.'

'With the exception of bear cub,' Anders says. The meat as succulent as roasted lamb.

Wanny quietens. 'Poor little wretch.'

It niggles him, her softness. As if trapping equates to villainy.

'When we get home,' the woman starts on her list of cravings. Anders's mind drifts. His gaze shifts to the land. He can see a long way inland, back to Hansbreen's frozen tributaries with their dark lines of moraine snaking through the mountains, coalescing into a broad frozen river. He has lost count of their crossings with the sledge. He hacks through seal meat, half listening to his companion feasting on fresh fish and smoked salmon, on drinking an entire jug of fresh cow's milk, *an inch of cream on top*. Anders tussles with the shape of the future, his and her place within it. Home is at least two months away. Svendsen instructed them not to expect a ship before the fifteenth of June. Two months is two months too soon to think about next season, to respond to her hints about whether he and she might work together again. He feels himself bristle at being pushed before he has fully thought things through. Call it bloody-mindedness: he will not be pressured. With another fellow, talk of partnerships is hallowed, reserved for the smoky confines of Mack Ølhallen and a skinful of beer, each trapper in the beer hall reflecting on the season gone, weighing his options for the next, quietly surveying the room to assess the prospects. A woman has scant understanding of trapper's lore. It is the downfall of their sex, he decides, the need to have each i dotted and t crossed, before the words are even written on the page. She would do well to remember she is a mother to boys. That she is still a man's wife.

He watches her stacking seal along the floorboards of the boat. Even to navigate such conversation fills him with unease, reminds him again of why he favours a simple, solo way of being. He is not one for words of love or of loathing. He and Othelie shared hard truths only at the point when it was too late to mend things. He learned a thing or two from those exchanges: do your uttermost to avoid a woman's tears; steer well clear of her wrath. Anders carves off a flipper. Enough that Wanny shares his bed, reaches for him in the night.

He passes each flipper down to her. He grows overheated in his heavy woollen sweater. Anders looks around. The fjord has stilled. Stretches of ocean have frozen into grease ice. No breath of wind, no movement to keep the water from freezing. Wake up, man. Alarm prickles his skin. 'Quickly now,' he calls down. 'Finish up. We need to get a move along.'

Wanny yanks the anchor free of the icefloe. How the ice crumbles these days, her feet breaking through the crusted surface. Anders talks about spring melt, the sea ice disintegrating from the underside up. She feeds the painter rope into the boat, stows the anchor, takes her place at the middle thwart, her feet seeking out a footing amid a ballast of seal meat. The boat sits low and heavy in the water. The

Chief takes the bow. He doesn't wait for her to start, but rows with long powerful strokes. Wanny gauges his concern. She twists to search toward their home shore. At midday the channel was inked with open water. Now, a crystalline carpet stretches all the way to shore. She hears the rhythm of the Chief's oars and works to match his furious pace. With their backs to home, Wanny feels they are moving at a barrelling pace. She visualises the shore growing close. When she turns to look, well, yes, it is somewhat closer, but still they are a vast way out.

The rowing rapidly grows harder, the boat sluggish. The Chief pushes his oars so far down into slush that the blades collide with hers on their way back up. It feels like they are rowing through porridge, struggling to make headway. Ice scrapes against the bow, the slush extending further down than an oar can reach. She hears an odd squeaking sound, like a cork being wound into the neck of a bottle. Ice binds around the boat. It rises up toward the gunnel.

'Anders,' she says.

He looks at the diminishing freeboard. 'Lighten the boat.'

She cannot argue, determined not to count the dreadful waste. Piece by piece they discard the *storkobber*, until in the boat's wake lies a half-submerged rubble of blubber, flippers, the seal's fine pelt, a quantity of meat that would have seen hunters and dogs and each and every *selvskudd* through to the end of the season.

Ivanna. None of it matters.

With each discard the boat rises. The freeboard increases. With each discard she feels the boat list. They move their body weight to the far edge of the thwarts to tilt it back to level. The heavy strip of meat is all that remains of their catch. She hears the Chief say quietly, 'We keep the steak for as long as we can.' A marker of hope.

Her oars make a futile attempt to pull through ice. How much pressure can an oar take before it snaps like a matchstick? 'It is no use!' she cries. They change places, he at the middle thwart, she kneeling at the front facing forward, leaning over the gunnel to shovel away slush with her hands. She feels the boat jerk forward. They make headway. Yes. 'We are on the move,' she cries. She hears the Chief heaving on the oars. Too soon the squeaking starts up again. Ice girdles the boat. She pushes it away with all her strength though there is hardly a space to move it to. The surface is a tidy jigsaw puzzle, pieces of ice locked together. Wanny tries to lift and stack small pieces which prove to be many times bigger than they look bobbing on the surface. One piece almost drags her from the boat. Their efforts count for something. They inch forward, the Chief grunting with effort, she perspiring with the strain of hurling and shovelling, her hands without feeling inside sodden mittens. She looks to Hansbreen, turned the colour of rose gold, the cloud above the glacier a blush of pink. She looks back toward the south. The sun tracking low. A few more hours and it will be night.

The Chief halts to catch his breath. He turns to look to shore. He drops his head. 'Wanny,' he finally says. He looks defeated. 'I am sorry. I don't know that we can make it.'

Never before has he spoken this way. 'It will be all right,' she says. 'You will see.' The same phrase he uses in troubled times to reassure her. 'We are within reach of the big berg. Let us try for that.' Normally they would give a wide berth to a berg that might topple unannounced, crushing everything in its path. She is pushed back to her girlhood at Sommarøy, pulling nets with her father in weather turned foul. Her father had gestured toward Håja. So long as the island's pyramid of mountain remained in view, they were never too far from home. 'We can do it, Chief!' she cries. The berg ahead is Håja.

An hour of fighting slushy ice. Metre by hard-earned metre they close the distance to the berg. From there a kilometre more stands between the berg and shore. How can two small people win against the might of nature? Wanny pictures her boys with a deep rush of sorrow. To lose a father and now their mother. It would not be like her own father, his fishing boat retrieved, his body laid out in the boathouse, she forbidden to enter its doors. She and Anders neglected to leave an entry in the logbook at the halfway hut, not even a sentence to say when and where they have gone. Whoever comes to find them, months hence, will have to piece together the puzzle of their disappearance. Their rowboat missing. Their sledge blown to kingdom come, not staked down, so sure were they to be back by afternoon. Their faithful dogs will still be tethered to their chains – she cannot bear to think of it. Images veer and bounce. They settle on herself and Anders approaching the headland, before them the strewn timbers of the *selvskudd*. The slain cub. A mother's effort to raise her young. *A bear is devoid of human feelings*, the Chief stands firm in his belief. No. Wanny has seen it for herself. A bear that strikes a heavy *selvskudd* to the ground does so with a madness borne from grief and rage. She looks to the berg ahead, her eyes smarting from cold, her vision swimming between grief and rising fury at the monumental struggle it has taken them to reach this far and still all their efforts might amount to nought. The faces of her children. Her frozen hands. She tears at the ice to free the boat's path.

They stop dead, twenty metres between boat and iceberg. Anders ruminates. He contemplates the range of gear aboard, pays a nod to whichever close call from the past taught him to always stow copious lengths of spare rope beneath the back thwart. Two sets of oars. He studies his boots. The woman is half his weight. The risk. He takes a breath, needing to keep his voice buoyant. 'What do you say if we lay the oars down across the ice between here and there? Have you pull yourself across?'

She hesitates. 'The berg is too far for the oars to reach.'

'I will lash them together. Like a kneeboard. You pull them along as you paddle with your hands.' He shakes his head. It is a ludicrous idea.

She looks to the berg. 'And if I get there?'

'*When* you get there. You will have this length of rope secured around your middle. You take it and tie it fast around that tumble of ice blocks. Check that it won't slip off. We get the boat secured. Lighten the load. I follow and then we pull the boat in.'

'And then?'

He has no answer for *and then*. 'Wanny,' he says. 'One step at a time.'

Again she looks to the berg. A furrowed brow. 'All right.'

All right. He lashes a set of oars and eases them down upon the frozen surface. A bowline around her waist. He feeds out the rope as she climbs from the boat down upon the oars. She perches on her knees upon what amounts to an unstable, unseaworthy raft. She paddles full speed with her hands, more shovelling a path through the frozen sludge, her balance steady. She pauses to pull at each mitten with her teeth, each saturated article dropped upon her knees. 'Are your hands working?' he calls. She doesn't answer. He feeds more rope. She is close to halfway. Forward she goes on the pair of lashed oars, nearer to the berg. She is an oar's length away. She reaches for the raised ledge of ice, tips, rebalances herself in time. He hears himself sigh. She shifts her weight from the oars to tread upon a lip of ice that takes her weight. She pulls herself up onto the lip, the flat of the berg covered with a cushion of snow that offers good traction. She clambers to her feet, turns to face him. He sees her victory cheer.

'Mrs Woldstad,' he calls across.

'What now?' She shakes out her hands. They will be frozen.

'You are one hell of a woman.'

He has enough rope he can join to span plenty of extra distance between boat and berg. A short drop rope he hangs from the line to lash loose items weighing down the boat. Their rifles. Two rucksacks, he feeding out the line as she pulls the rope at her end. Each article lurches across until it reaches the berg. She takes an inordinate time to unknot the tie. Even at the best of times, her fingers suffer the cold more than his. She raises her arm and he hauls back the excess length of rope. The last of their belongings to be ferried across is the heavy slab of seal. Does it count as a necessity? he asks himself. Far from it, but as long as they have that choice cut of seal in their hold, all is not lost. All the wasted meat and effort burns hot inside him. Makes him more determined. He gets the rope tied around himself, the loose end behind him tethered to the dinghy's bow ring. He sees Wanny hold her end taut as he tests his body weight upon the oars. He is considerably heavier than her, the lashed timbers bowing beneath his bulk. He sinks below the sludge, wet from knees to groin as he furiously shovels a path across. He can hear himself snorting. He ignores his hands turning cold and stiff as wooden paddles. If she can do it, so can he.

She helps him up onto the ice, his fingers and joints turned wooden. She clasps his hands to her chest to help thaw them. 'I am all right,' he says. Wanny scrambles through her rucksack for the thermos, spills coffee, the snow splattered brown, as she fills the mug. Her hands look as cold as his feel. She helps wrap his hands around the cup's warmth. He takes such great gulps that the steaming liquid scalds his gullet. He tears at a corned bear sandwich, the bread and meat frozen through. He has lost track of the last time he ate.

Together they pull the boat across, the tips of his fingers throbbing with pain as the feeling returns. He loops the boat's anchor around an ice boulder.

Anders feels sure the berg is grounded, confirmed when he surveys its landward side. A reef running toward shore, beside it a line of semi-open water. The channel peters out at the fast ice, a flat expanse clinging to the shore. That expanse of ice is bound to be rotten, but still strong enough, he prays, to take a body weight, to haul a boat across.

Once more they take to the boat, reload each belonging, push and pull the hulk to reach the open channel. They row an exhilarating one hundred metres, buoyed by the rate of movement, the sensation of real progress.

They step from the boat onto the sheet of fast ice. He feels it move beneath his feet. He grips the boat's gunnel to balance as they yank the vessel upward to help lift it, praying that the edge of the fast ice will not shear off beneath its weight. Anders stands ankle deep in water to heave the boat clear. The long slow haul of dragging the beast shoreward, expecting any moment to step straight through the ice. He is the first to break through the crust, wet to his waist. Out he clambers, his clothing doubled in weight. He tightens his grip on the boat. The ice should take the woman's weight but when she plunges to her armpits he halts, tying a rope around her waist in case her fingers lose their grip. Their mittens gone, somewhere back there lost to the slush. If they should run out of strength or willpower. If they are forced to abandon the boat to save themselves . . . No. The boat is their lifeline, no matter the burden of dragging it. Tug by arduous tug, hands red raw, fingers white with cold, they shunt it across rotten ice.

It is long dark on a moonless night when the first crunch of gravel scrapes beneath their boots. Seven hours to cover the longest two kilometres of his life. Wanny looks near to tears. 'Last push,' he tells her. One last wearying time they empty the boat and pump it free of water to lighten the beast, each taking a turn. 'It is helping warm us up,' he tells her. Anders finds a slender length of driftwood and drags it along the shore. It is all he can manage to dig a trench with his hand and boot and to wedge the wooden pole beneath the bow, enough to help roll the boat a meagre distance up the beach before surrendering. Wanny throws the anchor up the beach without looking where it lands. She is past caring and he not far behind. Too tired to lift her spirits, to make light of his relief to be finally onshore, this raw, numb state of being. He summons the feeling of a warm fire, a hot drink to propel them both onward for the mile-long slog east to the halfway hut at Isbjørnhamn. A march through deep snow, every layer they wear a leaden armour frozen to their bodies, their boots weighing down their steps.

He is too weary to greet the dogs, the three of them delirious and set to choke themselves on their chains. The effort of unbolting the hut door with wooden fingers and stumbling inside, he doing no better than her at pulling another new match from the box before dropping it to darkness. The numb, hit-and-miss clumsiness of striking the match tip against its box without breaking the stem into splinters. At last they get the firebox alight. The laborious task of yanking off sodden layers, cuffs and bands caught around his neck and wrists, the tang of sweat and sheep as they stand in wet woollen underwear steaming before the stove. Anders resorts to using the palms of his hands as tongs, he cannot flex his fingers to lift the emergency cognac from its shelf. His teeth to free the cork. He takes a sizable slug, the brandy's warmth igniting a flame within his stomach, flooding his chest. He hands the bottle to Wanny who has no taste for cognac but takes as big a slug. She wipes spillage from her chin. She makes a face. 'It tastes like water.'

They make a large pot of hot chocolate sweetened with a full tin of Viking milk – at any other time a wicked extravagance. They down three mugs each and call it dinner, their fingers thawed by the warmed enamel of the mugs. They collapse into sleeping bags and plunge into dreamless sleep, woken twelve hours later by a fierce thirst and the whining of hungry dogs. They pull on clothes, nowhere close to dry. Silently they pack belongings on the sledge, trusting that on the way home to Hyttevika, the hallowed slab of steak will still be waiting in the boat. That the boat itself will still be on the shore. He cannot remember the state of the tide or how high they hauled it.

Before Anders bolts the hut door, Wanny turns. 'Wait,' she says. She returns inside, sits at the table and opens up the logbook. He follows her in, stands at her back, his hands resting on her shoulders. Her pencil moves clumsily, her fingers as raw and swollen as his. By tomorrow their hands will be a crop of chilblains. She holds up the book for him to read her account of their day on the fjord. A single line. *Unsuccessful, laborious and not entirely without danger.*

'A faithful account?'

He rests his chin on the crown of her head. 'You have it to the letter, Mrs Woldstad.'

FOX

new life

THE MOUNTAIN SQUEALS with birds, the air ruffled and tumbled as guillemots heavy with fish arc in and land beside their neighbours. Kittiwakes alight on higher cliff sites, old mates surveying last season's nests, first-timers charged with industry. Birds flutter and swoop to pluck building matter from snow-patched surrounds. Skuas use their rigid claws to scrape a shallow bowl of gravel protected from the worst of the wind; other pairs nest on the leeward side of a rock, their dappled eggs blended to Fuglefjell's earthly palette of stone and lichen.

The young blue vixen, attuning to the sensation of new life within her womb, draws in the cloying air, the scent thick with bird, the territory sharp-edged from the growing flush of daylight, from myriad sensations that slowly gather into the onset of summer. She turns her ear to the trapper leaving the hut. She bounds into position to watch his effort of heaving a rigid contraption up the hill. She sits tall, her head cocked, making sense of its arrival as he sets it down amongst rocks, a sharp clang reverberating across the hillside. He stands upon the thing, splaying its hoops flat to the ground. The young vixen smells the intoxicating whiff of fresh ptarmigan held within its grip, a flavour she breathes deep into her belly. She waits for him to leave then makes her way down the hillside to sit before the contraption. She tests it with her whiskers, dabs her snout upon its frigid steeliness. The ptarmigan head rests inches from her reach. Her tongue laps as she inches closer. She hears a sound, distracted by the scent of her brown- and blue-eyed mate, in his hold a fresh, plump kittiwake. Away she gallops to greet him. Their first catch of the season.

The older vixen crosses to the lookout, a ritual that sees her tip her muzzle toward the fjord, her search for her own mate a waning urge with scant expectation. Daily, she weighs up her prospects, her hold on the den, a new season's litter that once born she cannot raise alone. The vixen waits for the trapper to return to his hut – one door, a second, claps behind him. The hut issues a duet of muffled voices, an aroma of meat, the reek and whine of dogs tethered outside to their chains, halos of dog hair parting from their winter coats. The vixen follows her nose to a new waft of ptarmigan. She circles the steel hoops, familiar with their form. She covets their prize. She draws in the scent of her offspring who has been here ahead of her, leaving the ptarmigan morsel intact. The older vixen sprays the ground in a marking of territory then sets herself down. She is a canny fox. But also a pregnant mother without a mate, a fox grown lean with hunger.

In the older vixen's absence, the young blue and her mate take up position at the entry to her den. Wariness comes from habit. The blue remains on watch, aware of her father's long absence, pondering the shift in prospects with a mate of her own. Young dog fox disappears down through the opening of the rocks. He surveys the breadth of the den, satisfied it is plenty enough for his new family of fox. He reappears through the furthest exit, his scent sprayed through the den.

Across Fuglefjell's headlands and valleys, the wooden jaws of fall traps remain agape but for a single trap clamped down upon a passing white, the clatter of stones heard across the landscape, the hind of the trapped fox soon set upon by the older vixen.

With the lengthening days, the trappers spend greater time outdoors, the woman stripping the white of its mauled coat, the man kneeling on the roof, hammering new coverings over those the young blue has worked to pull free. The woman clucks at the bodiless white coat, too torn and damaged to stretch on a board, a few salvageable strips its only value. The flaying completed, she pads along the cobbled beach to crouch beside the runnel with her knives, scouring blades and handles with loose sand, cleaning her hands and forearms in tepid spring water.

Surrounding the hut, the perimeter of dog excrement grows pungent with the melt. The woman circles the hut, a timber paddle clutched in each hand, gathering the rank deposits and walking them down to the ocean. The man and the woman break from their work to rest on blocks in the sunlight, set between them a wooden barrel, its lid topped with food and two large mugs steaming with heat. The trappers sit with their backs to the throng, surveying a fjord unravelling with thaw.

The man finishes his drink with an *aah*. He sets down his mug, collects his rifle and leaves the hut to climb the slope and trek amongst the jaws. He stops partway to kneel before the contraption, the ptarmigan head untouched. He inspects the surrounds, two sets of paw prints crisscrossing the snow. He takes in the depression beside the trap where a fox has lain long enough for its body heat to melt the snow. *Got you.* The trapper looks about. He catches a glimpse of a blue patrolling beneath the bird cliffs. No mistaking those markings, Little Blue now fully grown and too canny for fall traps. But, yes, indeed, Anders surveys the crisscross of fox prints, that young rascal is tempted by the scissors. He dwells on the prints with a fancy that there is not one but two blues, a pair who could soon produce a litter of fine blue cubs. He debates the short-term reward on setting the scissors in the thick of the breeding season; argues whether he should instead let nature take its course. He pictures an entire family of blues settling in their terrain, primed for next season's trapping. He calculates their worth and issues a whistle. He reins himself in. He has not hauled the scissors halfway around the mountain to surrender to idle fancy. He is a betting man and they are due a blue. *Tomorrow*, he commands the scissors. These days at Fuglefjell are their last gasp for trapping. Once April turns to May the season is too far gone, the plush winter coat yielding to the moult.

While the older vixen patrols the bird cliffs in view of the trapper, the young blue sits below the hut before the woman, taunting the three dogs tethered to their chains. The roof of the hut is no longer accessible, the snow ramp reduced to a lopsided hillock leaking braided trickles of snowmelt. The woman casts about scraps of dried fish, one each to the brawling dogs who whine and yelp relentlessly. The young blue sits poised, the last piece of fish diverted her way.

She trots beside the woman to the top side of the hut. She crunches on her fish while the woman rubs at windows until the glass squeaks. The young fox rises with alarm at a blue fox eating inside the windowpane. She seizes her fish and bolts uphill to settle and eat a safe distance away.

She licks her muzzle and whiskers clean of fish. She licks her paws to wipe her ears. The fox halts. She stands tall and at alert. She knows the scent even before the polar bear comes into view, the animal ambling along the coastline toward the trappers' hut.

14

Fuglefjell, late April

WANNY SLOWS FROM cleaning panes of glass. From the other side of the hut where the dogs are chained, Mira's barking outdoes the Alsatians. Wanny pictures Little Blue parading on the hill within view of them, as bold a fox as a cheeky monkey when it knows the dogs are tethered to their chains. 'Shush!' Wanny calls. 'Mira, quiet!'

A crunch of gravel. A new thought's shard of caution scrapes at Wanny's shoulders. She drops the window cloth, rounds the corner of the hut to look along the shoreline. Right there on the beach, its heavy pads digging into gravel. The bear momentarily halts, raising its snout to seek out the hut. To home in on *her*. Wanny stumbles when she breaks into a run. She pulls the hut door the wrong way and with it the handle comes away in her hand. The dogs shriek and yank at their chains. Wanny heaves her shoulder against the door to loosen and push it free. She seizes her rifle from the corner of the portico. She thinks to move into the inner room of the hut. Wait there and hide. Mira, Karo, Storm. Three dogs defenceless on their chains. She eases herself back out, the portico too tight a space to properly wield her weapon. She has both hands clutched around the stock, the butt of the rifle pressed against her abdomen as if she were some fast-shooting cowboy from her boys' comic books. The bear strides toward the hut with a quickening pace. A hungry bear who has her firmly in its sights. In panicked haste, Wanny swings the barrel in a loose arc to fire, the bullet whizzing over the dogs, the recoil shunting her off balance. She lands hard on her elbow and forearm, the rifle loosened from her hold. The bear barely slows at the sound. It angles upward from the shore. Wanny scrambles to retrieve her weapon. A second useless shot from where she lies twisted on the ground, another bullet wide of the mark. She can see the bear's flaring moist nostrils as it paces toward her, readying to spring. Ten more paces and those teeth and claws will be undoing her flesh. She is somehow on her buttocks, wedged firm against the hut. She crooks both knees to shield herself, moves the barrel between them. No time or need for sights. She lifts one knee to her chest to raise her aim to that broad, buttery chest that holds the bear's beating heart. She squeezes the trigger, the bear's head blocking out the sun. Involuntarily, Wanny's hand thrusts the bolt forward again, her ears throbbing with the pulse of her blood and the crack of a final shot. She closes her eyes to a starburst of red, to a surrender of breath and a warm stream wetting her trousers.

The Chief pants, his eyes fixed on her. 'Are you hurt?'

She shakes her head. She cannot find her voice to speak above the ringing in her ears. She is seated on a makeshift stool of driftwood, not trusting her legs to hold her upright.

Beside her, the bear lies a body length from the door of the hut, its indigo tongue hanging loose, an edge curled in on itself by its canine. The chest is branded with a round badge of carmine, the shoulder smudged scarlet. Wounds that look too meagre to kill a big bear.

The Chief breathes hard. His face glows. 'I heard the shots,' he says. He will have raced across the slopes to reach her. He looks about but doesn't ask what happened. The sorry tale is laid out before them: a trapper caught unawares; a trapper within inches of losing her life to a bear.

'Four shots,' Wanny whispers. He kneels down before her. She doesn't care that he sees the wet of her trousers. The sensation of bones dancing loose within her body refuses to settle. She wishes the Chief would hold her.

'Let me see.' He unwinds her fingers from a grip, which she only now registers as bracing her forearm. Her woollen shirt is ripped at the elbow from her fall, the fabric stained with blood and gravel. The newly freed elbow starts to throb.

With a gentle hand, he folds up the ruined sleeve to inspect the gash. 'You will live. We'll go inside and clean it.'

'I wasn't prepared,' she says.

'But you managed. On your own and under pressure.'

Managed? 'Barely.' Her rifle was propped in the corner of the portico, she going about her domestic chores as if this were a day of spring cleaning in Tromsø. Two loose aims bound to miss their mark and squander precious seconds. A third that winged the bear's shoulder. 'The bear was at the far end of the beach. Then it was here.' She gestures with her head. 'It moved so fast. The noise of the rifle didn't scare it at all.'

'You pinned it through the heart.' He looks to the bear. 'A young one. Thin and hungry.'

'He was upon me. What if I had missed?'

He rests his hand on her knee, his face inches from hers. 'Listen to me, Wanny. Even the best and most experienced trappers have their share of close calls. Our life comes with risk. We all get the jitters. A trapper's life cannot dwell on *what ifs*. We learn what we can from each encounter to keep ourselves alive.'

Wanny searches Anders's weathered face, the lopsided nose, lips chafed from dry and cold, an expression that often seems to verge on mirth. A partner with a sharp tongue and a warm heart. His scant offerings of praise mean all the more for they are gifts in truth. She places her hand on his, her skin as rough and dry as his, fingernails blunt and jagged, her chest swamped with a realisation. She loves Anders Sæterdal. She does. A different kind of love, one she hadn't known existed. She cannot compare this to Othar. She could not have loved a man more. Had he survived, their life was preordained, neatly mapped out along a well-trodden road. In her younger self she carried expectations no different to any other young wife and mother. Yet the wish for something more lay dormant, biding its time until now to waken. Here in Hornsund, she is looked upon by Sæterdal as a compatriot, more or less an equal. With that partnership her world feels limitless. A bear is dead beside her, with no room for defeat. In Anders's eyes there is only learning. She holds dear these simple days with the Chief – the clarity of purpose they share, their industry, their days and nights inextricably entwined. Wanny draws breath against a stab of feeling that has been smouldering for weeks. A future they do not speak of. She has no claim on Anders Sæterdal. He shows none to her. Another two months and their time will be over. Wanny blinks. *We learn what we can from each encounter.* Does he see a future, with her, here, doing this together?

'Mrs Woldstad. You are looking far too broody,' he says brightly. He stands and gives a sharp rap to the lid of the barrel. 'Finally you have provided us the intended use for our coffee table.'

Mrs Woldstad. A married woman. Two boys waiting for their mother's return. It is impossible for a woman to have it all.

The dogs drool as the Chief flays the pelt, the two Alsatians rigid as they wait for the next scrap of blubber to be flung high in the air. He is a devil to those dogs, seemingly deaf to their piercing barks. He seems unbothered by the cries and screeches from the countless birds living on the mountain. Their noise pervades her thoughts, punches through her sleep. Even the ringing in her rifle ear is overwhelmed by birds.

The insatiable Alsatians wolf down each offering. Her Mira sits subdued, the blubber at her feet promptly snatched away. Mira's teats have distended, her body heavy with pups. Hard enough that a dog falls pregnant in such a place where it is relied upon to work. What would a woman do? She has lost count of the months since she has had a proper cycle. Svalbard has its way of dealing with such matters. She speaks above the screech of birds. 'How much longer can Mira pull the sledge without risking her pups?'

'She will let us know. Hopefully she will be good for this last trip across the glacier.'

'This will be our last?'

'The last time on foot,' he calls above the noise. 'You saw it yourself on the way here. Crevasses and moulins opening with the thaw. The glacier becomes too menacing. We'll do another trip out here in the boat. Dismantle the traps, take back bedding and gear to stow at Hyttevika, get everything ready . . .' His voice trails off.

For next season. Talk of which invariably comes to an abrupt close. What of her? she wants to ask. What of them? A year ago, the prospect of driving her own taxi, the financial independence it offered at a time when even domestic work was hard to find, was all she dared ask of life. She skirts around the subject. 'Are you happy with the catch so far?'

He waggles his head. 'Not the worst. Nowhere near the best.'

'I make this our thirteenth bear. Twelve and the cub, if the young one counts.'

'My word he counts,' he says. 'We have done very well with bears. But only thirteen foxes of value to date, all white. By now I would have liked a dozen more, blues amongst them.'

'We are running out of time.'

Yes, the Chief nods.

'We will still spend the last month on the islands?'

'That is the plan. Eiderdown. Duck and gull eggs.' He drags the pelt free of the bear. 'Will you scrape? I will start on the butchering.'

'Of course,' she says. Wanny is weary of bear. Of cooking bear. Of eating bear. What she would give for a banquet of halibut or freshly smoked salmon. She drapes the corner of the pelt across her knees, instantly warmed by a coat as weighty as a carpet. After flaying a fox's delicate skin, it takes several strokes to adjust the pressure and angle of her knife. The task of scraping the underside free of blubber will take the best part of a day, an effort that leaves her hands throbbing. She has learned the painful way to glove her hands for the salting, though still it permeates through to bite at nicks and grazes. Even a young bear like this will take their combined effort to fold in the edges and roll the pelt to fit the barrel. A top-up of brine before the lid is sealed.

'Plenty of fox spoor around the scissors this morning,' says the Chief. 'I spied your Little Blue wandering about the bird cliffs.'

Her Little Blue was here at the hut, at least until the bear arrived. 'He shares himself around.'

The Chief taps his nose. 'I have it on good authority that we shall have that fine blue pelt to add to our tally. I will lay a bet upon it.'

'I will not,' she says. Nor will she indulge him with praise for the scissors.

He looks across to her, his expression inscrutable. 'Wanny, you are too soft to be a trapper,' he says quietly. He is deadly serious.

A sting of words. Are they true? Her defence rises above the birds. 'I have said before, I do not think it soft, or sentimental, to favour a fair battle between hunter and hunted. Out in the open. On even terms.'

He gives a soft grunt. 'What of your morning encounter with the bear? I do not hear you proclaiming it a victory?'

Victory, no. More a sombre reminder of fallibility, that she is nothing at all without a rifle. She sees it now through Anders's eyes: his kindness toward a woman breaking down before him, wetting herself from her lone encounter with a bear. She has forfeited her right to name herself a trapper.

'What is it, woman?' he says. 'You are out of sorts.'

Wanny takes a breath. 'What of you, Anders?'

He breaks from the butchering. 'Me, what?'

'Next season. What will you do?'

He gives a shrug. 'I will come back here to Hornsund. So long as I can meet my loan.'

'Who will you bring?'

He grips his knife, slices along the backbone. 'If fox numbers stay low, it will be the devil's job enticing anyone of choice.'

The reek of flayed bear barely registers against the acrid vapour from bird guano raining down from the mountain.

'Chief,' Wanny says, scrabbling for the right balance of words. 'Do you think that you, or even another trapper, would take me on? As a partner?'

His brow furrows. She wills him to say, *You are who I want.*

His face is unreadable. 'I will make my own plans,' he says. 'I cannot speak for any other trapper. Or your home situation. Those are your concern.' He turns his back to her, gets on with the butchering.

❉

Together they climb the hill to check the fall traps. Early morning at Fuglefjell is Anders's favourite time of day, late April on a day of utter still. Sun streams across the mountain face. Dovekies in their hundreds circle the air, the light glancing off their wings. The flock settles on the water. The fjord mirror calm, dotted with drifting ice. Not a zephyr. Below at the hut, skuas and glaucous gulls fight over scraps of bear meat and blubber that the glutton dogs, asleep on their chains, now find too meagre to trouble themselves with. The Villa porch is stacked with sacks of bear meat that must wait for the dinghy and good weather; a big, heavy load to ferry back to Hyttevika. He has learned the hard way not to leave meat in huts to thaw over summer. Perfume to a fox's nose.

Wanny interrupts his reverie. 'Should we take the flag from its case? When we get back to Hyttevika.'

'It is not forgotten.' He does not need reminding. 'I get it done on time every year. I will check the flagpole, dismantle the Signal line.' No animal has come close to the Signal. It irks him her urge to have things ready for departure before need be. Let them get done with this season. Let him settle on next year's plans in his own time, at his own pace. 'Is it not enough to live for now?' he snaps at her. 'You will be home with your family soon enough.'

She gives a wounded look.

'I am sorry,' he says. He is harder on her than on any other he has worked with. Small wonder she feels restless. She likely craves new faces and bright conversation in the way she hankers for fresh food, the trappings of home. On leaving Hyttevika she had stacked her letters to mail on the table beside their journey note. *In case a passing ship calls in,* said she.

'You will be missing women's company,' he ventures.

She shrugs. 'Of course it would be nice to sit down with a friend. But that is not a need for women's company over any other kind.'

'You are a strange one, Wanny.'

'Does that mean you are pining for another man around the place?' No mistaking the feisty tone.

He gestures to his dogs. 'I have two, perfectly pitched to my tune. Those numbskulls usually have something to say on a broad range of topics.' A clap of steel. Anders turns. 'You hear that?'

Wanny concentrates. She shakes her head. 'All I hear is birds.'

He takes the binoculars from their case, scans the slopes below. 'It could be the scissors.' Then again, he may be fantasising. 'I will walk down and take a look,' he says.

'No,' she says sharply. Her face has turned quite florid. She takes a breath. 'May I go this time? Please.'

'Away then,' he snaps and continues on. She is impossible to fathom.

From where Wanny crosses the ridge, the distant steel trap resembles a swan's neck shaped into a lady's brooch, an elegant curve to pin to a lapel.

The creature's body is arched to the curve of its hoops, as if it were set to leap along the breadth of steel. Even the tips of the fox's silver coat share the same metallic hue. The scissors might have seized a foot, but no, the small fox is lifted clean off the ground, its throat held between the interlocking pincers, front paws dangling loose, the animal's glassy gaze fixed on the ptarmigan bait below.

Little Blue is dead. Why set it free? It is no more. Cart the whole contraption back to the hut and let the Chief deal with it. The number of warnings, the cautionary tales he issues her about the perils of the scissors.

Wanny straddles the trap as she has seen Anders do. She has to raise the back half of the fox – the silky softness of its coat, the body still warm – to reach the lever with her foot, her other foot weighing down the opposite end. Her boot pushes hard upon the stiffened lever to prise the hooped jaws open. She reaches for the fox, takes it by its neck folds. Should she lose balance, if her boot should slip, the pincer jaws will snap shut and take her hand off with it. She lifts the fox free, sets it down at her feet, gingerly eases off the spring until the pincers lock together.

She shakes off the racing in her chest. Why should this one matter? She is immune to every white fox she pulls from the fall traps. She is held by a fug that eddies through her gut, seesaws into numbness. This is just another fox caught in a trap. Another to bolster their numbers. Their reason for being here. But her body will not be placated. Her skin prickles. Her hands fumble, all nerves and jitters. Why?

Why, Ivanna? Because you are too soft to be a trapper.

Not an ounce of softness did she afford her aging husband. For Martin there was nothing but the steely determination that sustained her through the ache of childhood robbed of a father. The same bone ache at Othar's death. With the prospect of this singular, miraculous chance to come to Svalbard, she held no care for who she wounded. Nothing would stand in her way. *They are too much for you*, she had argued with Martin at sending her boys to board with her friend, her husband already despairing at her year's absence. *You are of an age to be their grandfather,* she reminded him, *with scant understanding of their needs.* Gentle Martin. He had stood before her as the accused before the jury, shaking with anguish at what was being taken from him. It was a turning point, their future together thrown to the winds. Wanny had offered no gratitude, had shown no contrition as Martin pleaded his case. Was he not as fit and active as any man? Hadn't he supported her independence, he himself securing the bank loan for her taxi? Each time she drove her cab he had been there to care for little Alf and Bjørvik, day and night, when their mother had not.

A woman deserving of nothing.

She gathers up the little body. She cannot bring herself to tie its paws and sling it from her rucksack. Held in the crook of her arm, Little Blue stares up at her with amber eyes, their sheen already dulling. Wanny studies the fox. Even the dearest face is stolen by a stranger in death. She studies the familiar pale markings. The extraordinary pelt of silver. Tips dusted with coal. Beneath the plushness a framework of protruding bone in contrast to a belly round and firm. 'All those treats,' she speaks to it.

Nor can Wanny bring herself to carry out the flensing, to strip the creature of its final dignity. 'It is our only blue,' she argues with the Chief. 'God forbid I punch a hole and ruin the thing.'

Does he register the distress she is trying hard to quash?

The Chief flenses outdoors. Wanny peels potatoes, the tip of her knife circling the eyes, swollen nubs readying to sprout. She checks each potato, cuts out spoiled flesh. They are down to the dross. She dices a turnip, a limp, lifeless thing, blackened at the end, doubtless with a taste to match. She parboils the vegetables then sets them aside, the stove sized only for a single pot. She heats a pan with dripping to sear diced bear. A simple stew the Chief never tires of. Would she feel the same for Anders Sæterdal without this place? This common purpose to their lives? She gets on with the meal, fumbling with the mug to mix the gravy paste. *At sixes and sevens, Ivanna. Over a fox.*

The Chief returns inside, his hands scrubbed clean in the hot spring. Nature's warm trickle of water is their greatest luxury. He reaches for a towel. She hears him sigh. 'You are not pleased?' she asks.

'You were right,' he says. 'Little Blue was a vixen. Skin and bone. Still managing to carry five kits.'

'Oh,' Wanny utters. She leaves the stove. Sits on a stool. Little Blue. The rounded belly. A mother with young. *A small blue fox to melt this frozen heart.* She deflects her fluster. 'The coat is good?'

'She lived a warrior's life,' he says. 'Skin so pocked and scarred I wouldn't have bothered if it wasn't a blue.' Meat sears in the pan, beads of fat splashing across the stovetop. The Chief takes a fork to turn the meat.

'If we had known,' Wanny says.

'If we had known,' he says. 'They would likely have settled here. Blues amongst them. An entire family primed for next season.'

A new season without her or Little Blue, both sent upon their way.

Tomorrow they leave this place to return to Hyttevika.

One more day, little fox. If only we had waited.

15

Hyttevika, May

AN AFTERNOON OF rest for she and Mira. Take a break, the Chief insists, two new white pelts drying on the line to set him grinning, each of them recorded in the book. He has turned manic, off to check the trap line a second time today, another twenty kilometres, a last gasp before the traps are dismantled. Time to herself. No housework or baking. No mending socks or scrubbing floors. No sharpening knives or cleaning rifles. Clothes that can wait another day before they insist on being washed.

The flag flies at full mast atop the pole she still thinks of as the Signal, the home colours vibrant against the May sky. Hornsund's rightful occupants are in residence, that pennant and its halyard jiggles and clanks to the world. Too early for ships, the Chief sounds so sure, ice in the fjord a loose impassable sheet that drifts with current and tide. But here on land is an afternoon of brilliant sunshine, eight, nine degrees.

Wanny sits on the outside bench, her back against the hut wall. Mira lies at her feet, her dog heavy and sluggish, ready to drop her pups at any time. Wanny closes her eyes. Lifts her face to the warmth and a surge of resentment. The Chief has as good as told her he will bring another partner next season. She will show him. She will take out her own trapping lease here on Svalbard, bring her boys and teach them how to trap. She gives an audible sigh, shakes the thought from her head. *Empty dreams, Ivanna.* She knows from her taxi that no lender will give a woman a loan. Even the name on her banking account – money she alone has saved – falls under her husband's name, her husband's governance. *Shackled by your gender.*

Her eyes open with a start to scan for bears. After one close call, she doubts the art of catnapping can ever be hers again. She tries once more. Closes her eyes. She lasts less than a minute. 'It is no use,' she says to Mira. To be idle in the daytime feels too strange. 'Shall we take a little walk?' Mira, heavy with pups, has slept the morning away, but with a personal invitation she thumps her tail, hauls herself to her feet.

Inland they hike, a slow and easy amble for Mira's sake, Wanny's rucksack and shotgun strapped to her back. She turns and looks upward to the sound of geese, the sun in her eyes, their haunting calls quickly fading. The tarn is thawing, changing by the day. The surrounding landscape has transformed into rivulets, clusters of grass and reeds piercing up through snow, a black quagmire concealed beneath. Insects. It takes a moment to register their low throng, to see the movement of tiny wings amongst the vegetation. Wanny sets her belongings down. Mira circles her tail then settles down to nap. Her dog pants. Small sandpipers, bristling with industry, are light enough to totter unhindered across the boggy ground, seeking out titbits. A pair of larger birds, white-faced, yellow-billed – phalaropes, the Chief calls them – wander close by, undeterred by her or Mira's presence. The brightest in the pair is a vivid chestnut, its mate subdued. The water birds fossick amongst snow-free patches of tundra.

The return of so many kinds of birds. Pairs readying to nest, feeding up, prospering in Svalbard's endless daylight. A frantic summer race to raise their family before the sun turns its back and slides away. In this place, life and death are given and taken by the ice. By its circle of thaw and freeze. A cycle bigger than her small life, a constant that will surely outlive her children, and her children's children. In that, she thinks, is reason to have faith. To be thankful. 'Yes, girl,' she gently strokes her dog. 'We should like to soak up this place forever.'

Anders has cause to whistle a tune, to burst into song: another two white foxes to bolster their final tally. He inspects the pelt, combs his fingers through its fur, a tuft pulling loose in his fingers.

He turns to his dogs, proffering a small speech to thank them for their hard work and willingness to cooperate. He gives each a vigorous scratch. 'You are a handsome boy,' he says earnestly to Storm and then praises Karo. From a fine mother, who fell last season to the lightning blow of a bear's front paw. Tossed like a rag through air.

When he reaches the hut, Wanny races out. 'Last for the season!' He shows off the foxes.

'Anders,' she interrupts him, bursting to speak. 'We have increased our personnel count.'

It takes him a moment. 'Mira.'

'Eleven pups.'

He shakes his head. Eleven will sap Mira's resources. He still needs her to work.

'No sooner had we got back from a walk,' Wanny says, 'than she waddled inside and set herself down in her box of hay to nest. She turned her back as if wanting to be left alone. Next thing – do go in and see them. They are precious little things.'

He crouches before Mira, strokes her soft ears, pups latched to her teats, loose pups wriggling and jostling to lever across the others. Storm and Karo have followed him in. They sit a distance away, each with a worrisome expression at the sharp cries and whimpers, the room high with milk and puppies. Half of these pups will amount to nothing. 'We should choose the best five or six,' Anders says. 'Prospective sledge dogs.'

'Oh,' she says.

He looks to Wanny. 'Sooner rather than later.' He reads her expression. She grasps the fate of those not selected. 'This is no place for a dog unfit to pull its weight.'

'I see,' she says.

'I will take care of it.'

Her voice takes on an edge. 'You will take the best ones as your own? To bring up here next season?' Sometimes she has a way that brings Othelie to mind. He feels himself wading out of his depth, headlong into current.

Anders cogitates. 'We shall see,' he says. He busies himself inspecting each of the pups. His actual thought, which he will not admit to now, is to keep two or three pups and sell the rest back in Tromsø. A lineage of good sledging dogs can bring a tidy profit. But he is beset by women's voices ringing through his head. *Ought Mrs Woldstad not have a say in Mira's pups? Are they not hers as much as yours?* A choir made up of his ex-wife, his older brother's wife who as good as raised him, and the lilt of that sweet and gentle voice which he conjures once in a great while to be wrapped within her grace. Anders draws a puppy to his face, takes in its scent, strokes its small, soft head. His own Emilie named in his mother's honour. He returns the squirming puppy to its box. 'We will wait and see,' he says again to Wanny. He is no good with these troublesome kinds of binds.

16

Fuglefjell, May

FOUR DAYS AFTER whelping, Mira joins the brother dogs to haul the sledge from Hyttevika to the halfway hut at Isbjørnhamn. The outbound load is light with bare essentials, Anders's goal to bring back a full load of gear and bedding from each of the two satellite huts and stow them in the main hut over summer. Secured to the sledge is a box lined with hay, its six small residents oblivious to the perils along the way.

At the big river, he and Wanny grow wet to their waists in the rush of muddy meltwater, dogs and sledge carried metres downstream before they regain a purchase and clamber onto land. The woman does well to steer the sledge across without it toppling. Anders questions the crossing on their return journey, how they will navigate the rising torrent when each new day sees ice loosen its grip, new rivulets burbling into streams and dumping melt into the fjord.

Bit by bit, the mountain tiers yield more to rock and less to snow. Spring has sprung earlier this year than last. He finds it a muddling feeling, this part of the season, finishing up, being sent upon his way as if it were nature, not man, who has the final say. The same wrench as last year in packing away the traps; for all the season's hard-won gains, something of himself is dismantled in the process. Now it seems the hills are as sprinkled with polar foxes, as if the landscape has been given a liberal shaking of pepper. Those elusive rascals appear only long enough to taunt him. He has a mind that the foxes sense the time is near to reclaim their land and roam unhindered before next season's trapping. His own life is this ebb and flow. A balance to it all.

He looks across to his partner, still not his equal in height though she stands on the sledge to steer. He senses an unnerving shift in Wanny Woldstad. He cannot place his finger on it. She is subdued though not unhappy. That is only part of it. There is a distance between them. He sees a quiet dignity about her person which leaves him feeling stranded. Perhaps a boy's losses are what sets a man ill at ease with change.

The puppies on the sledge wake and whimper, their bleating growing louder. Mira, at the rear, frets and causes havoc when she twists in her harness and upsets the pace. A family who will wait no longer. He calls the party to a stop, a sack laid out on snow, the youngsters reunited with their mother to feed. Snuggle time, the woman calls it. She is quite taken with it all.

An overnight at the halfway hut, mattresses and bedding damp from condensation, the inside walls dripping, the hut's perimeter of snow reduced to mucky slush divulging all manner of bone and excrement. This hook of land is a cesspit.

His boat pump is a rudimentary assembly made from lengths of old pipe, a shortened mop handle to plunge and draw up water. Anders shifts his weight to the edge of a thwart to lean the boat and pool the last gallon of meltwater, a frozen sheet beneath the running boards through winter, now swimming about the boat. A blood-brown hue pulses from the spout, with it the rancid whiff of slaughter. Winter hides a multitude.

❄

Wanny and the Chief swap their sledge for boat and oars to make the onward journey to Fuglefjell. A final journey to the farthest hut. They set off after dinner, the breeze petered out, Wanny's favourite kind of evening. Mira stays low in the boat to be beside her pups. Karo and Storm commandeer the back thwart, their paws draped over the gunnel, gazing about like a pair of princes while she and the Chief heave on oars. East past Hansbreen. Around the slopes of Fannytoppen. Beneath the painted cliffs. By land or by sea, Wanny knows every footfall, every mile of the route and its many varied landmarks. She sits at the bow, oars raised. She twists around in her seat to look. Any moment the Villa will come into view.

They pass by a small berg glistering in evening sunlight, its angled face a molten sheen, its skirt a tinkling trill of water. Wanny softly sings the nation's anthem to the rhythm of the oars. The Chief joins in, this their national day. A newfound sense of calm to match the stillness of the evening. A poignancy. Her first thoughts are of her boys and the dear ones at home who will have cheered the parade, music playing, drums beating, the crack of children's poppers, the trumpeting of car horns. The brightness to the sky seems in keeping with their own small song of celebration, sung in a boat on a fjord in a place where nights are now as bright as days. Who would fathom that harmony can be found in a setting where life's only surety is the changing of the seasons?

Wanny blinks away regret. She has to put away her feelings toward this unlikely man. It has taken a conscious swing in outlook, helped along by physical exertion and days steeped in nature, to meet with a feeling of peace. She feels a sense of calm, knowing that her time up here with Anders Sæterdal is drawing to a close. She will not live a future that wallows in regret for a life that is not hers to have. Water burbles from their wake, rippling out through a flock of dovekies settled on the mirrored surface. There must be a thousand birds bobbing about, as small and buoyant as bath toys. Wanny smiles. She has spent a good deal of time in this boat looking through the back of the Chief's head, his shoulders and arms heaving on oars, her own oars keeping pace. Anders Sæterdal gifted her this marvellous chance that no one else would give. He taught her how to read the land. Trusted her to manage herself and carry out her share of work.

'Are you still drawing air?' he calls over his shoulder.

'Have I slowed?'

'You are quiet, is all. The dogs are concerned.'

'Tell them I am fine. All is well.' *And that, Ivanna, is truth.* Perhaps the talk around Mira and her pups, with it the Chief's unquestioning air of proprietary, helped set these dominoes in motion. She had added a letter to her stack on the table before plucking it away again. Rethought her stance. Returning to Martin would be the decent thing to do. Her husband is a good man. Has always been a kind man. A man she has given the most vulnerable years of her life. A letter is inadequate. Atonement must come once she returns to Tromsø, she and he together in a room. She wants Martin to know how grateful she is for the home he has provided. She needs him to acknowledge that, through these years, she has fully met her pledge to him. For better or worse Wanny is laying aside the security of marriage, thankful that 1933 is not the same helpless world it was for a widow when Othar was taken. She has a future in Tromsø, standing on her own. She runs her own taxi. She has the means to cover the loan. She has a way and a will to manage on her own at a time when others are struggling. How many women can say that?

Sæterdal is not at fault in how he views the ownership of the puppies, in who he chooses as his working partner. Life. People. The things we say and do. We are what we are. All that came before still lives within us to give us our shape. Each in our own way is beholden to another. Women and men alike.

❄

The Villa is crammed with bodies. With the reek of dog hair and puppies and regurgitated milk. With grubby tea towels and dirty cleaning cloths and threadbare woollen socks drying on the line. With scrapings of dried cod and rice set in a dish on the floor. The stove hisses, the room altogether too warm for Anders's liking, the ceiling raining condensation. Mira and her young sleep on a sack by the stove, Anders having to sidestep across them, avoiding the bowl of leftovers, to reach his bunk.

Wanny sits at the table writing up her journal. He hesitates. 'Will you join me?'

She looks to him. Shakes her head. 'Not tonight.'

For his own sense of pride, he makes light of the refusal. He poses before her in threadbare long johns, mismatched patches and odd-coloured thread holding the wool together. 'How can the lady resist?'

She smiles at the spectacle and returns to her journal.

He brushes it off with a laugh as he swallows the taste of rejection. Once more, he is left with an agitated feeling of abandonment. She is telling him that this part is over.

A new day. Their final at Fuglefjell. The brother dogs know when a treat is in store. They flank Anders's feet to follow him along the trap line, watching intently each time he heaves stones aside to dismantle a trap. Wanny dismantles traps on the opposite ridge.

Anders frees a wizened ptarmigan head from its bait stick, hides it in his pocket until he has another, one to throw to each dog. 'There you go. One for you, too.' A crack of bone. A crunch. Down it goes, ready for the next. Several traps are still buried in snow, not one of them hiding a fox. Something makes Anders look up to the mountain, to a white fox peering down at him, perched on a perilously narrow ledge amongst the bird cliffs. How do these creatures not come to grief? He is tempted to take a shot to its head with his rifle. If he could retrieve the wretched thing. By the time he takes out his binoculars for a closer look, the little devil has vanished. He waits, his eyes scanning the cliffs. Minutes later it reappears, higher still. He homes in with the glasses. The thing stops and turns, gives him the evil eye as if it knows he is onto it. Odd eyes. Look at them. One ice blue, the other amber. An aberration he has seen in pure-blood sledging dogs, never in a polar fox. The white issues an unblinking glare before turning tail, its concentration turned to guillemot fledglings which shuffle and shriek upon their ledges. 'Off with you then,' he tells that odd-eyed fox, though he surmises it is he, Anders, who has been dismissed. 'I will have you next season. See if I don't.'

❄

Together she and the Chief roll and drag two heavy lengths of driftwood to prop against Fuglefjell's hut door. 'Not that it will stop a determined bear,' the Chief says.

'They are here on land in summer?'

'Their goal is to head north to the pack ice in search of seal. One or two can be stranded when the ice blows out. Youngsters mainly. If they are lucky, they will find enough onshore to keep them through the summer, scavenge a washed-up whale carcase, take an old or injured reindeer. Trappers at the north end say the bears follow glacier trails, moving over the island to the north-east corner. There is always sea ice up there; there always will be. A cold current, summer and winter.'

They shutter and bar each window, the pointed ends of nails facing out. Wanny looks to the mountain. She scans the slopes.

Keeps the thought to herself that there is no small blue fox to usher them on their way. 'Goodbye, then, Villa. You are as clean and scrubbed as you can hope to be.'

'You have done well, Wanny.'

'I know how to clean.'

'I don't mean just that. You have done as much as a small man. On all fronts, you are *riktig*.'

A quaint expression particular to the Chief's home district. Clever. Capable. He calls her *riktig* with a rifle, *riktig* with her cooking.

Not *riktig* enough. She cannot bring herself to acknowledge the compliment.

Together they roll the barrel, heavy with bearskin and sloshing with brine, down the gravel beach and onto a ramp. They tilt it upright into the boat. Sacks of semi-thawed bear meat cushion its drop. Bedding, mattresses, sheepskin liners, the Chief's old clogs, gear and rope, his favourite saucepan, a canvas bag of odds and ends fill the boat to make a huge load, burgeoning with the extra weight of two people, three dogs and a family of squirming puppies. They try to row out, the tide low. 'I will get it,' Anders says, but even without his weight, her own weight grounds the boat.

'You are too feeble, Sæterdal,' she jests. She unlaces her boots, pulls off socks, climbs out to help push the boat to deeper water, never mind an injured elbow.

They take their places at the oars. Out beyond the rocks the sea looks calm but Wanny feels the rhythm of a lazy swell rolling in from the west, carrying loose sheets of ice. Two inches of freeboard. Regularly the Chief rests his oars and takes up the water pump. He seems entirely unbothered by the leakage, suggesting they bypass the halfway hut and row the extra miles to Hyttevika. 'We can travel out to Isbjørnhamn another time to collect the sledge, bring home the hut bedding.'

Which is better? she thinks. To cross a raging river with a sledge, or row a laden boat, its upper planks leaking after standing so long on land, across an angry ocean. Neither option fills her with glee.

The swell grows stronger, water and ice slapping the wood and washing over the gunnel. Wanny gives a cry of surprise when a pod of belugas surfaces alongside, a dozen or more, close enough to see their bulbous heads, to smell their fishy blows. As quickly, their milky bodies vanish. She and the Chief revert to their original plan and heave on the outside oars to turn the boat in to Isbjørnhamn. The boat sits sideways to the swell, rocking precariously until they reach the lee of land.

Anders tethers a plank of wood to the sledge for the homeward trek from Isbjørnhamn. Lashed to the sledge is bear meat and bedding, a boxful of puppies. The barrel of bearskin, other heavy items, can wait to be retrieved another time. He hears the big river roar well before it comes into view. He chooses a narrowing and lays it across the river's cleft of ice, just inches above the water, the plank not long enough to reach the full distance from one dry bank to another. He watches water douse the wood, thrown up by the torrent below.

'Are you certain about this?' Wanny calls above the roar of water when he sets himself down on hands and knees to crawl across. 'Faint heart never won fair lady,' he skites more boldly than he feels. The plank is all they have. An iron grip, a show of bravado and a plea to Lady Luck inches Anders across the plank, his face and clothes showered with water. He scrambles up the ice and onto land to stand upon the Hyttevika side.

Back on the far side, the three dogs are harnessed single file to the sledge, Karo in the lead. 'March on!' Anders shouts from his side of the big river. He waves to entice dogs and sledge across.

Either his voice and actions are lost to the rush of water, or the dogs are stricken with fear. He sees Wanny urging them. Mira may be willing but Karo and Storm refuse to budge as if they are being sentenced to the gangplank. Gangplank is what that length of wood will become if it dislodges and gives way.

'Sons of Satan!' he curses at the top of his lungs. It is no use. He gestures to Wanny to forget about the dogs and sledge and get herself across. She stares at the torrent that divides them and for a moment he thinks she may also refuse. But she is not short on courage, his Wanny. He holds his end of the plank firm as she advances on hands and knees, only once at the worst part of the river pausing to peer down to the turbid water below. It gives her enough of a fright that the rest of the way her gaze remains firmly fixed on him, startled and wide-eyed. She reaches safety. 'Well done,' he says. 'You hold the plank steady for me.' He starts his crawl back to the Isbjørnhamn side with the intent of wrangling the blasted dogs. At the river's fiercest part, he pushes back the thought that a six-inch width of wood is all that keeps him aloft; God help him if either end gives way.

The brother dogs turn a deaf ear. They sit on their sizeable bottoms, suddenly intent on licking their paws, nibbling their claws, far too occupied with dog grooming to find the time to pull a sledge. He frees all but Mira from the harnesses. She he can convince, not for the sledge alone; it is her puppies that she will not leave behind.

Mira strains to move the load without the brother dogs. She won't give up. The force of motherhood, Anders thinks. He crawls onto the plank behind the sledge, shunting it forward with his shoulder, only the central base of the sledge making contact with the plank. The sledge runners have turned outriggers, hanging out on either side. He keeps the sledge level and in control lest the whole thing rams into Mira's rear and pushes her off balance, she and the sledge toppling from the plank. A drowning for mother and pups. The roar of water deafens his thoughts. Inch by laborious inch he manoeuvres it forward. Mira is more than halfway across when she stops, angling to turn and check on her pups. His yells and pleas are lost to the water. He sees Wanny crawl out from her side. He begs for the plank to hold their collective weight. She reaches out to her dog with an arm. Finally she has Mira's attention, holding the plank single-handed, the other enticing her dog onward. Mira takes a step. Another. Forward they go. Below, the incline of ice comes into view, the silty river cascading over it. Ice meets a shoulder of gravel. A final push and the sledge runners lift and grate against solid land.

The woman lavishes Mira with praise while her dog's focus is on being untethered to check on her young. Mira leaps up onto the load, her paws on the lip of the haybox, reaching in to lick each pup, her family dry and safe and none the wiser of their adventure. Back on the Isbjørnhamn side the brothers pace back and forth along the shoreline, agitated at being left behind. 'I will fix you two,' Anders says. The Alsatians study his actions, their ears pricked as he harnesses Mira to the sledge as lead dog. Affronted into action, the brothers leap one after the other into frigid water. They power forward, immediately swept downstream by the current. 'You idiot pair.' Anders shouts a few more choice words. The torrent will likely take them all the way to the lagoon down along the shore. His two are tough and brawny enough to survive their icy swim. 'Pinheads, the pair of them,' he says to Wanny.

'What now?' she asks, stroking her dog, Look at that creature, no mistaking her happy face. Mira, the hero of the day.

'My two will find their way across.'

17

Hyttevika, June

ANDERS STANDS BEFORE the hut mirror, shaving mug and brush in hand. He tilts his face to the window, lifts his chin, lathers his throat. He was never one for a full beard, this ragged stubble his concession to the cold, kept at bay with rusted scissors that have given it the finish of a balding coir doormat. Scissors will not do today. He sets down the mug and brush, works his fingers to keep his skin taut. He draws the razor around his chin, toward his ear. Stroke by stroke the blade peels away the ragged growth, the feeling of air on bare skin a naked sensation. Will Wanny like his fresh new look? She has outdone even herself this week with the volume of boiled water, has bathed more than once, her hair washed and brushed until it shines. She spends time buffing her fingernails, holding out her hands and sighing at the state of them. He is not inclined to ask why she no longer wears her wedding ring. Why she no longer comes to his bed.

Anders's thoughts turn to his son and daughter, the charge of excitement he dares not let himself feel at seeing them again. Both will have shot up, his boy of an age that he may hold back in the way Emilie did last year. Looked on by his girl as a stranger. It could break a man's heart. His marriage, the fragile reach he clings to with his children, the ache of missing out on their lives: these are the greatest costs of the life he has chosen.

He sees Wanny through the window, perched outside on a stool harping the eiderdown, freeing it of every leaf and stick. 'You are cleaning away our profits,' he calls through the glass. She does not hear. She wears a set of clothes he has not seen before, her old bib and braces packed away. *Today might be the day*, she says. He is doing his best to look respectable. He does not need those on the ship to think that while she keeps lofty hygiene standards, he has gone to the pack, a trapper turned feral.

Anders feels his first wild thirst for beer. About this time each year he starts hankering. He smacks his lips. He can taste it. His fancy sets him propped at the bar of Mack Ølhallen, the room crammed with this season's trappers. Young, cocky trappers will commandeer the first round of babble, outbidding each other with their death-defying bear battles, their close calls with crevasses. Othelie's voice chimes in his head: *You were just the same*. When the talk settles and Anders's turn comes, he usually draws a crowd, never short of a story bolstered with levity and his own theatrical flair.

He rinses the razor, taps it dry. He starts on his other cheek, imagining the taste of that chilled *blanding* and the talk of this year's dealings with the traders. Gone are the days when a premium fox sold for a good month's wages. *Twenty years too late for that, boy.* No matter. He need only settle his loan, make good the one ahead.

Plans and lease holdings, prospective partners, assessing who in the place is fit or unfit for the task. His trapping compatriots will quiz him on how the woman fared. Most will think him turncoat or fool for taking her; either way he is damned. He can hear the jeers and mockery. Did she manage to shoot anything? How often did you need to save her? The only memorable rescue was she hauling him to safety after his unceremonious slide down the mountainside. Anders draws the razor along his jawbone. The feel of her hand placed around his, not a word spoken, with it a solemn reverence for the nature of the place, acknowledgement at how close he had come to losing his life. He taps the blade free of shaving cream and whiskers. Enough rounds of beers and the talk will edge toward their private arrangements. He sighs at the thought of these two disparate worlds, a foot in each of them. He wants to be part of that timeworn club of fellow men. Its sense of belonging. Yet to do so comes with its own tacit rules in favour of his fellow sex, at odds with the richness of this season. This last year he has lived the place anew, a softer, more civil way of living. Those in earshot will want to be told that having a woman to bed can be the only plausible explanation for taking her along. Where does it leave him? Anders has no wish to be shunned. To comply affords an easy road to redemption in the eyes of his peers. Plenty of mileage and laughs to be had. He hears his own ribald banter. Anders pulls back at the sting of a nick from the razor blade. He takes a handkerchief, holds it firm against his cut skin. The side of his face held to the light is so deeply tanned above his beard line that it looks grubby. The pale fan of lines around his eyes, creased across his forehead, gives him an altogether wizened look. He has always fancied himself a young man. A ladies' man. He studies his weathered skin, his misshapen nose, the profile of his face held in shadow. *Who are you, Sæterdal?*

Wanny balances the down harp across her legs, the hewn wooden frame laced with rawhide strung as tightly as a snowshoe. The sieve-like contraption, like other makeshift working tools around this place, has been cobbled together by some bygone Hornsund trapper. Perhaps Mr Rudi himself. She will ask when she gets home. She takes a new handful of down, the clump matted with debris. She spreads it out across the harp, runs the wooden fid across the strings, teasing loose the down; twigs and leaves and eggshell raining to the ground. The song of strings turns the ear of Mira at her feet, the puppies leaping over their mother's back to catch the fallen debris. Her Mira is a sweet and patient mother. 'Aren't you, girl?'

The collection of down is an arrangement to suit all parties, Wanny decides. The eider's nest, lined with the mother's own breast feathers, had fulfilled its need, her brood ready to be taken to the water. The outlying islands form a fox-free sanctuary, the surrounding skerries a winter moat that somehow hampers the formation of a bridge of sea ice. All the islands of Dunøyane sit within their leasehold. A fortnight of camping out, rowing back to Hyttevika at intervals to bring back bags of down and check on the dogs. The work came as a welcome change, reward for hard winter months.

Wanny plays the strings back and forth, the fid rounded at one end, tapered to a blunt point at the other, any other time their tool for splicing rope. She has a temperament suited to harping work, more so than the Chief, not because he is less capable, but he has small patience for this task that demands a fine touch and dexterous fingers working hours at a time. He is a man of contradictions. Hand him a bearskin and he will scrape all day without complaint.

After harping, the down needs hand-cleaning to pluck every last fragment of seaweed, every tiny willow leaf and speck of vegetation. Wanny closes her eyes and opens her palm to a handful of newly cleaned down. There is no sensation of weight, none at all, only the merest hint of touch when the down is ruffled by air. She closes her fingers around the magic, its golden glow of warmth. Five dozen nests to make a single winter duvet. 'Only the finest households,' she whispers to Mira. She weighs the sack of down still to be cleaned and packed away, determined to finish it all before the ship arrives.

❄

July arrives and still they wait, though there is no shortage of passing ships. At each dark smoke plume lifting from the horizon, Anders races up the hill with binoculars; Wanny beelines to the hut to fix a fresh pot of coffee. Before long there will be no more coffee, a dire situation he does not care to dwell on. Anders peers through the glasses, past the breakers, until, yes, he spots a cargo ship destined for Advent Bay to deliver supplies, collect a shipment of coal. Twice he makes out the shape of a tourist liner, bringing well-to-do Europeans for a taste of the north. Anders pictures those wide-eyed onlookers braced at the ship's railings, cosy in their fine furs, marvelling at the mountains and glaciers of this 'cold coast', Anders mouths the English of Svalbard's well-earned title. A stop at Advent Bay's postal hut to mail a card from The Wild. The concept of a vacation, the very idea of sailing across a heaving ocean all the way to Svalbard simply to gaze upon it, he finds an altogether amusing enterprise.

Everything is ready for departure. Sacks of down stacked in the porch. The last bear pelt salted and barrelled. All but the clothes on their back and coats on their hooks folded and stuffed into duffle bags. Five days pass. Eight days. Ten. Where is the damn ship? Anders studies the sky, breeze ruffling the water, a stretch of ice lying close to shore, beyond, looser floes at a slow rate of drift. He comes indoors and taps the barometer. A steady needle. 'Let's get ourselves ready,' he announces.

Wanny startles. 'The ship?'

'Thermoses and lunch. Let's row to the southern side, see if Hanssen and the Italian are still about.' If they have left? Anders asks himself. Then he will be none the wiser.

❄

The breeze reduces to small flurries, the sun high, the journey slow with each zigzag to skirt around an icefloe. Somewhere in the distance the deep whoosh of a whale blow. Something big. Wanny pauses from rowing.

'There,' the Chief points to a whale's tall plume of vapour. 'A fin whale.' The exhalation loosens to a sheet that momentarily shimmers with all the colours of a rainbow.

'That is something,' she says.

'Might even be a blue. The biggest of all.'

At the three-hour mark they are halfway across Hornsund's great waterway. Wanny's fingers are stiff from gripping oars, she thankful that the skin of her hands has grown too calloused to invite new blisters. They stop for coffee and *smultringer*, the doughnuts crisp and fluffy, cooked fresh that morning. Wanny's fingers are painted with oil, tinged with the aromatic sweetness of cardamom and hartshorn.

'Look at us out here in the deep,' the Chief says, 'scoffing coffee and doughnuts.'

Indigo water laps against the clinkers, the summer sun warming her back. *Remember this, Ivanna. Being fully present. Want for nothing more.*

The Chief takes a third doughnut. 'These are no good for my health,' he says. His look turns sombre. 'You realise we are nearly out of flour?'

She does. 'We will make do.'

'That is what you would say.'

'We will not starve, Anders. We have no shortage of eggs.' Buckets' worth gathered from the islands.

He wipes his hands across his trousers. 'I have finished writing up the record book. We both need to sign it.' The tally of their year's catch to be sent to the Sysselmann of Svalbard.

'How many?' she says, having already done her own calculations.

'Thirteen *bjørn*, seventeen *kvitrev*, not counting ruined skins, one *blårev*, some *storkobber* and *snadd*. I estimate forty to fifty ptarmigan, geese, of course, good eggs and down.' He waits for a response. 'You are not pleased?'

She is pleased, yet somehow that simple list does not reflect their year of effort. 'Two people could not have worked harder.'

'We have worked well.' He turns back and pulls on the oars. 'And now I am quite ready for a vacation abroad. Perhaps a voyage south.'

'You say the silliest things.'

Which is preferable? Anders asks himself. To live and work amongst the magnificence of mountains and glaciers lining Hornsund's northern shore – *their* shore – or to gaze upon the spectacle each and every day from a somewhat featureless southern shore? Beauty, they say, is in the eye of the beholder. He imagines Schønning Hanssen will be no different to him in his affection and guardianship for his realm. It is part and parcel of working a place, of knowing its ins and outs and the cycle of its seasons.

Hanssen's hut sits locked and empty.

'They are gone,' Wanny says. She looks bereft.

'Yes.' It takes Anders only a minute to pick the lock, step inside to an orderly hut, the stove set with kindling, a pair of matches protruding from their box. He reads the note left on the table. 'They left some weeks ago,' he calls.

'We didn't see a ship.'

Anders shrugs. 'The mouth of Hornsund is a broad stretch of water. A small ship could easily pass without us noticing.'

'What does it mean for us?' She sounds more glum than anxious.

'Do not worry yourself. The ship will come.' He speaks with more knowing than he feels. 'We are here now,' he says. 'Let's at least take the time to enjoy it. I will show you around.'

The trappers' hut sits on a hummock of gravel. The remains of whale skulls and vertebrae, walrus skulls, their tusks long gone, crown the surface. 'It looks built on the backs of sea creatures.'

'In a way, that is exactly how it is,' Anders says. 'This was once a blubber oven. It would have processed whales. Some walrus by the looks.'

'The Pomors?'

'Long before the Pomors. During the sixteen hundreds, newly discovered fishing grounds for Dutch and English whalers.' He walks her around the low jagged wall, tarlike and circular, that rises rough-edged from the gravel. 'It is where the boiling blubber spilled from the cooking pots and fused with gravel and sand.' The rubble is speckled with fragments of old red and yellow bricks that once formed the ovens. If he looks hard, he sees sharp edges of broken pottery. With the toe of his boot he unearths the bowl and shank of a clay pipe.

'So bare and bleak,' Wanny says. 'It has an odd feeling.'

He has felt the same about other old whaling sites. 'A place can do that.' Not helped by a surround devoid of tundra but for patches of moss and lichen. Along the shore is a broad river delta, its numerous courses spilling meltwater into the fjord. 'This place delivers its good share of foxes,' he says. 'Gåshamna serves Schønning well.'

They walk across the landscape, over hexagonal stone circles where permafrost has pushed stones up to the surface, the cycles of thaw and freeze forming a patterned land. Stones are not the only objects the permafrost releases. Beyond the remains of old dwellings, rough-hewn planks jut clear of the soil at haphazard angles, ancient remnants of whalers' graves. Ahead of them, a large lake is home to families of geese, its waters fed by Gåsbreen. 'The small glacier we see from across at Fuglefjell.'

Wanny crouches down. 'See here,' she says. 'Even in a barren place there is life, if you really look.' She points to a dwarfed tuft of saxifrage, its star-shaped flowers unlike the saxifrage from their shore, as if the creator has dabbed a spot of colour at the centre of each pale petal.

Anders checks his watch. Looks out across a mirror calm *sund*. 'Time to get a move along. It will be close to midnight before we reach home.'

'So.' Wanny stows the anchor beneath the bow thwart. 'It seems we have been forgotten.'

'We are not forgotten. Don't you know that a man is a man and his word is his word?'

She mumbles something he fails to catch. The tide has dropped. Anders hands her his rifle, gestures for her to get in and shift her weight to the stern. He lifts the bow and heaves against it with his shoulder. 'You are too fat,' he says. The keel scrabbles across gravel until the boat lifts with the shallows.

GUILLEMOT

water cry

FUGLEFJELL'S MOUNTAIN SHRIEKS with bird calls. Fulmars wheeling high, kittiwakes in nests, each square foot of cliff ledge crammed with Brunnich's guillemots. Within the feathered crowd nests a smattering of Black and Common guillemots, every pair racing to rear their chick. The midnight sun tracks golden in the sky, days drift one into the other without dawn or dusk, yet the birds along these cliffs are in accord with the summer slide, the incremental shift in light that has fledglings issue a shrill new cry, their water call, the signal that they are readying to take to the water even before they have the capacity to fly.

Mother birds leave the cliffs and track their way south; fathers stay to show their young the way.

On a high ledge at midnight, a parent preens, his feathers tattered and worn. The young chick beside him has grown from a ball of down to a glossy juvenile, all but its flight feathers grown in. The fledgling stands. It opens its beak – its strident water cry new and unsettling to old and young bird. It flops back down. It frets. It rises. It circles on the ledge. Its father rises and calls, stretches its wings, agitated, expectant. In turn, the young bird shakes its own wings in clumsy imitation.

The moment.

The fledgling shuffles. It baulks. It teeters forward, stumbling from the ledge, nothing for two hundred metres but air and the pull of gravity. A flap of wings and the father is airborne, diverting his path to stay close to the young bird. Down they go, parent and chick, an implausible drop to the water. The fledging is light in weight. It does not spread its wings to fly so much as make a frantic attempt to glide. It spirals down, stricken at the movement of water racing up to meet it. The fledgling plunges to the ocean seconds before its father, fully dunked in an unruly baptism. It bobs to the surface as buoyant as cork, shrieks its cry in a mad frenzy of escape. The small bird paddles at speed, turning loose circles, doused from splashes, struggling to rid itself of this wet new sensation. The father lands neatly on the water, his feet angled forward in a measured skid. He scans for glaucous gulls that, without him here, would take his fledgling in a gulp. The father calls repeatedly as the fledging beats a clumsy path across the water. In moments the two are together, wing against wing, father and young. Their time on the mountain is over. Their life on the water has begun, a father water-bound for the time it will take his own flight feathers to moult and refresh. They will spend these last months of summer side by side, he showing this young bird the ways to dive and forage, to thrive entirely on its own.

18

Hyttevika, July

WITH EACH PASSING vessel, Wanny's yearning to see her boys grows sharper and louder. Which isn't the same as wanting to leave. It is the not knowing when or how that churns inside her. Why has the ship not come as they said it would? She folds away her good clothes and returns to wearing patched bib and braces. They can take her as she comes. If they come at all.

The Chief seems entirely at ease with it all. He busies himself collecting and chopping firewood. Fuel for next season. Normally he would seek out her help. Other than cooking meals, and the day-to-day running of the hut, Wanny is largely without purpose. She has given up shooting geese that forage on the lake, the perimeter of bog too irksome to deal with. Last week she stepped through reeds and moss to retrieve her catch, only to sink to her thighs in fetid black sludge. They have geese hanging on hooks, ready to be plucked. Enough to see them through.

Each day, foxes trot across the landscape, their white winter pelts overtaken by tawny summer coats; a different animal, scruffy by comparison to the elegance of their winter being. The foxes slow their pace to sniff at dismantled traps before moving on, a spring in their step as if to say, yes, things are as they ought to be.

The sight of a whaling factory ship steaming north sends her thoughts to a friend's father from years ago, a skipper on an Arctic sealer. Wanny had asked about his hunting life. In return he had given her a shrug, as if to say there was nothing worth sharing. She prised from him an image she has never forgotten. He spoke of hundreds of seals sleeping on the ice, their coats glossed by morning sun. 'It is all still in here.' He had tapped his head. 'It seemed very sad to disturb the idyll. Such are the needs of we working folk.'

The slaughter. Of that he would not speak. Only that each of those pelts put food on a family's table.

Her entire adult life has been a struggle for existence. Has charged her with a will to make her own way. Now, without exaggeration or embellishment, she can call herself a trapper. Her name in the record book, signed alongside the Chief's, to verify thirteen bears, seventeen white foxes, one blue, some ringed and bearded seals.

Perhaps the defining stamp of a Svalbard trapper is the need for independence. Every trapper she has ferried in her taxi has talked about a life of his own making, the sense of peace in being master of his own frozen realm. In quieter moments, the Chief shares his worry that if the price of pelts continues to slide, if fox farms flood the market with pelts, if the demand for fur should slump, the day may come when trapping is no longer viable. What, he asks, will he do with himself? She cannot picture Anders Sæterdal as happy doing anything else. *In America*, he says with concern, *the big store catalogues are filled with the new mock furs.*

Wanny had scoffed at the notion. *Who would buy a dressed-up fur?*
Those who cannot afford the real thing.

People such as them.

She startles. The *pelskåpe*, forgotten, still folded in its wrapping and pushed so far back beneath the bunk she neglected to pack it. She has not worn the wolf coat once. Why? The collarless style is hardly reason. Nor that she has still to pay for it. She is as deserving as anyone to own a costly garment. She knows the reason why. It is because a man, once again, sees it as his entitlement to determine what is best for her, without consultation or agreement. A brand of benevolence to wield control. If she were to explain the subtlety to the Chief, that the *pelskåpe* would not have been arranged so had she been a man, he would think her petulant. Cutting off her nose to spite her face. Even another woman would likely deem her ungrateful and ungracious. At twenty years of age, starting out with Othar, she'd have thought that of herself, too well-behaved back then to challenge a man's word. At forty, her life reshaped to fit, she has earned the right of contempt.

Anders spreads the map of Svalbard across the table. Fifty miles, eighty kilometres, he calculates, to row from Hyttevika to Bellsund. He has marked a circle around potential stopping points. 'Given fair weather,' he says, 'it takes four or five hours up through the islands to Kapp Borthen.' He taps the map. 'A rest stop here if need be. We plug on another two or three hours to the old hut at Dunderbayen. Camp there overnight. The next day, a big day, around to Calypso Bay at the mouth of the *sund*.'

'Who or what is at Bellsund?'

'Beluga hunters, here, down this arm of the fjord. With any luck they will still be in residence. If we row across the bay at Recherchefjorden, it takes us to within reach of their cabin.'

Wanny studies his markings on the map. 'If they are not?' she says. 'In residence.'

'Well.' He scratches his head. He turns back to the map. 'We would think about continuing on. North along the coast to Advent Bay.'

She spans her fingers across the gaping mouth of Bellsund. 'Anders. That is a vast stretch of open ocean.' Far greater than Hornsund.

'No, look,' he says brightly. 'We would cross to here, this eastern headland that divides Bellsund in two. Follow a course up along this long low island. Here at Camp Bell, the north side, I know of a trapper's cabin.'

She stares at the map without speaking.

He cannot blame her reluctance. He could easily talk himself into deciding against the idea. No. He has thought the plan through. Weighed up the risks. 'Wanny, I am fully expecting Lady Luck to be on our side. We will find the beluga hunters and their ship right here at Bellsund.'

She looks to him. 'What about the dogs?'

No. He shakes his head. 'We cannot take nine dogs. They would need to stay here. Feed them up before we leave. Leave them water and food to make do.'

'They will scoff it all before we have oars in the water.'

'They will not starve. We have left them before. We would expect to be back in one or two weeks.' His dogs will survive on the line with water and a hearty feed. Beyond that time? He would not trust his two with six plump puppies.

Wanny puts her head in her hands. 'We could stay, Anders. Stay and wait for our ship. It could come any day.'

'We could wait. And we will,' he says gently. 'If that is what you wish.'

'What has happened to it? Have they come to grief?'

He is more seasoned to these kinds of unknowns, to happenings beyond his control. 'Could be any manner of things. A delay leaving Tromsø. Engine trouble. They may have sailed first to Advent Bay, or further north to pick up other trappers.' His guess is as good as hers.

She looks at the map.

'What do you say, Wanny?'

'I suppose we have to do something.' She raps her fingers on the edge of the table. 'I am trying to muster enthusiasm. The ocean here is so much fiercer than at home.'

'I understand.' He does. He does not relish the task of rowing fifty miles. He does not welcome the formidable distance more if their luck runs out at Bellsund. What he would give for a decent motorboat. 'If you say no we will stay. If we go, we should both agree. That is fair.'

She counts the date out on her fingers. 'They are six weeks overdue.'

Yes, he nods.

She sighs. 'We would need to pick our days. Promise each other not to take unnecessary chances.'

He draws an arm around her shoulder. 'On that we are agreed.'

※

A casserole of goose soup. A second of roasted goose. Their sleeping bags and rifles. The old emergency tent normally strapped to the sledge when they travel across the glacier. Cooking pots. A wooden board to set the primus upon should they need to cook onboard. The Chief has baked bread, she a sponge cake of all things, split and flavoured with a spread of strawberry jam, never mind the lack of cream. Let them be thankful for fresh eggs and sugar, into the mix their last precious shakings of flour.

Wanny's foreboding rises when they set off in wind, the dogs chained to their long line and howling as she and Anders push the boat from shore. Left off their leash all but the puppies would vanish in search of food and human company, never to be seen again. She cannot dwell on their fate should a bear pass by.

'The sou'westerly will blow us north,' the Chief says cheerily from his place at the middle thwart. Every half hour he halts from rowing to pump out water; a greater volume, it looks to Wanny, than slops in with the chop of waves. How much seawater can a boat hold before it sinks?

Within the span of the morning her mood lifts. It feels much like any journey east to Fuglefjell. Wanny and the Chief fall into an easy pattern, a familiar rhythm of oars pulling through water, her back and shoulders strong. The ocean calms to a millpond. Where else but Spitsbergen does wind fall away as suddenly as it arrives? Her focus turns to the new stretch of coastline, its backdrop of mountains and glaciers. Was there ever a more beautiful place? 'This is my furthest north,' she says to the Chief.

He gives a nod. 'I said you would get to know the place. I offer no end of travel and adventure.'

She laughs. 'You kept your pledge. And I am thankful to you. Really I am.' Wanny halts from rowing. She looks around. 'I have been here almost a year and I still ogle at the might of the place,' she says. 'Does that ever fade?'

'If it does, you are reminded of it soon enough. This land shows no care for a person who forgets that their hold here is conditional. Who would we be without a rifle in our hand? How long would we last out in the open?'

'Perhaps in that lies the heart of the wonder.'

'No doubt,' he says. 'No doubt.' They row on, silent in their reverie. The Chief lifts his oars. 'Each time I come here, when I look across the water at a cabin set upon the landscape, I have the same sensation inside my gut. That has never faded.'

'What kind of sensation?' Wanny prompts. It is unlike the Chief to speak in such a feeling way. She doesn't want him to stop.

'I suppose akin to reverence. Not for God,' he says. 'For human endeavour. For perseverance in all its forms, from the first men who laid eyes upon this place. The old explorers. The early whalers. The Pomor trappers. Our two local men from forty years ago. Those

Tromsø seamen stranded up here for winter would have thought themselves the unluckiest men on earth.'

'They lived to tell the tale?'

'More. They were the first from our lot to set up camp ashore, find a means to live off the land. The pair earned themselves a small fortune with their year's haul of fox pelts and bearskins. That set the rest of Tromsø thinking.'

'Some day,' Wanny ventures, 'Svalbard could be bustling with towns and people. With all manner of industry.'

'Never,' he says. 'No. The climate, the ice, the nature of the place puts paid to that. The wild will win out long after the likes of we mere humans come and go.'

Set on a low-lying headland is the hut at Kapp Borthen, if its dilapidated shell can be called a hut. It has been many a year since this hut was cared for and tended, warmed with a stove, a welcome refuge for its trappers. The hut offers nothing more than a reprieve to stretch their legs, look around, confirm their bearings on the map.

Another four hours across still waters, whale blows out in the distance, the whoosh of their spouts skating clear and loud across the surface of the ocean.

'What if a bear should pass by the hut?' Wanny says to him. It takes Anders a moment to pick up the thread. She is fretting about the dogs.

'They are on the long line. They will fend for themselves.' He cannot bring himself to tell her otherwise. He has made the best of a bad situation. 'Should the ship arrive, the skipper will read our note and make his way to Bellsund to meet us there. They will know to feed the dogs, take them aboard.'

'If your two let them get near.'

'Mira will lead the way. She keeps the boys in check.'

'She is a good dog,' Wanny says. 'I knew she would do well up here.'

'Did you now?' he says. 'I had my doubts to begin with.'

'You had your doubts in both of us.'

'We have come a long way.'

They row into a small, inviting bay with easy access. Once ashore, Wanny lights the primus to heat the soup. A group of eiders nest metres away, unperturbed by their presence. 'They are late starters,' she says.

'My word they are. Too late for their young to make it before winter sets in.'

The tundra is dotted with a carpet of delicate red and white flowers, different from those at Hyttevika. Already, the leaves of Arctic willow, trees no taller than her calves, show a blush of autumn colour. This change of seasons, near on a year ago, is when she first entered this high Arctic world.

The Chief rinses their soup mugs at the water's edge, takes gravel to scour the pot. He collects water from a rivulet to boil coffee, a half-strength brew to stretch their diminished supply. He refills the thermos then pours enough for two mugs, scalding coffee to warm gloved hands.

The Chief takes a noisy slurp. He makes a tortured face. 'I may as well be drinking tea.'

'Here,' she says, breaking off a hunk of cake. 'This will help.'

Out to sea they gaze upon an endless ocean, the evening sun causing her to squint. 'It feels a very long way away from Hornsund,' she says.

'Can I tell you something?' the Chief says.

Wanny nods.

'I was, well, impressed, that you agreed.'

'To this?'

'Some men I know would have baulked at the idea.'

She cannot decide if he is paying a genuine compliment, or confessing to having hoodwinked her. 'Does that mean I am gull-ible? Or that you are not to be trusted?'

He downs his coffee in gulps. She cannot drink it so hot. 'I suspect it means you have no shortage of pluck. That you are as good as anyone I know to help us succeed.'

Once she would have glowed at the praise. Now, it feels as empty as a placation.

The Chief picks at crumbs of cake caught in the folds of his trousers. 'Not to mention you are Svalbard's premium cook.'

He is trying so hard. 'Thank you,' she says.

Anders stows the primus and pots in the boat while Wanny disap-pears behind a hillock of tundra. Late July, the air thick with the drone of insects, the midnight sun a perpetual flood of daylight. They need to make all the distance they can while the weather lasts. It would not be unheard of to wake tomorrow to pea soup fog. His watch reads ten at night when they push off in the boat, the ocean gilded, swarms of dovekies weaving low across the water. He trusts the hut at Dunderbayen will offer better shelter.

Anders's hands and body soon protest at this night-time effort of rowing atop a full day at the oars. His shoulders ache with tightness, his arms feel leaden, the pads of his palms are chafed from gripping damp, salt-laden oars. He chastises himself for not donning gloves throughout the day. He will pay for it tomorrow.

'Airy,' Wanny describes the petite residence at Dunderbayen whose window frames hold not a single pane of glass.

'Clear views of the sky.' He peers to the gaping hole in the roof bereft of its stovepipe. A hut without a stove is no hut at all. A good part of the floor is missing, which they block as best they can with lengths of driftwood. They plug the roof with a weighted-down pot lid. A mug of coffee from the thermos at midnight, both too weary for talk. They crawl into bed, their reindeer bags covering the floor space.

Anders ought to be as dead to the world as Sleeping Beauty but his mind whirrs. He tells himself he has no cause for concern. They have made good time; they need another good day tomorrow, ten or twelve hours to reach Calypso Bay that could all end up a wild goose chase. He wills himself to sleep but he tosses and turns inside his reindeer bag, the breeze getting up, the air damp. Amber light streams in through the unheated hut, the roof and walls groaning and squeaking as if annoyed by their presence. Beside him the rise and fall of Wanny's breath. Look at her. She sleeps as deeply as a child. He studies her face, the curl of her lashes, the flaps of her hat pulled down to keep her ears warm, wisps of sun-bleached hair trailed across her cheek. It seems a lifetime ago, no, the life of a different man who shared a bed each night with Othelie, who learned to be a father to two small children. He wishes he had done more by his wife and family, seen how hard Othelie was trying, been a better, kinder man. Not once can he remember saying he was sorry. He struggles to picture Wanny as a mother. This year has been he and her, no other, every day together. He feels a nip of envy to hear her say she longs to hold her boys.

Anders knows of no other man who can claim this arrangement with a woman. He and Wanny, it strikes him as . . . modern. Yes. The kind of thing you might find in the big European cities, not here in his time-steady world. She is a novel woman. A working partner, his friend and compatriot. She is chief cook. She *was* his sometime lover. She is different to women he has known, as tough and resilient as gentle and giving, a combination that should no longer feel at odds but still strikes him as a marvel.

Anders tries to conjure a memory of how it was last season, the season before. With another man you didn't watch your p's and q's.

You were not expected to put in the same effort keeping the hut spick and span, adding these womanly touches that have come to feel a part of every day. Was it more carefree back then? Would he have shared the same daft ramblings as he does with her? The feeling of coming home to the hut; not once has he felt the want for something inexplicable that punctuates his other seasons. His skin shivers with cold. He rests his face down against hers and ponders the uncanny softness of a woman's skin. She rouses to his touch. For the first time in weeks she draws him close.

Wanny wakens to the cry of loons, their calls so human-like they could be a traveller in grave distress. Above the rush of wind, she hears rain. It picks up tempo until the noise turns to nails driving themselves inside this ramshackle shelter. Water is dripping on the Chief's face and he stirs beside her. 'Are the sleeping bags wet?' he mutters, half asleep. 'You stay warm. I will find the tent.'

'It is quicker with two.' Together they drag themselves out to pitch the tent inside this forsaken hut, moving their sleeping bags under cover to dry. 'Is it morning?' she asks. With no dusk or dawn, no hint of darkness, there is no telling what time it is.

'Early, still. Come back to bed.'

They might have forged on after breakfast if it were only rain to contend with, but beyond the shore the ocean turns steely and mean, a biting wind whipping up the waves. Resigned to a day ashore, the Chief claims that he will spend the entire time napping. Likely chance. She knows him better than he knows himself. After breakfast he begins to patch the hut, Wanny helping block the worst gaps in the walls, sourcing slender lengths of driftwood to split, picking through the least bent and rusted nails scattered on a shelf.

It is midday the following day before wind and rain eases. They have eaten all their prepared meals, a situation that once she would have worried over. They each have a rifle and ammunition, the ability to find their own food when the need arises. Should the fuel for their primus run out, they will make an open fire, these bays and headlands a catch-all for driftwood, for dried seaweed and stalks of tundra to start a flame.

It takes a morning of weaving around skerries and reefs, the Chief rowing, she kneeling on the bow thwart crying out directions to lead them safely through the narrow channels. Seawater washes over the bow and douses her leather coat. Breakers frill the shore.

The wind blows from the wrong direction. The current is against them. For ten hours they row without stopping, neither hungry so much as parched for thirst. So as not to lose headway, one continues to row while the other takes a mug of coffee from the thermos. Relieving herself over the side of the boat – the Chief turned the other way for the sake of her dignity – amounts to an acrobatic feat, crouched on the gunnel, holding on for dear life, her rear exposed to the ocean, the wind creating havoc. 'Oh, to be a man,' she shouts to the sky. They reach the headland of Bellsund, then three more wearying hours to make the sheltered waters of Calypso Bay.

Wanny has her first taste of Svalbard's mining industry, a coal seam exposed near the beachline which the Chief says proved too small to last. The whole enterprise abandoned. The bay is dominated by one large building with a cluster of smaller dwellings. 'The size of it,' she says of the main building. She nearly utters, 'How did they heat it?' but catches herself in time. Outside each dwelling sits a hummock of coal.

A railway winds along the waterfront. They walk past a barge perched high on the beach, part-buried in gravel; hairy lichen and moss greening the lower planks. 'That old tub looks in better condition than our boat,' she says.

'Rubbish, woman.'

The Chief points to a small cabin a distance away. A hut built of driftwood. The door framed with reindeer antlers. The roof lined with tar paper. A sledge strapped on top. 'Trappers!' she cries.

'Shall we see if they are home?'

She races to match his pace. The girl-like thrill, a charge of nervousness at the prospect of finding trappers in residence, of seeing new human faces beyond their own small realm.

The curtains are drawn. The door bolted. She hears the Chief sigh. He kneels to pick the lock. 'I feel sure they will forgive us the break-in,' he says.

Inside, the accommodation is positively palatial compared to Hyttevika. Linoleum on the floor, several walls papered, the kitchen painted a cheery shade that brings to mind pale margarine. The windows here are twice the size of their main hut. Wanny pulls back the curtains, their hems and tie-backs meticulously hand-stitched. A flood of light. A shield of warmth radiating from the glass. The hut, its surrounds, are all order and cleanliness. Outside lies a quantity of coal that would serve a pair of trappers through the harshest winter. A real house for overwintering, its realm reserved for men who she rates equally as capable as her, perhaps more so, at keeping a well-run hut. She stands at the blackened stove – not a skerrick of rust, not one ring warped, the firebox tidily set and ready to light. She feels newly swamped with failure. A heightened sense of lack. No matter what she does, how hard she strives to earn a place here, nothing she can do will be enough. On the wall above the washbasin hangs a calendar, July the third circled in pencil. Beside it: *Home to Norway*. Wanny clucks. 'The ship has collected every other living soul on Spitsbergen.'

The Chief ignores her. 'These chaps won't mind if we spend the night, leave things as we find them.'

She feels like Goldilocks, tentative at first, then testing out each homemade stool, trying out the different bunks, inspecting the array of pots and pans, the assortment of crockery and cutlery. 'They even have a cake skewer.'

The Chief emerges from the hut's storeroom with a full-sized tin tub that he has to steer ahead to manoeuvre through the door.

'The size of it!' she cries.

'I thought Mrs Woldstad might like to take a soak,' he says. 'Cheer herself up. We have no shortage of fuel. Plenty of water. I am your manservant at your beck and call.'

'Anders. Yes.'

The exquisite luxury of lying back in steaming water, wet hair floating across her face, her ears immersed, tuned to the slow thudding of her pulse. She revels in the simple joy of being clean from top to toe, the sliver of dishwashing soap taken from its caddy a precious commodity at this moment. The Chief delivers a pot of warm water to rinse her hair. A nailbrush. He sits himself at the table with a fresh mug of coffee, staring at her. He shakes his head and grins.

She laughs, splashing him with water.

'If this is what it takes to see you smile, I shall have to order a bigger tub for Hornsund.'

She stops, the air turned brittle. Is he teasing her? 'What are you saying?'

He shrugs. Then silence. 'Well. I thought, perhaps. Next season. Once you sort things out at home.'

She wipes water from her face. Draws her knees to her chest. 'Are you asking me to join you?'

'It seems. I suppose. I am. Yes.'

Was this the intention all along? To make her wait until she had surrendered hope of ever coming back. Would he be so cruel? She tries to read his face. Smug.

'When did you decide on this?'

He shrugs. 'This very moment.' He looks flummoxed. 'Which is why I asked you. Isn't it what you want?'

She rests her chin on her knees. Why she should feel this surge of white fury, she cannot say. She reaches for a tea towel, the only cloth available to dry herself.

'Look away,' she yells at him.

'Can I not sit with my coffee, enjoy the view?' At the set of her face he complies, turning to face the window.

She addresses his back, her voice tight. 'For months, Sæterdal, you have been telling me I am not cut out to be a trapper. You are too soft, Mrs Woldstad. You are too this. You are not that.'

'That is baloney,' he talks to the window. 'You forget all the many times I praise you. That you are *riktig* with a rifle. A fine cook. That you work hard. That you have become capable in every way.' He huffs. 'But none of that counts, does it? You prefer to be hard done by. The suffering widow.'

'Do not . . . that is rubbish. Uncalled for and insulting.' She dries her feet on the tiny towel to dress. She brushes her hair with her fingers. 'You want a trapper of your choice. You are always saying that.'

He turns to face her. 'That is true. As is my right.'

'Another man, is what you meant. So why me? Why now when I have needed to think and plan a different life ahead?' Wanny knows her face is fierce.

He doesn't answer her.

'Well? You are never usually lost for words.'

He throws up his hands. 'We get along, don't we? We talk. We laugh. We are good with one another. We work well as a team.' He takes his empty mug over to the bench, studies his feet. 'It feels right. Do you not feel the same?'

She drapes the towel over the line. 'I cannot say how I feel. Only that I need to consider what is best for me and my boys. They are the most important people in my life.'

'You do that,' he says, reaching for his coat, marching out the door.

Anders stamps along the shoreline, his rifle on his back. He needs to clear his head of irritation. He gives her exactly what she says she wants and now she doesn't want it. He tracks the open seam of coal. He glances out to sea. This blighted place. A lack of viable coal was not its only shortcoming. Any trapper, even a numbskull, could have told them that every other day nature would beat them. A north-facing beach entirely exposed to weather and swell. No skerrick of shelter. Landing a barge, getting coal out to a ship would have been the devil's job. Anders boggles at the infrastructure, the vast wealth of the few, the crowns poured into audacious hopes and dreams, a telegraph house and mast, a narrow-gauge rail line, the cluster of substantial buildings, even a barracks. And yet, he cannot help but pay a nod to men's vision and temerity. The world would be a meagre place without such plunges of boldness. He looks about at empty buildings, the sense of abandonment. What strikes him keenly is the sight of laden rail carriages, hillocks of coal, with nowhere to go. That moment of realisation when purpose and optimism turned dark with dismay, a shiny new enterprise, silenced and still.

Early morning, the sun high and dazzling, the water an eye-smarting lake. Anders pumps water, a trail of dirty froth in their wake. At the bow, working the oars, 'It looks like a postcard,' Wanny says brightly. 'We are lucky with this weather.'

He grunts. After yesterday's altercation his foul mood is not inclined for chatter.

'And we are making good time,' she says.

They are a seesaw in motion. Should he grow quiet or glum, she feels the urge to pep him up. Anders cannot help the slow churning in his stomach as they row across Recherchefjorden. Not even the far shore will render the moment of truth for they need to either row or trek overland another two Norwegian miles to be in sight of the Bamsebu cabin. If they gaze upon that stretch of fjord empty of a ship, a dwelling deserted, it will confirm his fears that the beluga hunters are gone, with their only remaining option to row all the way to Advent Bay. This is what troubles him. He has not broadcast his concerns about their boat, that each day he pumps out an alarming increase in water. Their battered dinghy has lived a long and strenuous life and now it is barely seaworthy in calm conditions.

They row for two hours until a breeze gets up, rising to a headwind. Wanny favours his idea of bringing the boat ashore, trekking overland the rest of the way to Bamsebu. 'It is a fine day for a walk,' she says. 'This has to be the most tranquil place.'

'Tranquillity within earshot of a glacier is a dangerous illusion.' Anders carries slender lengths of driftwood in the bottom of the boat to act as rollers when they come ashore. He has a block and tackle if they get stuck, though driving a holding stake into Svalbard's unrelenting ground is easier said than done. What he would give for the dogs' hauling power.

At the far shore he and Wanny heave the beast a boat length over rollers before the wooden lengths bed down in mud and gravel, a beach with so little incline that it is likely to be swamped by tide or wash. He feeds out the full length of anchor line which she marches up the beach. Together they weight the anchor with the heaviest stones to be found. The glacier shimmers. From somewhere deep within, the ice issues a report of grumbling. Therein lies his other big concern.

He checks the anchor, feels it give. He searches far along the shoreline for additional weight. The boulder he chooses is so heavy he is forced to walk bow-legged, hears himself grunt ape-like with the effort, a weight too great to crook his arms and lift the stone against him. The last stretch he drops the thing to roll. He unstacks the anchor stones they so neatly assembled, only to begin again.

'You are going to a great deal of trouble,' she says.

'A big calving,' he nods to the glacier, 'will send a series of waves right across this bay. I don't intend to come back and find our only means of transport washed away.' He gives the anchor a hefty kick. 'Better,' he says, as satisfied as he is likely to be.

They set off, his field glasses slung from his neck, their rifles and rucksacks firm against their backs.

They meander along beachlines and pick their way through cobbled shores. They trek over undulations of tundra, bone dry underfoot. They walk for an hour then rest at an inviting boulder, sized to seat two hikers with their coffee. He peels off a woollen layer and stuffs it in his rucksack. He downs his coffee. 'No cake?'

'Gone.'

He sighs. 'Shall we forge on, then?'

A short way inland they deviate to a high point. 'Let's see what we can see from the top.'

Partway up they turn back to a sharp crack, a deep boom from the glacier. 'A calving,' he says.

'I don't see anything.'

'The sound takes seconds to reach us. By then the action is over.' Through his field glasses he spies a wall of deep blue ice where the glacier has calved. Broken ice bobs on the water. Kittiwakes flock around the site, swooping down to collect small fish stunned by fallen ice or carried to the surface in the turbulence. They wait and watch for a second calving but all is quiet.

'The glacier has returned to sleep.'

Near the summit of the hill comes a shrill commotion of geese. On the downward side stands a line of barnacle geese. It takes a moment for Anders to realise the cause of their distress, a fox slunk low on its haunches, trying its best to stalk the gaggle. The fox waits and watches for a break in the line. Just before it lunges, the geese take the upper hand, a united shield, charging forward with a raucous babble, their formidable bills hammering at speed until the fox issues a yip and skulks away. 'Well, I never,' Anders says. 'Mikkel Rev is off to find himself a safer meal.'

Anders grips his field glasses to keep them steady. Slowly he scans the empty fjord, trying to magic up a ship. The raised shore-line beside the Bamsebu cabin gleams as white and lustrous as a treasure trove of pearls. Anders turns his focus to the cabin, the two smaller shacks, still and silent, each door closed to hope or optimism.

'It is not as I wished.'

'They are gone?'

'It looks that way.'

'May I see?'

He hands her the glasses. 'The cabin is halfway along, just back from shore.'

'The sand is pure white.'

'It is not sand.'

'Gravel, then.'

'You are looking at the slaughter site.'

She looks again. 'Belugas?'

'Their bones. The money is in the skin and blubber.'

He has not heard her squeal before. 'Anders,' she cries. 'I think ... is it? ... Yes ... Oh Lord. It is! It truly is!' She waggles her hand ahead of her. 'Look. There. You see?'

'See what, woman?' he seizes back the field glasses. An open door. Is it? Yes! A figure moving between the cabin and shacks. A second figure. 'My word if you are not right.' He turns and hugs her. 'It is people. With a telegraph. A ship.'

Wanny laughs. She kisses his nose. 'People,' she says as if the very concept is a miracle. He holds her tight. He feels her startle.

'People. Look!' She spins him around to face the fjord. She jumps and waves. She hollers like a mad woman. Directly below, a whaler steams down the fjord to Bamsebu. Clasped to its starboard flank, a loose necklace of pearl white whales. From the stern a frothing trail of scarlet, the bloodied wash purpling the fjord.

FOX

the mountain alive

THE TRAPPERS' HUT sits empty and still, curtains drawn, its door bolted and propped with lengths of driftwood.

Food is still plentiful, the mountain alive with fledglings.

Behind the hut, dog fox tracks across the slope, a plump juvenile kittiwake clutched in his jaw. A reindeer stag saunters below, ignoring the fox, slowing to graze on lush summer growth.

At the entrance to the den, a blue vixen keeps watch over her kits who romp and play, tumble and nip. An undersized family of two tawny kits, a third kit stillborn. The largest has its father's odd, arresting eyes.

Dog fox splits apart the kittiwake. He stands back as kits clamber over his paws, snuffling and snorting, their snouts buried in the kittiwake's open carcase. They yank at feathers, tug at fascia and guts, too young to understand the value of the gull's oily flesh.

Dog fox and vixen keep a sharp hold on their territory, on the alert for trespassing foxes. Their den is extensive, generations old, familiar and comforting, the place where the vixen was born a runt, where her mother and mother's mother each were reared.

Her father is lost to the ice, her mother taken by the trappers' jaws that reverberated loud and lethal across the mountainside. The young vixen had slunk down the slope, approaching with caution to nose her mother's limp body, the tongue hanging free, the belly swollen with pups. She had retreated to watch the woman prise apart the trap that clamped her mother's throat.

She sets herself down beside her mate, her muzzle resting on his back. She nips at his neck. He turns and licks her brow, paints her eyelids with his tongue. She wears a charcoal summer coat that traps the full warmth of Arctic sun, that soon has her overheat. She leaves her mate to guard their young. She saunters through tundra rough and cool beneath her belly. She skirts around the reindeer balancing its headdress of antlers. She prances over dismantled traps, undeterred by the lingering scent from aging bait sticks. She knows well enough of traps. The young vixen stops to lap at a puddle of snowmelt. She rolls to scratch her back then chews on twigs of willow. She climbs to the headland to sniff and leave her mark at the base of the wooden cross. She sits tall and alert. Her senses are tuned to the volume of bird calls, the quality of daylight, the imminent change in seasons. The small fox looks down upon the trappers' hut, pondering the man, the woman and her handouts, measuring the trappers' absence. She watches the moving waters of the fjord, alert to movement, turning her ear to a far-off thunder of calving ice. Her senses remain primed to the squeak of rowlocks and trill of oars moving through the water.

The young blue vixen bounds back to her den. She licks the ears of her two small kits who yawn and nip and tussle. She leads them into the cool of her den and sets herself down, teats swollen and heavy with milk. Her kits scramble across her, their needle claws and milk teeth nipping at her belly. Little Blue closes her eyes, licks at air, two mouths nuzzling and snuffling against her to feed.

19

Tromsø, early August

WANNY CANNOT STOP beaming. She grips the ship's railing. She cannot stop looking about. She is a child on national day, giddy from the sights and sensations as the ship steams through the fjord toward home. Never has she so utterly understood *green*. Wild fields. Verdant pastures. Trees. The height of them! The slopes of the fjord are dotted with shorn sheep and plump cows. The smell of home.

Nearer to town the foreshore gives way to smartly painted houses, their window boxes a floral rainbow of colour. She draws in a strange new smell and realises it is Tromsø. Her town. She tunes her ear to its arrangement of sound. The town feels big and busy, brimming with industry and movement. The clang and clatter of the port. A ship's horn. A line of trucks and cars. A town too orderly, too . . . civilised. Suddenly, stupidly, she hankers for the Arctic wind, the wild. She feels disconnected from her body. Her skin turns pincushion at the familiar toll of the town's church bell. Somewhere in the distance children are playing. A man is whistling a tune. The remarkable heat of Tromsø's late summer sun.

A motorboat ferries them to the quay. Wanny baulks at having to hand in their rifles to the no-nonsense Customs men in uniform.

She walks onto the pier, her back free of its rucksack and rifle, her muscles twitching with the sense of having mislaid something vital. She looks to the end of the pier. Her heart jumps. Is it them? She is walking on air. She stumbles. She is on one knee holding out her arms. She cannot stop hugging her boys, holding each precious face in her hands, gazing upon them, exclaiming, 'Look how you have grown! And you have filled out!' She strokes their hair. Feels stubble on Bjørvik's chin. She holds his chin in her hand, brought to tears by how much of his father he holds in his features. 'I have missed you!' she cries. She plants Alf's head and face and nose with kisses until he squirms and gasps for air.

The Chief joins her and, in turn, the boys shake his hand. Look at Bjørvik, talking with the Chief man to man, Alf wanting to learn about his year. She hears her name spoken. 'Your mother is a fine trapper,' the Chief says to her sons.

'She's not bad with a gun,' Bjørvik tells him.

'She taught me and my brother,' Alf says. Her heart is at risk of exploding with pride and joy.

'My baby,' she strokes Alf's hair, which causes his cheeks to flush with embarrassment before the Chief. 'You are almost your brother's equal in height.' They are good boys. Happy boys. Bjørvik chortles at her trapper's hat. In her eldest son, Wanny hears his father's joy. Alf insists on wearing it, pulling the flaps down around his ears and flicking them from side to side. Oh, to show these two the north. An elderly man ambles past and throws up his arms at the sight of her youngest clad in leather and fur on this sweltering summer's afternoon.

The Chief does not stand close. He does not place his arm on her shoulder. The old easiness feels even more strained than onboard the ship. He tells her he must leave to speak with the buyers: the sale of their pelts, the eiderdown. 'I may see you Thursday,' he says. 'More likely Friday. Once I am sorted.' He nods and walks away. With this, Wanny feels a thud within her empty chest. In these twelve months she has not spent a single day or night apart from Anders Sæterdal.

Her boys have brought a bag of freshly picked farm strawberries, fruit so shockingly red and ripe that she can do no more than gaze inside the bag and draw in the fruity redolence. She picks out a berry and turns it on its stem. 'Will you look at it,' she exclaims to her boys.

In the blink of an eye she has been transported across an Arctic ocean to a homeland both dear and alien. Already, their hut, the landscape, the very name Hornsund, feels distant and unreal. As if these past twelve months, the waiting and worrying for a ship, their long rowboat journey, is nothing more than a delusional dream. Had they not decided to row to Bellsund, waited instead at Hyttevika, their ship would have arrived within days, having first diverted to the north of Spitsbergen to deliver a new season's trapping team and collect another party. All her imaginings of the ship having sunk, of she and the Chief being overlooked, amounted to ordinary delay and made her feel naïve when the captain simply shrugged and told her, *par for the course here in the Arctic*. True to the Chief's word, the captain had followed the directions in their note. He and his crew had wrangled the dogs and taken them aboard, then full steam ahead to Bamsebu to collect Wanny and the Chief. Her Mira, even the Alsatians, shrieked at the sight of she and the Chief climbing onboard. The dogs emaciated. Two of six pups unaccounted for. The palaver of towing their leaking dinghy all the way back to Hyttevika. A frantic day at the hut to ferry a mountain of gear and boxes and barrels aboard. Wanny taking Mira ashore to scour the territory for the two missing pups. A year ago, the voyage north, the Alsatians showed her their disdain. Climbing back onboard to sail home, the missing pups in mind, she could not stand to look at them. Wanny had no chance to farewell the place, just a poignant, parting look as they motored out through the islands. The stamp of those snow-tiered mountains. Their treasured hut dissolving into land.

She and her boys wander to the centre of town where Wanny's taxi is parked. How entirely foreign, another woman's life, to sit upright behind a wheel again. The smell of leather and tobacco. The volume of traffic. The speed! The driver of the car behind toots his horn to overtake her. She drives the boys to the dairy where they sit on a bench in the warmth of the sun. A pint of cold, fresh milk rich with cream.

Her first days in Tromsø pass as a blur. People. Martin, her husband resigned to their fate before they even spoke. He sounded tired as he traced through his notes scribbled on an envelope, wanting to voice each matter he needed to share. Affirmations. Disappointments. A need to understand. If their start together could be likened to a business contract, so too could its closure. New arrangements for her loan. A plan for removing her belongings. The ending settled.

❄

Day turns to evening, soft autumn light, the twilight buttery. She drives slowly through town to Anders's lodgings, butterflies in her stomach. She would like to tell him how she has missed him. She feels confused by how distantly he behaves. To preserve her honour, she tells herself, though she doesn't care what people say or think.

When she arrives, Wanny feels a welcome return to the old way when the Chief makes a play of choosing whether to sit in the front or back seat of her cab. He gets in alongside her, closes the door. An exhalation of breath. Here in this private space it is just the two of them. He looks full of himself as he hands her a bulky envelope.

'What is this?'

'What do you think it is, woman?' He grins. 'It is your earnings.'

She peers inside the envelope. 'My.'

'It may look substantial,' he cautions, sounding exactly like the Chief. 'Keep in mind this represents an entire year's labour and . . .' He waggles his head. 'If you should choose to join me it will need to keep you for another year.'

She locks the envelope in the glove compartment. 'In fact, I am decided. Yes, I would like to go back.'

'Is that so?' He grins. He searches her face. 'Your home situation?'

'In that regard I am sorted.'

'What of the boys?' he asks.

She has no answer.

'They are fine young men, Wanny. Good and strong. As eager to learn the ways as any I have known.'

She looks to him. 'I would give anything,' she whispers, not daring to speak the words.

He gives a nod. 'We will talk about it later.'

She turns over the engine, so full of happy jitters she grates the gears. 'Where to, Mr Sæterdal?'

He rubs his hands. 'Where else?'

She pulls the cab up outside Mack Ølhallen. Not a thing has changed. A group of weary women, one with a toddler, waits on the pavement outside the beer hall. Wanny slides out from the driver's seat, props on the running board and holds her open door. 'Shall I collect you later?'

'No need. You are coming in with me.'

He is deadly earnest.

'Anders,' she scoffs. The obvious seems lost on him. 'I am a woman.'

'You certainly are,' he says in his serious voice. 'It had not escaped my notice.'

She gestures to the steps of the beer hall, a rowdiness of voice and men's laughter spilling onto the street. 'Go on in,' she says above the din. 'I will call back for you later.'

'In there?' he says. 'On my own?' He holds his hand to his chest, stupidly bereft.

'Off with you.' She shushes him. 'I have plenty to keep me busy.'

'Are you not a trapper?'

'What am I to say to that?'

Anders turns to the women waiting on the footpath. 'Is this the trappers' bar? Am I in the wrong part of town?'

A young girl giggles. The others look to one another, bemused by his banter.

'Anders. Go,' she urges. 'Mack's would never serve a woman, even a trapper.'

'I am sure they would not,' he says, full of himself. 'I have no doubt they will not if you should order a glass of milk.'

She shakes her head. 'You are a clown.'

'Wanny,' he says. 'I have never been more serious. You are a *fangskvinne*. My working partner and compatriot. If you refuse to go in then I cannot go in. And you must live with the consequence of denying me a much-needed pint of *blanding*.'

'Sæterdal.'

'I will not take no for an answer.'

She takes a ragged breath. Anders moves to the front of the cab. He extends his arm. 'Please,' he says. 'Come with me.'

She looks to the heavens, takes a deep breath. 'One drink,' she says.

'One drink.'

Wanny closes her cab door and draws herself tall.

EPILOGUE

Sørkjosen, northern Norway
26 October 1959

WANNY CLIMBS DOWN to the curb, the young driver not hiding his irritation at running late. 'Be quick, now.' His fingers strum the bus's oversized steering wheel as he waits for this doddery woman to pad across the road to post her precious letter. Wanny's new bouclé coat is buttoned against the weather, the strap of her brolly slung from her rifle shoulder. Old habits. She feels the first spikes of sleet, imagines last night's ice still clinging black and hazardous to the shadows of the road, the air shrilling into storm and lively enough to tear a perfectly good umbrella inside out. She could tell that driver a thing or two about storms. In her handbag she keeps a plastic rain bonnet, a tidy invention that folds away to nothing, though she dare not scratch about for it now. She hears the rumble of the bus's motor, draws in its fumes, marches herself further along the footpath. A cautious step out onto the road, stopped by a line of oncoming traffic motoring around the bend. The driver will have to exercise his patience.

She is on her way home to her housekeeping post on Senja, a contrast to the attraction she has become in Tromsø, the papers naming her a celebrated author, *First Woman Trapper on Svalbard*; her Oslo publisher talking of a reprint.

Last week's public talk at Tromsø still niggles her. *The gall of the woman*, Wanny has written to Anders, the letter in her handbag ready to post. A fiery young woman with free-flowing hair, a Frenchie by her accent, had held up Wanny's memoir and waggled it before the crowd. *Did you stop to think about that mother and her cubs, the families you turned into fur coats, the rights of all those defenceless creatures?* A disdainful smack to the back of the book. Wanny's book. *Her* words. The woman had said something more, not loud enough for her to catch. The host beside her had heard it well enough, his head ranged down, the hall grown stiff with discomfort. In these twenty-odd years of giving talks she has not been shown an ounce of ill feeling. No shortage of good people wanting to hear about her Arctic life as a *fangskvinne*, the first female trapper, never mind the day it took to bus from Senja to Tromsø to speak about her book. Another day of travel here to Sørkjosen to spend time with her youngest and his family.

No. She will not apologise for the living she sought, the life she earned. *There seems to be all manner of trouble and disharmony in the world*, she wrote to Anders, *the old values turned inside out*. The unrest feels not dissimilar to their final year of trapping, Europe brewing for war, the price of furs no longer worth the effort of flensing, insufficient to repay their loan. Even here in Norway's quiet north, the sixties hurtling toward them, she sees change all around. A new way of life with crowds and noise and traffic, everybody loud and in a rush. It maddens her to feel this way, old and left behind.

Wanny has not shared her life with Anders Sæterdal for several years, he happy to remain in his old home county of Mo i Rana, farming fox and tending his cattle. Perhaps without Svalbard to share, perhaps the change in how they saw themselves – she floundering to find a new purpose, wanting to be nearer to the boys – had gently eased them into separate grooves. She will cherish Anders Sæterdal until the day she dies.

These closing days of October will not be lost on the Chief, he as primed as she to the change in polar seasons. At Hornsund the sun will be drawing down for winter, *mørketid* bedding in. She still thinks of the polar night as a world turned blue, a time alive with bears, foxes parading in all their winter finery. *Never underestimate a fox*, the Chief would say, words no truer than on their first return to the north. Little Blue had reappeared at the Villa, astonishing them both, a small blue fox sitting daintily outside the hut, waiting for a handout.

Animal rights? The Chief would laugh aloud at the notion of a wild animal having entitlement, having value beyond the price it fetched. He and she never entertained such indulgence. *A time of simple needs*, she has written in her letter. *We depended on ourselves and we got on with it, made do with what we had.* Through five Hornsund winters she felt utterly alive. The miles they travelled, the foxes they trapped, bears laid across the hut floor, evenings and blizzards spent scraping skins. The joy of giving her two boys and Anders's young ones the chance to learn the life, Bjørvik becoming a trapper in his own right. Up there, it was about simple meals cooked on a stove, fuelled by the wood they gathered. The goodness of a flank of seal, the delicate meat of a cub.

Any answer to the French woman eluded her. Even the principle Wanny had lived by, that a hunter's skill with a rifle represented an equal battle with a bear, suddenly struck her as out of time, too tenuous to voice. A bounce of long hair as the woman marched her indignation from the hall.

The rumble of the bus shifts octave as if the motor itself is losing patience with her. She cannot slow the Monday morning traffic. On the opposite side of the road, a mother with a child on each arm hurries from the post office, a small family braced against the wind. Wanny blinks away the cold. The hood and cuffs of the little girl's jacket are edged with blue fox. Even from here she knows the genuine article. Somewhere, packed in a trunk, is her first white fox skin from decades ago. The most exquisite gift anyone has given her.

The mother at the opposite curb draws her children close, leans down to speak to them. The small girl looks to Wanny and returns her wave. Wanny moves forward from her side. The family steps out to cross. She wishes she had offered the French woman something meaningful. Something bigger than herself. She steps away from the curb to an icy blast, a gritty wind straight from the north. Wanny shields her eyes. No thinking human could spend five winters in the north without a deep respect and understanding for its creatures. Without a love for the land. Perhaps *awe* is too grand a word, but awe is the way she thinks of it: reverence, a thread of fear, a deep regard. She could have spoken to that woman of bears, of fox, the mix of tenderness and fierceness with which they raise their young. She could have talked of the Pomors who came before, whose wooden crosses paid homage to the land, who honoured the creatures they trapped and the spirits that watched over them. She could have shared the fortitude required for any Svalbard creature – animal or human – to survive an Arctic winter. She and the Chief braved everything that nature dealt them, saw it as their dues for eking out a lightly trodden life in tune with the land.

A sharp cry. The mother, her little ones halted on the road. Wanny turns her good ear. From the edge of her vision a shimmer of white. She reaches for the strap taut on her shoulder, sees a white lorry barrelling toward her in a wail of brakes, tyres skidding on a slick of ice. At the moment of impact she feels an unearthly warmth. Time slows. All these years and now the bear comes knocking. The white envelops her, gathers her up, a patterned tread of broad black paws and white heel guards. A creature of immense bulk that shunts her forwards, airborne and timeless.

Glossary

Andresens—an equipment store and gunsmith established in Tromsø in 1870, initially providing equipment for whale and seal hunting. Andresens still operates as a popular outfitter and gunsmith.

Bamse (Bamsebu cabin)—an affectionate term for a bear such as a teddy bear

bjørn—bear

blanding—a beer blend of 40 per cent Mack Pilsner and 60 per cent Mack Bayer, specific to Mack Ølhallen and popular amongst the trappers

blårev—blue fox

breen—glacier

bukt(a)—bay

dovekies—little auks

Dunøyane—Down Islands

fangskvinne—female trapper

fangstmann—male trapper

foehn—a warm, dry wind blowing down the side of a mountain

formkake—pound cake

Fuglefjell—Bird Mountain

Gåshamna—Goose Harbour

God Jul—Happy Christmas

God morgen—Good morning

Hartshorn—'baker's ammonia' (ammonium carbonate), a rising agent used for baking cookies

Henry Rudi—Norwegian trapper (1889–1970) who worked in Svalbard and East Greenland from 1908 to 1947. Coined 'King of the Bears', Rudi shot 713 polar bears throughout his career. During World War II, Rudi and fellow trappers became founding members of the North-East Greenland Sledge Patrol which operates today as Sirius Patrol.

Hilmar Nøis—Norwegian trapper (1891–1975) who overwintered in Svalbard a record number of seasons from 1909 to 1963. Nøis's second wife Helfrid, whom he married in 1937, thrived on the lifestyle and brought many homely touches to their huts.

Hornsund—Horn Sound. *'They brought a piece of a Deeres horne aboard, therefore I called this sound Horne Sound.'* – Jonas Poole, English whaler, 1610.

Hyttevika—Hut Bay

Isbjørnhamn—Ice Bear Harbour

Juletid—Christmastime

koselig—cosy

Kragen—short for Krag-Jørgensen. A centrefire rifle used by early Svalbard trappers for shooting polar bear.

kvitrev—white fox

Lano—a Norwegian brand of bath soap

Maiblomsten—May flower

Mikkel Rev—Mister Fox. A character in a traditional Norwegian children's book.

mørketid—polar night (24-hour darkness). In Hornsund the sun sets on 30 October and does not rise again until 13 February.

Norwegian mile—10 kilometres

ølhallen—beer hall

overvintrer—a trapper who spends the winter and best part of twelve months living and working in Svalbard.

øre—a Norwegian coin, akin to pence or cents.

pelskåpe—fur coat

polfarer—polar traveller

riktig—right; correct (colloquial)

rype—ptarmigan

selvskudd—a self-firing bear trap invented by Svalbard trappers that comprised a sawn-off shotgun placed in a wooden case set on wooden legs. Seal bait was placed at the open end of the case, then fastened to a string secured to the gun's trigger.

Sjefen—Chief; Boss

skåles—cheers; toasts

smultringer—doughnuts

snadd—ringed seal

Sommarøy—Summer Island

Sonja Henie—Norwegian figure skater and film star (1912–1969). Sonja won more Olympic and World titles than any other ladies' figure skater.

Spitsbergen—the largest island of the Svalbard archipelago. Spitsbergen translates to 'pointed peaks'.

storkobber—bearded seal

sund—a large ocean inlet, wider than a fjord.

Svalbard—an archipelago of which Spitsbergen is the largest island. Svalbard translates to 'cold coast'.

Sysselmann—Governor of Svalbard

toppen—peak, summit

valmuefrø—poppy seed

Viking—a brand of condensed milk

Acknowledgements

A LOVE OF the Arctic and an admiration for Wanny Woldstad are the reasons I wrote *Cold Coast*. Having worked seasonally in Svalbard and north east Greenland for many years, the evocation of landscape flowed easily. In contrast, writing Wanny Woldstad's story came laden with deliberation: the responsibility of a novel based on real lives from a country and culture other than my own; wanting to present an authentic 1930s mindset toward trapping and hunting before the disparate views of a contemporary reader. My hope is that *Cold Coast* honours Wanny Woldstad and Anders Sæterdal's lightly trodden lives, without apology for their outlook or means of living. Through their experiences and observations, I hope readers may feel as ignited with the magic of the Arctic as I do, at the same time as we reflect and act on its tenuous future.

A heartfelt thank you to those whose generous contributions assisted the research: Australia Council for the Arts for support to carry out research in and around Tromsø and Longyearbyen; Ingrid Crossland for providing an unofficial English translation of Wanny's memoir *Første kvinne som fangstmann på Svalbard* (*First Woman Trapper on Svalbard*); Ingrid's mother Sidsel Woxen for assistance and follow-up thoughts on Norwegian culture; Anne Oyasaeter from

Oslo for translating archival material about Wanny; Rune Solhaug from Tromsø who shared insights into hunting; glaciologist and polar adventurer Heidi Sevestre who provided expertise and maps of Hansbreen's two-kilometre glacial retreat since 1933, along with an understanding of crossing the glacier on foot; shipmate and historian Carol Knott for onboard lectures and conversations about Wanny and the trapping era. From 2001 through 2019 I worked annually in the Arctic for Aurora Expeditions aboard MV *Polar Pioneer*. Those diverse and cherished experiences, for which I am so grateful, allowed me to know the marvels of the Arctic and to immerse myself in Wanny's world.

Sincere thanks to fellow writers and friends for invaluable feedback and encouragement through the writing process: Keith Feltham, Donna Mazza, Vahri McKenzie, Rachael Mead, Richard Rossiter, Leslie Thiele.

On the publishing front, alongside the steadfast literary agent I have in Fran Moore, it feels so rewarding to be amongst Ultimo Press/Hardie Grant Publishing's debut season of authors, with thanks to Alex Craig for her tremendous support and editorial input, Robert Watkins and James Kellow for welcoming *Cold Coast*, and to all at Ultimo Press whose mighty efforts send a book at its most elegant and eloquent out into the world. My appreciation goes to editor Deonie Fiford for her sensitive editing, and to Rebecca Hamilton who meticulously proofread the novel. Thank you. Sandy Cull from gogoGingko has designed a cracking cover, while the fine typesetting is the work of Simon Paterson and Bookhouse, Sydney. Shipmate, naturalist and artist Heidi Krajewsky created the two delightful hand-drawn maps at the front of the novel.

The marathon effort of researching and writing would be far less joyful without the support of loved ones at home. Thank you, especially, to my partner Gary Miller.

NOTABLE MEMOIRS AND biographies from the trapping era in Svalbard and in North-East Greenland:

Adams, Paul (1961). *Arctic Island Hunter*. George Ronald.

Howarth, David (1957). *The Sledge Patrol*. Collins.

Maxwell, A. E. and Rund, Ivar (1976). *The Year-Long Day*. J. B. Lippincott.

Ritter, Christiane (2010). *A Woman in the Polar Night* (translated from the German, originally published 1938). Greystone Books.

Woldstad, Wanny (1956). *Første kvinne som fangstmann på Svalbard*. Tanum.

About the author

Wild places form a big part of Robyn Mundy's life, and her novels. Robyn has wintered and summered in Antarctica, the setting for her first novel *The Nature of Ice*. Her second novel, *Wildlight*, is set on remote Maatsuyker Island, home to Australia's loneliest lighthouse where she spent ten months. For over twenty years Robyn has worked seasonally as a ship-based tour guide in Svalbard, Greenland, Antarctica, the Norwegian coast and wild Scotland. Her numerous visits to Svalbard led to the writing of *Cold Coast*. Robyn lives in Tasmania with a penguin biologist and a Blue Heeler. Visit her website at www.writingthewild.net and Instagram at robyncmundy.